What You Meant For Evil

Theodore R. C. Cox

Cover design by Alex Reimer

Cover font by Wahyu Eka Prasetya

ISBN: 978-1-7376970-0-8

For Abdullah, whose bravery inspires me.

This is a pre-release version of *What You Meant for Evil.* It's very close to the final version but still probably contains a mistake or two. Hopefully not many more than that because all of the editing is exhausting. Whew! :)

When you're finished with it, please pass it on to a friend. Or — even better — buy them a copy of the final version. Details are available at: www.WhatYouMeantForEvilBook.com

Thanks for reading.

Theodore D. C. Cox

one

Samira: Dreams

Winter 2011

The bus jounced along a barren stretch of highway. Dust rose in faded clouds of umber. It obscured the landscape, giving a dream-like aspect to the already alien terrain. Samira stared out the window. Her mind was a furious tumult, trying to make sense of what she was seeing. This was not her home in Latakia, Syria. She was somewhere else. And everything felt wrong.

The bus hit another bump. Shocks creaked and thumped. Samira nearly hit her head on the glass and that's when she saw him. A stranger sat in the seat beside her. Caramel colored skin around eyes twinkling with… something terrifying. He was staring at her. She turned, looking around the bus. Everyone was staring at her, she realized. The entire bus was watching.

A slow feeling of dread prickled over her skin. It rose like a hot flush. She reached up, horrified, feeling her hair. Loose. Uncovered. Strangers were staring at her uncovered head. Her stomach lurched. Modest women did not travel about with uncovered hair. *How did I wind up on a bus in the middle of nowhere with my head uncovered?* An empty, sick feeling cramped her abdomen. *What will my father think?* It was a wild cry in her mind. Her hands clutched awkwardly, trying to cover herself, but they were too small. There were so many of the dark locks. They defied her with an attention seeking shine and curl they'd never had before. Swirling with thoughts of family shame, her head filled with self-accusation. Long black hair was everywhere. Every eye was staring. She quivered. Dishonor burned her cheeks. She wanted to scream and throw up. To disappear somehow. It got worse.

Beside her, the strange man with his laughing eyes, reached out his hand. *He's laughing at me,* she reasoned. His thick, callused fingers steered toward her hair, as if he was going to stroke it. A male stranger stroking her hair was unimaginable. Awful. Such an intimacy could not be allowed. But she was only seventeen, and he was at least thirty. He was powerful, muscular, and she felt small. *How can I stop him?* Her heart was feral, pounding and growling chaotically. *In some Syrian families, we could be married.* That thought unsettled her in a different way. His hand continued moving toward her. It was a familiar gesture like a husband might make to a wife alone in their bedroom. *Like when I was a girl and my father would stroke my hair as I went to sleep.* She pulled backwards, her head pressing against the glass of the window. Relentlessly, his hand approached. She slapped at it, struggled against it. Struggling made no difference. She spun her head this way and that, looking anywhere except into those bottomless, kind eyes. *Why is no one helping me? Why do they all just watch as he assaults me?* Her gaze met his for a second time and she knew him. The fight went out of her.

His hand touched her hair. It was the softest, gentlest touch. Calm rolled through her like a wave. Suddenly, everything was better. Her hair was neatly coifed in a stylish hijab. No one was staring. Her dignity was intact. Her heart still thudded in her chest and she felt breathless, but her panic and fear were gone. She knew him. She welcomed his touch.

The stranger smiled at her, his eyes sparkling with warmth. There was a promise in those eyes. He saw her as she truly was. He understood her value. Her lips curved upward and her teeth broke through.

"You will come to me," he said. "And I will exalt you."

Samira awakened, her eyes snapping open. She tore at confusion, like cobwebs on her face. Everything was a jumble. *Where am I*?

A violin trilled quarter tones in time with a thick, pounding bass beat. The sound was thin and tinny filtered through the speaker of her mobile phone.

The dream flashed through her mind, a hot stab of shame. Little flashes of the bus and people staring jeered at her. Her hands jerked up to her hair. It was uncovered. Splayed all over her pillow. *My pillow.* Her eyes darted around. She lay in her bed. *It was just a dream.* She took a deep breath, slowly letting the tension exhale away into nothingness. *Or... maybe more than a dream.* A lazy smile quirked at her lips. Mischief sparkled in her eyes, a mirror of the stranger's delight in her. She reached for her phone. Sitting up, she turned off the music and casually tossed her phone on the bed.

Her eyes scanned across the room. Like always, her side of the bedroom was immaculate and spare. She was not addicted to possessions and thought excessive decoration was a useless vanity. Things needed to have value and purpose. Her nightstand contained a single lamp and a copy of Dominic Erbach's seminal business masterwork, *Power to Change.* Even the charging cable for her phone disappeared neatly behind the nightstand when not in use.

A dresser away, the room transformed into a chaos of teddy bears and discarded clothing. Yasmeen, her ten-year-old sister, slept like an angel. It was hard for Samira, sharing a room with someone else's mess. She had an image of herself which was not compatible with teddy bears and discarded piles of clothes. But their father insisted. It was normal, ordinary even for the girls to share a room. Sharing would build a bond between them. As was nearly always the case with Yacoob Masoud, he was right. Samira adored Yasmeen, at least when the girl wasn't driving her crazy.

Samira rose quietly. Her expression soft as she watched the little girl sleep. Without thought, she scooped up a pair of pink, flowered pants from the floor before kneeling next to Yasmeen's bed. Gently, Samira caressed the girl's hair. Yasmeen was a treasure. As she touched her sister's hair, she felt again the sensations of the dream. The sudden peace warmed her and she smiled again.

"Yasmeen," she cooed, softly. "Precious sister. It's time to wake up."

The little girl's chest slowly rose, seemingly undisturbed by Samira's attention. Samira's mouth curled downward. Yasmeen opened one eye coyly, and then made a pouty face when she realized her sister had caught her peeking.

Laughter broke Samira's stern facade. She stroked Yasmeen's cheek with an idyllic smile. "Mother used to do this," she said. "She would curl a finger in my hair," Samira twisted her finger into one of Yasmeen's locks. "'Susu,' she would whisper, 'beautiful Susu,'" Samira found raw emotions just under the surface. The nickname, Susu, always seemed too childish, but the dim memories of her mother were so precious. Mother kneeling by her bed, gently waking her like this. Yasmeen would never have those — not of their mother.

"Did mother look like you?" Yasmeen was all big eyed empathy, and Samira realized she'd gotten lost in a moment of grief. She took ahold of herself. Their mother was gone a decade now, it was past time to put the pain behind her. She smiled at Yasmeen.

"A prophet spoke to me in my dreams this morning." Her voice was liquid and creamy.

Yasmeen's eyes opened wide and she sat up suddenly, her question forgotten. Her little sister's enthusiasm was almost enough to mute the feeling of loss.

"Like *the* prophet?" Yasmeen queried urgently. The little girl was practically panting with sudden enthusiasm.

Samira rose slowly. It was an effort to remember the excitement of her dream, to let her mother's memory fade. She turned away from Yasmeen, automatically folding the pants she still held in her hand. She moved to the dresser. As she reached the heavy wood surface, she paused. She could feel the taut drama of Yasmeen's anticipation stretching between them. Cutting her eyes back to Yasmeen, she gave a tiny shake of her head and grinned.

"Moses?" Yasmeen demanded. "Jesus? Joseph? Which prophet? What did he say?"

Samira laughed and set the folded pants on top of the dresser. She loved Yasmeen's enthusiasm. *What would I do without you, little sister?* She wished everyone in the family could look to Samira's leadership as Yasmeen did. That put a crease on her brow, but she sighed it away and turned back to her sister.

"He said soon," Samira's eyes sparkled, "I will be the boss."

The words felt sweetly ominous as they rolled from Samira's mouth. She reveled in the joy of them, but Yasmeen drew her attention.

The little girl's hand went to her mouth. She spoke in an excited whisper, "of Mahmoud?"

Samira continued smiling, but she felt her eyes harden at her brother's name. Moving back to the bed, she perched on the edge. She turned her head away from Yasmeen, gazing at nothing. Her mind spun with the myriad possibilities. "I will exalt you" echoed in her mind. At last, she turned back to Yasmeen.

"Of Mahmoud, of Father… of everyone."

two

Mahmoud: Favorite

Mahmoud watched his baba and worried. Yacoob Masoud sat hunched in a chair. A blanket wrapped the old man's legs. He looked frail. Tired. A shadow of the powerful tycoon who'd raised Mahmoud. Mahmoud loved the old man, fiercely. He understood the obligations of a son to a father. But he could also see the time had come for Yacoob to rest. Mahmoud could run the business now. Yacoob had earned the break.

The old man's legacy was everywhere. The living room was expansive. A magnificent Persian rug sat in the center of the polished marble floor. The couches and chairs were fine leather. The tables and chairs, hand-carved wood by master craftsmen. Declaring success without being overbearing or vulgar, that was the Masoud home.

Yacoob tilted his head rapidly upward, making a pop with his tongue. Then he returned his gaze to his wrinkled palms.

Mahmoud wondered, *when did he get so old?* In his mind, his baba was a powerful man in his prime, not this shriveled old husk.

Mahmoud turned and paced away. He saw himself in a gilt-framed mirror. His own dark face was lined, his fifty years evident in the gray at his temples. He looked tired. Every grey hair seemed to have a weight and a cause. He slumped. *Why must everything be a fight?* Squaring his shoulders, he turned back to his father's chair.

"Already, you mistakenly promoted this woman," he lectured. "Now she is making more trouble for us."

It was hard for Mahmoud to keep his tone respectful. Exasperation ballooned his words. Yacoob's time had passed. It was hard to accept, but his savvy was years behind him.

The old man didn't react to Mahmoud's words. He sat massaging his temples, his eyes closed. *Did he even hear me,* Mahmoud wondered? *Is he here? Or is his mind slipping away as well?*

"Mahmoud, my son, this is not about one woman." He opened his eyes, looking up at Mahmoud. "We have a reputation."

The word struck like a blow. Mahmoud froze. *Does he really think I don't care about our family's reputation?* He tried to hide the hurt in his eyes as he met his baba's gaze. Maybe he succeeded. Maybe not. Nothing showed on Yacoob's face. In the background, a television program babbled senselessly. Mahmoud barely registered the noise. The television was always on.

Yacoob turned away, his face transformed. Life and energy returning to his eyes. He smiled, wide and beaming. Susu swept into the room. Mahmoud grimaced. She nearly skipped in an abaya of their finest silk. Her hijab was bright and stylish. She was beautiful, graceful, and mercilessly foolish. Making things even worse, the old man couldn't see her as she was.

With a creaking of his ancient bones, Yacoob levered himself painfully from the chair, throwing his arms wide to embrace the girl.

"Good morning, Father." Susu gave him a tender kiss on the cheek. Stepping out of the embrace, she cut her eyes to Mahmoud, giving him a cold glare. "Brother."

"Susu," he greeted her politely. Her glare grew even colder. *Of course, she wants to be Samira now. As if a grown up name will make her ideas less childish.*

No words came to him. He didn't want to spar with her. Yacoob would take her side no matter how foolish she was. It was better for him to leave and resume this conversation with Baba when she was elsewhere. He turned, moving toward the door.

"You are the most precious jewel, Samira."

Mahmoud squeezed his eyes shut, his jaw tightening painfully. For years it had been this way. Mahmoud was heaped with scorn for keeping their business alive while foolish Susu was lauded for rising from a chair or walking across a carpet.

"Of all the riches Allah has showered on me, you are my greatest treasure."

Mahmoud steadied himself with his hand on the door frame. Tears came into his eyes and acid burned his throat. *Does Baba not think of me at all? He praises her and makes me nothing.*

"Mahmoud and I were just discussing a problem at the silk farm," Yacoob continued. "I would hear your wisdom."

Mahmoud froze in the doorway. This was a disaster. He could count on his sister to ruin everything. She was obsessed with some European computer magnate, and thought somehow everything she read about a different business in an alien part of the world was fully applicable to the business their family had spent generations building. Escape was no longer an option. He turned back into the room. It was critical that he cut this short before she could do any damage.

"Do not trouble—"

Susu cut him off, "Of course, Baba. Whatever you wish."

Her smile to Yacoob was innocent, but then she turned to Mahmoud and her grin was all malice.

"Laila has become pregnant," Yacoob began. "Her husband visited me last night. They would like—"

"She is demanding—" Mahmoud spoke over Yacoob. But the old man cut his words off with a look.

"Laila," Yacoob resumed, "will not be able to work for several months. They wish to know if she will still have a job after the baby is born."

Mahmoud inhaled sharply, ready to make his case. He froze. There was a faint hope here. Susu didn't know what Mahmoud had suggested. Perhaps she would choose his side without realizing it. Mahmoud held his breath.

"Your brother believes," Yacoob continued, eliciting a defeated exhalation from Mahmoud, "we have no obligation to her."

Susu nodded sagely, "But you are concerned about our reputation in the community."

Of course, Mahmoud thought bitterly, *she knows his mind intuitively.*

Yacoob nodded, his face disappearing into a wrinkled mass as he grinned stupidly at her. It was all Mahmoud could manage not to slap his own forehead. The trouble was that whatever these two invented, Mahmoud would be expected to implement. It would not be Yacoob or Susu at the farm or on in the factory.

"Laila has a tender heart," Susu began. "When she holds her baby, she will no longer wish to return to work."

Mahmoud looked up at her in surprise. Was she taking his side? Did she actually think about the business and not merely her desire to gainsay him? She met his shocked gaze, confident and calm. He felt a surge of hope. She quirked an eyebrow at him and then turned her smile on Yacoob again.

"But her husband is… unreliable. He will lose another job, and they will need the money. She will come back to us."

Mahmoud sighed. It was too much to hope. She never took his side. If he said fire would destroy the silk, she would light a match and declare him a fool.

"We offer her an unpaid leave of absence," Susu continued, "up to one year. She will think we are being generous, we will gain goodwill in the community and it will cost us nothing."

Mahmoud tried to keep his mouth shut, but he couldn't. The truth of the matter exploded out of him, propelled by his frustration.

"And who will manage her work during the staff shortage?"

"I am certain," Susu gave him a wolfish grin, "you have the spare time to handle her work, brother." He'd walked right into her trap.

Mahmoud fired back, "I barely see my sons as it is—"

"Perhaps you should go home to your wife instead of spending your nights in a bar soaking in arak."

His jaw dropped. The accusation should have been expected. It was always something with her. She would take things he'd done and present them to Yacoob in the worst possible context, but… this was completely false. Mahmoud never went to bars, had never consumed any alcohol in his life.

He shifted his gaze to Yacoob. The old man's face was turning purple.

"It's not true. I have never touched alcohol," Mahmoud protested. He could hear it. The desperation in his voice made it sound like a denial. But it really wasn't true! "It is a lie, Baba. I would not shame the family—"

"A lie?" Yacoob's voice was quiet and cold. For all the anger shaking his frame, he held himself in tight control. "And was it a lie last week when Samira brought news of you visiting cafes with young women who are not your wife?"

Mahmoud's mouth opened and shut silently. How could he explain? It wasn't as bad as it sounded, but… it wasn't wholly innocent either. His best friend, Nabil, was — for all of his fine qualities — a man of unsavory appetites, and he often led Mahmoud into compromising situations with young women. *But it isn't* my *fault!*

"You were supposed to be at the farm, watching over our business."

Mahmoud's head dropped. He reached up, his hands clasping hold of his cheeks. He pressed them together, pulling downward, stretching his cheeks, trying desperately to feel something other than burning shame.

"Please," it dribbled out of his mouth, a broken whisper. "I did leave early. And I was at a cafe with…" his voice failed him. It took him a moment to compose himself and continue. As he spoke his voice gained strength and indignation. "With a girl, but — I did not — I have not been drinking at a bar."

Yacoob stretched out his hand, pointing a finger at Mahmoud. The younger man followed the digit to his own hand. To the heavy silver ring set with a fat red garnet. It was the heirloom of the Masoud family, the symbol of Mahmoud's inheritance.

"That is our family honor you are wearing. Was it on display at this cafe? While you laughed with a woman who is not your wife?" The questions sat a moment, unanswered by anything except Mahmoud's burning shame. What could he say? "You should learn from your sister's example."

Mahmoud's anger burned. *I hate her.* He watched his baba as the old man's head swiveled away from him, turned to Susu. Yacoob's anger faded. The old man's voice became smooth and lovely again. With an effort, he shifted in his seat, pulling out a long bolt of perfect silk. It was a riot of different dyes and colors. An artistic masterpiece.

"I have a gift for you, my precious Samira. It is the finest piece of silk we have ever produced. My greatest creation… after you."

Mahmoud shook with rage. *You mean the finest piece of silk* I've *ever produced.* It was not Yacoob who had stewarded its creation. *And it wasn't meant for Susu.*

With great ceremony, Yacoob rose and laid the scarf across her shoulders. Joy crinkled the corners of his eyes. The old man turned back to Mahmoud.

"You see? This is what it means to be a good child. Samira will always bring honor to our family. She will never break her promises, betray a husband or her family."

Susu gave Mahmoud a triumphant smile. Mahmoud blinked. He lost himself in a fantasy of smashing that wicked grin against the coffee table over and over — and then he snapped back to the conversation. Susu was still talking. Mahmoud's cheeks burned. He was not a violent man, and it shamed him to have lost himself in such thoughts about his own sister.

"That's just what I came to tell you, Baba. I had the most amazing dream."

Concern flashed across Yacoob's face. That was the one area where he could see her as Mahmoud did. Her ambition to be something beyond her birth or gender.

"It's not this dream about you running a company for that German businessman again is it?" Yacoob asked. Mahmoud felt a flicker of hope. Perhaps she would be set down today at least in one small area.

She laughed, raising her head and making a clicking sound with her tongue.

"No, Baba. It wasn't Dominic Erbach in my dreams last night. I dreamed of a future for our family."

Mahmoud listened in dawning horror as Samira described her dream and claimed it was a prophesy of Allah.

Hours later, sitting at his dinner table, Mahmoud was in a daze. Around him, his wife tried to corral their grown sons into chairs and lay out the many plates and bowls of food she had prepared. It was all just a wash of blurry action passing through him. His mind kept running back over the confrontation with his sister. She was so headstrong, so bent on ruining everything. After their father had finished reprimanding her for her foolishness about her supposed vision — *Ridiculous! Believing she would be the head of the family!?!* — He'd caught up to her in the hallway. As Yacoob sat wrapped feebly in a blanket, Mahmoud tried to salvage the mess.

"I know you mean well," he lied, "but reading books is not the same as running a business." He didn't think she meant well. In fact, he was convinced it was her singular goal to destroy him. "Constantly undermining me is hurting the business."

She glared at him. In private, she made no pretense of getting along.

"Maybe if you read one of Dominic's books, you'd do a better job, and I wouldn't need to step in." Her head popped up with a click of her tongue, disgust plain on her face. "And you are what is hurting our business!"

She turned to storm away.

He couldn't believe it. He struggled to control the rage that threatened to overwhelm him. "Did Father's words mean nothing to you?"

That froze her in mid-step. Slowly she turned back to him.

"Tell me, Mahmoud. You are so wise. Should I ignore a vision from a prophet because Father doesn't like what he said?"

That was the end of it. She'd walked away and he'd stood there, mouth working, but unable to form words.

"Mahmoud," Esma's voice was sharp. His wife didn't like him bringing his work troubles home.

He looked up and smiled at her. Her eyes were flat and accusing. The table was covered in a gorgeous orange cloth. Bowls of meat and vegetables dotted the surface. Bread steamed, warm on a platter. The smells of coriander and sumac filled the room. "Thank you, my precious one." The words were rote and empty. His boys watched him, waiting impatiently for him to serve himself so they could take their portions.

He scooped food onto his plate, hardly seeing it. A part of him was furious at his sister's presumption. Another part was filled with terror. *What if it's true?*

He swirled a bit of torn bread in the dark meat grease coating his plate, but never lifted it to his lips. Looking around the table, he roamed the faces of his boys: Ismaeel, Jaber and Ahmad. Ismaeel was shoveling his food away with an urgency to be somewhere else. Mahmoud wished he too had somewhere to be. It wasn't that Esma was a poor cook. The food had flavor. He just wanted a different life. He wanted the enthusiasm Ismaeel showed for action, the passion Jaber felt for women, the freedom Ahmad had from an overbearing father. His sons were blessed with something Mahmoud could barely imagine. Life should have color and flavor.

"I am late to meet Abdo." Ismaeel was halfway across the room. The boy would need to be settled soon. He was young to be married, but he was always out. Too often engaged with troublemakers. Abdo was often spouting hateful nonsense from Imams bent on getting young men killed.

"You've barely touched your dinner!" Esma complained.

"Can I come?" Jaber looked after his brother. Neither boy seemed to hear their mother.

"No," Ismaeel shot back, "stop trying to follow us everywhere."

The exchange was so familiar, it pulled Mahmoud back into memory. Long ago, he'd watched his older brother Omar rushing out the door, and his brother, Ali, trying to follow. He'd greatly admired his brothers then. Omar was powerful. He had a natural authority. Ali was a schemer. Somehow he always got you to do what he wanted. Mahmoud shivered imagining their fate for his own sons.

"Are you going to do something?" Esma's demand snapped him back into the present.

Mahmoud shrugged. *What am I to do?* He was not Yacoob Masoud. He would not exile or disinherit his sons for their bad behavior. Mahmoud sighed. *Why can't Omar be the one trying to save the business and deal with Susu?* It was never supposed to be Mahmoud.

Does Susu even know she has two older brothers? He was sure she must know. Omar lived in Latakia. Sometimes he even came to visit the factory when Baba wasn't there. He couldn't remember when Ali had gone to prison, but it was easy to place Omar's banishment. It had come only a few months before Baba's pretty second wife became pregnant with Yasmeen.

Yacoob hadn't been wrong. Not really. What Omar had done… and Ali… Mahmoud shuddered. They brought shame on the family. *How old was Susu? Five?* He couldn't remember. *How am I to live?* How was he to function? *The weight of everything is on my shoulders.* There was no sense of peace and safety in his life. At any moment, Yacoob Masoud could cast him aside, just as he had the two sons born before him. What hope was there for his sons if the fortune passed to Susu? She wouldn't take care of his family.

"You let those boys run wild!" Esma was ranting at him. He realized she'd been talking for some time and he hadn't heard. He looked up at her. She'd never been beautiful, but the years hadn't been kind. Frown lines pulled her mouth into jowls and there was a dark crease between her brows from scowling. "They need a father, not a lump in a chair."

Ahmad, who remained at the table, stared down at his food uncomfortably. Mahmoud had long ago given up on his wife's good opinion. Like his father, there was no pleasing her. But his relationship with his sons was important to him. He could not stand her berating him in front of one of his children.

"Enough," he said the word with quiet finality. His eyes met Esma's and the words dried up on her tongue. He placed his hand over hers, giving her an empty smile. It was all theater for Ahmad's benefit. "Ismaeel is in the prime of life. A good wife will settle him."

"And where will you find a woman of character to marry such a wild boy?"

Mahmoud patted her hand. "I am to inherit a great fortune, some women care more for money than happiness."

She stiffened. “Some women’s fathers perhaps.”

three

Samira: Sold

Spring 2011

Samira watched Mahmoud's back retreating down the street. Her brother moved with purpose and energy, but there was a tension in his shoulders. She rarely saw him looking relaxed or happy. He was always animated by anger, jealousy — some dark emotion. When he'd walked off the factory floor, she was certain he was up to no good. She followed him. After all, Baba had a right to know what his manager did when Baba wasn't there to supervise.

Sometimes she worried. Mahmoud's anger was her ally. It unmanned him, causing him to do foolish things. His anger proved again and again that he was unfit to run the company, that it should be hers. But she couldn't help feeling a tremor of fear as she followed him. How would he react if he caught her? What might his anger look like, unconstrained by the presence of their father, Yasmeen, or the factory workers? She wanted to believe Mahmoud wouldn't hit her, but she wanted to believe he wouldn't cheat on his wife, or publicly shame the family.

She paused in the street, letting Mahmoud get a little further away. Turning, she caught a glimpse of herself in a store window. She liked to imagine herself, not in an abaya and a hijab, but in a power suit, arms crossed on the cover of a book or magazine about successful people. She smiled, but gave herself a critical look. *Dominic Erbach says that success is all about preparation.* The scarf that she always wore now, wrapped and folded neatly like a hijab, was too striking. The gorgeous colors were too rich, too obvious. She hated to cover her precious gift from Baba, but… if Mahmoud looked back he couldn't mistake her for anyone else.

She looked around. The street was deserted and Mahmoud was disappearing rapidly. There was a bazaar a few streets over, but Mahmoud would be long gone if she rushed there and came back.

Moving cautiously, she followed Mahmoud, trying to stay close to doorways and alleys she could duck into if he turned.

He reached the end of the road, turning to the right. He looked back, and Samira jumped into an alleyway. Her heart pounded in her chest. She could imagine him, yelling and screaming in rage and then grabbing her, gripping her throat. Or perhaps it would be fists, raggedly striking her again and again. Her breath was coming too fast, adrenaline responding to her imagination.

She straightened her body, intentionally relaxing. That wasn't how it would play out. Mahmoud might hate her with every fiber of his being, but he was too afraid of their father to do her any serious harm. He would yell. Nothing more. She nodded to herself.

Peeking around the corner, she groaned. Mahmoud was gone. *Where did he go?*

"Are you alright?"

She whipped her head back the other way. A boy was in the alley, an armload of rags in his hands. She smiled.

A few minutes later, a drab abaya and an ugly brown wrap concealing her regular clothes, she watched as Mahmoud disappeared into a cafe. Finding him again had been a stroke of luck. If she didn't know better she would have sworn he wanted to be followed. *He thinks he's so clever.* She wanted to laugh.

She hadn't seen him in this particular cafe before. Was it unimaginable that so quickly after being called out by Yacoob, he would be meeting another one of his girlfriends? Samira thought so, but… Perhaps this would finally be his downfall. Baba would see Mahmoud for the dissolute scoundrel he was. He would give the business to Samira. She deserved it. She'd studied. Baba's obsession with birth order and gender was foolish! She could lead their family into the 21st century.

There were so many exciting ideas: new technology, labor and human resource strategies, social media marketing and direct sales — there was so much untapped potential for the company and their products. *Never leave a fortune on the table.* That was another Dominic Erbach quote. *One step at a time,* she reminded herself. *First I have to learn what Mahmoud is up to.*

She took a deep breath and slipped into the cafe.

So early in the afternoon, it was relatively quiet. There were two old men playing backgammon, but most of the tables were empty. She grimaced. *It's going to be nearly impossible to hide in here.* The waiter looked up and smiled and she slipped over into a corner, hoping that Mahmoud wouldn't notice.

He sat with his back to her. He was in an animated conversation with a man she'd seen before. *One of his friends,* she thought. Handsome, he was prematurely bald, in his twenties with a precise beard. *Mahmoud's friend is creepy,* she reminded herself. He always seemed to watch her when he came to the factory. *And why are they friends? He's young enough to be one of Mahmoud's children!*

She pulled out her copy of *Power to Change* and opened it. Pretending to read, she held the book just under her eyes, watching the two men over the top of the pages. She hoped it would obscure her face enough. If either glanced at her… *It's practically a burka,* she reassured her self. *All they can see are my eyes.*

Dice rattled across the backgammon table followed by a string of curses. One of the men had a hooked nose and a grimace.

Focusing on her brother's conversation, she leaned forward on her elbows. When Mahmoud had left the office, he claimed he was going to supervise a delivery. But there wasn't one on the schedule, and deliveries didn't happen at cafes. *Still,* she wondered, *is it possible this is business?* She had often seen this man hanging around the factory. *Surely, he didn't come just to stare at me,* she thought.

"I am pleased to hear there is mutual interest," the bald man said.

Samira raised her eyebrows. *That does sound like business.*

"Your plan is to marry and then travel?" Mahmoud was already diverting the conversation away from work it seemed.

Glancing over the top of her book, Samira noticed there was another man sipping tea across the cafe from her. He smiled and raised his cup to her. She looked down again.

"Yes. I think there is a good job for me in Aleppo, but…"

Mahmoud bobbed his head as though he knew exactly what the other man wasn't saying. What did any of this have to do with the silk business? *He's just here wasting time,* she thought.

"I have a cousin working in Turkey," Mahmoud's friend continued.

"And also an older brother in Paris."

Samira felt a little thrill. *Paris!* She'd always dreamed of seeing Paris.

"Paris? That should delight a young bride." Mahmoud's voice sounded malicious. Samira winced. She didn't like how closely his words had mirrored her own reaction. *I'm not going to marry,* she thought, *I'm going to run the business you're so keen to neglect.*

"What can I get you?" She looked over her book at the waiter, who smiled at her. She couldn't speak. Mahmoud would recognize her voice. She panicked. "Coffee." She barely whispered the words. The waiter nodded and moved away. Her heart pounded and her eyes were glued to the back of Mahmoud's head, watching his posture. She saw no indication he was on to her.

He looked strangely relaxed. It made her even more nervous. The friend was still talking.

"...stay in Syria. I'd like to be near my family."

"Of course," Mahmoud's voice was all exaggerated understanding. "But you have career prospects. You can provide. That's the important thing."

Samira smirked. This definitely was not about work. She took out a small pad and noted the time.

Another rattle of dice was punctuated with a triumphant cackle. It was the other player. He wore a pair of glasses and a broad grin.

"Some women," Mahmoud continued, as though he knew anything about women, "think they can handle everything on their own." *Some women can.* "They need a strong hand to disabuse them of the notion."

She rolled her eyes. Everyone knew Mahmoud's wife, Esma, was the one running his household. *Strong hand indeed.*

"I'm not afraid to be firm."

The dice rattled a third time.

Mahmoud chuckled. "I'm sure you're not."

Samira glanced up from her notes and met Mahmoud's eyes. He was turned around, looking straight at her. Suddenly, her hidden corner felt like a trap. Her eyes went wide, and she flinched back in her chair. Recriminations ran through her mind. *Why did I think he wouldn't see me? Hiding behind a* Dominic Erbach *book!* Mahmoud smiled. It was cruel, ugly with hate. She looked past him. His friend was also looking at her. Staring, really. Like she was... something he wanted to own. She swallowed hard. She felt suddenly sweaty, like she needed to bathe. She wasn't sure if it was fear or Mahmoud's friend staring at her.

"Join us," Mahmoud said. "There's someone I'd like you to meet."

At the backgammon table the man in glasses lost his smile as hooked-nose slid a final piece into position. The man in glasses started to reset the board.

She tried to settle her nerves. Mahmoud had caught her snooping. Backgammon tiles ticked like a clock out of time. She looked again at the other man sipping tea, the one who had raised his cup to her. He gave her another smile and this time she nodded back. The two old men didn't look up from their game, pieces clicking and sliding on the felt board. This was a public cafe. Mahmoud couldn't really do anything here. She was still in control. Putting her notepad away, she smiled, closed her book and rose, keeping her chin high. *I am composed and calm,* she told herself. As she rose to her feet, she slid the ugly brown rag off of her head, revealing her beautiful colored scarf. *Let Mahmoud remember exactly who I am.*

It was almost like they were playing a scene, being so polite and solicitous of one another. He invited her to the table and held a chair. She demurely accepted and joined them as though he wasn't a snake. The illusion was only mildly spoiled by the ugly abaya draped haphazardly over her clothes and the brown rag, clutched too tightly in her nervous fingers.

She looked down her nose at Mahmoud and smiled.

"I'm very interested to meet the man who has you sipping coffee in a cafe when you're supposed to be supervising a delivery. I'm sure father will be interested also."

The waiter set a coffee in front of her and she nodded to him politely. Cardamom seeds floated in the dark liquid. The smell rose, strong and comforting. She felt her adrenaline ebbing away. Glancing back at Mahmoud, she expected to see him looking annoyed, or better yet, worried. He was grinning like it was the best day of his life. Her heart fluttered. *What is he so excited about?* Nothing that made Mahmoud this happy could be good.

"But I *am* supervising a delivery, Susu."

She brought her coffee to her lips. Sipping calmly, she anticipated his fabrication. *I've got the upper hand here. There's nothing to be concerned about.*

Mahmoud continued, "Ata, my sister, Samira Masoud. Samira, meet Atallah Mohammed Tareq, your husband-to-be."

She choked on the coffee. It burned through her nostrils and spilled in an ugly mess on the table.

Mahmoud waited patiently for her to compose herself, grinning maniacally all the while.

While she patted at her face with a napkin, Mahmoud opened his hand, and Atallah handed him a five hundred pound note. She blinked disbelieving eyes. It was far too much to pay for the coffee.

Mahmoud was rising from the table, preparing to go. He was going to leave her with this Atallah. She started to get to her feet. It was improper for her to sit in a cafe with a stranger. Perhaps that was Mahmoud's game. Frame her for the same crime he'd committed. Trying to trick her with some story about a betrothal.

Whatever he's trying, this is ridiculous. There's no way I'm staying here.

"Baba will arrange—"

Mahmoud grabbed her shoulders, shoving her roughly back into her chair. It was shocking. She didn't know how to respond. She looked around. Dice rattled at the backgammon table. No one saw Mahmoud manhandle her. It was too quick. The waiter was chatting with someone in the kitchen. Across the way, the other man sipped his tea, oblivious. Mahmoud leaned over her, his breath hissing in her ear.

"Baba could never see you for what you are. But I will not let an ambitious woman tear our family apart." He looked up at Atallah. "She must never return home."

Atallah nodded. Samira was stunned. This was insanity. It couldn't really be happening. Mahmoud didn't really think she would stay, did he?

Mahmoud grabbed her scarf. The beautiful work of art, wrapping her hair, pulled tight around her scalp as his fingers closed on it. She reached up, grabbing it, trying to keep it from unraveling in his grip.

"Stop," she cried, "what are you doing?"

"I made this," Mahmoud hissed, "and it wasn't intended for you."

He pulled savagely, pins, hair and scarf tearing away in his hand. She clung desperately, but only wound up with a small square of ripped cloth in her fingers.

It hurt. Badly. But the pain was nothing. Her hair was uncovered in a public cafe. Shame flooded her body as blood rushed into her face. She felt it, like hot needles inside her skin. It was her dream, only, there was no prophet here to cover her. She couldn't look around the room now. Her eyes were trapped in her lap, but she was sure they were all looking now. There were no sounds from the backgammon table, no clatter from the kitchen. *Why do they say nothing?*

Hastily, she draped the brown rag over her head, struggling for some semblance of modesty, still disbelieving that her own brother would shame her this way in public.

"This isn't what's supposed to happen," she gasped.

Mahmoud turned, walking away, her scarf in his hand. She struggled to control her gasping, to restore her equilibrium, but she couldn't breathe. Tears started to form, blurring her vision. She didn't want to cry. Whatever happened, she didn't want it to be tears. She wouldn't look weak. Not now. She needed her strength, but it was gone, ripped away with her scarf and her dignity.

Atallah took her hand, gently. His fingers caressed the top of her hand tenderly. It was intimate. Inappropriate. Repulsive.

"I promise, it is not so bad."

She looked at him, disbelieving. Had he not seen what her brother just did? Was he some kind of idiot?

"They call you Susu, right? I like that. It's cute."

His eyes never left hers. They were warm, and there was something almost exciting there. A sense of passion just waiting to be unlocked. It intrigued her. But she wasn't going to be won over by small talk. There wasn't time for the mystery of this Atallah Mohammed Tareq. She needed to go home, needed to tell her father what had happened. Mahmoud needed to be punished.

The tears came anyway. They were running down her cheeks. She didn't want anyone to see them.

"My friends call me Ata," he said.

She tried to pull her hand back, but Atallah held it, his grip like iron.

"I will teach you to be a good wife, Susu."

Samira came to the horrible realization he wasn't going to let go, and there was nothing she could do. She thought she might scream. The waiter turned away when she looked at him. Hook-nose and the man in glasses kept their heads down, studying their game with new intensity. The other man, the stranger sipping coffee, he met her eyes sadly. But she could see that he, too, was not going to intervene. She realized she knew him. That's when despair took her. *I'm hallucinating,* she thought, *this can't be real.*

four

Samira: Married

The next few days were a whirlwind. Atallah whisked her off to his extended family in Aleppo where Samira was surrounded by people she didn't know. Everywhere she looked was an aunt, a cousin, a brother… family. Atallah's family. At first, she went along. *Baba will come soon,* she told herself. *When he arrives, he'll make everything right.* A girl, who Samira thought had to be two years younger than her, battered her face with a makeup brush as a heavyset older woman worked a curling iron on Samira's hair. The heavyset woman, who must have been an aunt, kept asking Samira's opinion. *What am I to say?* She wasn't sure. Samira was not a woman who read bridal magazines, or had a dress picked out. She'd never wanted to marry. Her dreams were of power suits and corporate boardrooms. *What do I care what my hair looks like under a bridal cloak I'm not taking off? Baba will come and end this sham wedding.*

She murmured non-committal responses to the woman's growing exasperation. Finally, this woman asked, "Where is your mother?"

Samira felt something inside her break in that moment. The years had resolved her to life without a mother — at least that's what she told herself — but she wasn't without family. Her reaction was involuntary, she'd looked at the door, looked for Yacoob Masoud. *Why is Baba not here?* And then she realized… *Of course he isn't coming. Mahmoud hasn't told him.* Won't *tell him.*

"What's wrong, child?" The aunt's voice was sharp. Samira realized her mouth was hanging open as she stared at the door.

"I can't go through with this," Samira said.

The young girl stopped her work with the makeup brush, her eyes large. The door opened and another girl peeked in from the hallway. The aunt glared at the interloper and she ran off, leaving the door ajar.

"What do you mean?" The heavyset woman asked, rolling another lock of hair onto the curling iron.

Samira hardened her resolve. "I can't marry him." She spoke definitively, only a hint of quaver in her voice.

The make-up girl was biting her lip uncertainly, but the older woman just patted Samira insincerely on the shoulder.

"Brides all get jittery. You'll be fine."

Samira pushed the woman away, getting her hair pulled.

"No!" She shouted, louder than she intended. "My father isn't here. He hasn't agreed to this!"

That declaration brought scandalized silence. Samira looked at the aunt, raising her chin. Her insides felt like quivering jelly, but she hardened her eyes. *I am in control,* she coached herself. *I am Samira Masoud. I will not bring shame on my family. I* will *be exalted.*

A glance from the large woman sent the girl scurrying from the room.

"We'll see," the woman said. "For now, hold still. I've not got the curls right yet."

Samira glowered. The curling iron twisting its way back into her hair seemed to be robbing her of agency. After a few interminable minutes, though, her patience was rewarded.

There was a tap at the door. The bridal cloak was thrown over Samira's head and an Imam entered. Samira didn't know him. Perhaps thirty years old, he had sharp eyes and a hooked nose. In some ways, he reminded her of a younger Mahmoud. That thought didn't fill her with confidence.

The Imam looked down his thin nose at Samira. His eyes narrowed. She tried to stare him down, a queasy feeling twisting in her middle.

"Your family has not consented to this match?" he asked. Behind him, an elderly woman appeared in the doorway. She was tiny, wrinkled and hunched but her eyes looked even sharper than the Imam's. Samira found herself staring a dazzling sapphire necklace the old woman wore.

"My father has not," she replied. Triumph swelled in her middle as she watched concern grow on the Imam's face. *He won't marry us,* she thought. *It's invalid without my father's permission.*

"The groom has shown me a wedding contract signed by Mahmoud Masoud," the Imam said. "He is not your father?"

The girl who'd been doing her makeup and the other girl who'd peeked in before were both in the doorway now, flanking the old woman.

Atallah has a contract? Samira hadn't seen any paperwork change hands. *How long was Mahmoud planning this? It doesn't matter.* "He is my brother."

The Imam's frown grew. The aunt, and the two girls looked shocked. Samira's eyes locked on the old woman. Her face was calm, thoughtful.

"Your father hasn't consented to the match?" the old woman asked.

Annoyance flashed through Samira. "No." *It's done.* She looked at the Imam. *Just say the words so I can go home.*

She could imagine Yacoob Masoud's face when she told him what Mahmoud had done. Her brother would never survive this. The business would finally be hers.

"Does your brother," the old woman asked, "hold a power of attorney from your father?"

Triumph abandoned Samira. She felt like the ground had disappeared from underneath her. Heat flared in her cheeks. She watched the tension drain from the spectators. The Imam's fingers stroked down his chin.

Can I lie to an Imam? She closed her eyes. Mahmoud ran the silk factory. He had a power of attorney so he could handle the family's day-to-day business. *Baba didn't mean for him to use it this way. By lying I would be righting a wrong.* The justifications fell flat on her ears. She knew exactly what Yacoob Masoud would think of lying to an Imam. She opened her eyes. "He does," she said.

The Imam nodded, the matter clearly settled in his view. An annoyed sigh shook through the heavyset woman. The young girls looked disappointed that the drama was over. Muttering something that ended in "saga" to the old woman, the Imam left the room.

The wedding cloak was pulled from her head again. Samira couldn't believe it. She'd been so close. One white lie and her "saga" wouldn't have ended in a wedding to a man she barely knew. *Maybe,* she admitted. All her hopes were built on an assumption that Yacoob Masoud didn't know what Mahmoud was doing. *Surely, he would be here if this was his intention….*

"You're quite a troublemaker, aren't you?" The aunt said, tugging painfully at Samira's curls.

"Give me a moment with the bride." It was the old woman. At her word, the room stilled.

"Of course, Haja." The aunt ducked her head and ushered the younger woman from the room.

Samira's body went tense. *Haja. Not saga.* There was a profound peace in the woman's eyes. Not a naive peace, rather a look that said I have endured all that life can throw at me, and I am still here. *Haja.* A woman who had made her pilgrimage to Mecca was called that — a wise woman who had learned life's lessons. Competence issued from the old woman in waves.

It wasn't uncommon for a woman to be the head of a family. Men often married younger women and those women tended to outlive them. One glance at this woman's eyes told Samira she was the matriarch of Atallah's family.

Shuffling over, the haja sat down on the stool the makeup girl had been using.

"When I was your age, I was nursing a baby."

"And I suppose you think that's how it should be?" Samira asked bitterly.

The old woman let out a slow chuckle. "I like you. Ata chose well."

Samira blinked, pulling her head back into her neck in confusion.

"This is the most terrifying moment of a woman's life," the haja said. She shrugged. "At least until your first child runs into the road."

Samira rolled her eyes. "You talk like this is normal. My father would never allow this."

"Because we are poor?"

Samira made some inarticulate sounds and the woman laughed again. Her eyes twinkled with mischief.

"We are all of us in a cage, Samira. Longing to fly free," the haja said. "Some are trapped by their fear, their obligations, or their social position."

Samira frowned. She could hear echoes of her baba's words coming from this woman's mouth.

"I think you will be someone very important one day," the woman continued. "But a woman is not a man to smash her way out of a cage. She does it with her innate grace and superior cunning. She makes her way one step at a time."

Samira snorted. "It appears my cunning isn't the equal of my brother's today."

"So much the better you be wed to Ata then," the woman smiled, "for your cunning will far outstrip his."

Samira grimaced. "But I don't—"

"You don't want to marry him?"

"I don't want to marry anyone!"

The old woman laughed again. This time she threw her head back and Samira couldn't help but smile.

"Marriage isn't so bad child. Husbands are frustrating, delightful enigmas."

"I want to run a business," Samira continued over the other woman.

The old woman frowned, a sad look in her eyes now. "You were born in Syria, Samira, not in the West."

Samira felt betrayed. For a moment, she'd felt connected to this woman. She'd thought they were understanding each other. *Is that what the years have taught her? The pilgrim's wisdom is defeat?*

"Why should that matter?" she demanded. "I am no less than a woman from Germany or the United States."

"No," the old woman agreed. "You're not. And perhaps, you will use your grace and cunning to make a world where your daughter can run a business." She placed a withered hand on Samira's thigh. Her brows lowered and her cheeks slacked, a sadness in her eyes. "In this, I… your mother… my daughters… All of us have failed you."

Samira flushed. *How dare she talk about my mother!* Just as suddenly, anger turned to understanding. The woman wasn't telling her this was right. *I shouldn't have to marry Atallah. But I am marrying him. What is right and what is real are not always the same thing.* Her shoulders slumped.

"It's not fair."

The old woman nodded, resting a gentle hand on Samira's shoulder. "That doesn't mean it's wrong."

Samira was taken aback. *Did I misunderstand her before? How can it be unfair and right?* Samira frowned and slowly twisted her three fingers in the air.

The old woman took Samira's hand in her own. "On my wedding day, I was terrified. I felt I was still a child. I didn't understand what my husband would expect… but I feared it." The haja gently peeled open Samira's fingers. "My mother brought me a gift. I meant to gift it to my son's wife," the woman's face twisted oddly, "but I did not." She slid something cool and heavy into Samira's palm. "It has always reminded me that there is beauty even in our darkest moments. Don't give up hope, child."

Staring into her palm, Samira saw an antique necklace. A network of linked golden bangles drew the eyes to a startling sapphire. Samira looked up. She felt an involuntary swell of expectation as she met the other woman's eyes.

"There is always room for hope," the haja said as she clasped the necklace around Samira's throat.

So Samira hoped. Short of grabbing a kitchen knife and trying to fight her way free, she tried everything — everything she could think of. But events continued to sweep her onward, relentlessly. Waves of Atallah's friends and family hemmed her in. Through the ceremony and the celebration… there was no escape. Everything brought her to this terrifying room.

Once elegant, the hotel room was decaying. The fourposter bed, was draped with a silk canopy, now moth-eaten and dusty. The wood furniture was as much chip as finish and badly needed polishing. What was created as opulence was made tawdry by disrepair. The air itself smelled of dust and mildew. One corner of the ceiling bore rings, like a dirty toilet bowl, a sign of water leakage years ago. It felt like a terrible metaphor for her life. All of her promise, her intellect, her business savvy, the opportunity of being born into a successful family… all of it left to rot. She was married now. Married to….

Atallah stood before her. He was so excited. He bounced on his toes. He grinned idiotically. Each time he looked at her, his eyes smoldered with lust.

Her mouth felt dry. Fear wormed through her. Yet, some darkness inside her tittered with excitement at those looks. There was something about being wanted. His desire for her had an aphrodisiac effect. It was all buried in layers of horror. She wasn't horrified by him. It was herself. She felt utterly betrayed by herself. Surely someone of her capability should have been able to avoid getting married against her wishes. All of her efforts had yielded nothing. Worse, some part of her was attracted to him. *Is that it? Has my subconscious betrayed me somehow? Do I want this?*

Atallah took a step toward her and she stepped back, trying to maintain the distance between them. He came on relentlessly. There was only so much room. She gave up the dance. He reached for her, lifting the bridal hood from her head and revealing her hair.

Pins and needles of shame stabbed into her cheeks. Her chest constricted and it became hard to breathe. This wasn't a bus full of strangers, it was worse. First, in the cafe, she'd been stripped naked as Mahmoud tore away her covering and now.... She was in a bridal suite with a husband she didn't know. A man her father didn't know. Coming from a wedding ceremony where none of her family had attended. And he was looking at her hair.

Her mind kept cycling back over and over to the wedding. She was married and her father hadn't been there. She'd never wanted to marry. There was no ideally laid out wedding plan in her head. Yet, even as she'd resisted her baba's attempts to see her married, she'd always believed that if she lost that contest it would only draw them closer. He would be an even greater part of her life because she followed his wishes and married. This third scenario, where he was far away and she was with a strange man — she'd never imagined it.

She reached up, trying to cover herself with her hands, but Atallah pushed her hands away. It was gentle, but firm. She still remembered the strength of his grip in the cafe. She didn't want to tempt that part of him.

Shuddering, her mind flitted to the error of judgment that had brought her here. That morning she'd been so confident she knew Mahmoud's limits. *I thought I was safe. If I don't know my own brother's limits, what hope do I have with this stranger?*

He stroked her hair. She shivered. At first it was horror, but then there was that other part. That part that wanted to be touched. *This is nothing like Baba touching my hair.* She told herself it was hormones. It was wrong. But he was handsome. His touch was gentle. His eyes burned for her. Her stomach trembled in a way which was both distressing and delightful. She looked away. There was something terribly erotic about his eyes. *He is so passionate.*

"Shhh," he said. "I—It's okay."

His voice was husky. She felt tension draining from her. His verbal stumble made him more human. His thumb caressed her cheek as his hand wrapped around the back of her head.

He leaned forward, his lips finding hers, soft, quivering. Pins and needles flared in her chest. That part of her that wanted him tried to drown her in the kiss. She jerked back and slapped him across the face as hard as she could. There wasn't any calculation. She didn't think it through. It was a purely instinctual reaction. He staggered back a step. His eyes flashed rage. He took a deep breath. The rage was consumed into that passion in his eyes. He smiled, rubbing the red mark on his cheek.

"I am your husband now." There was nothing sexy about his voice. The boyish stumble was gone.

He reached for her. Something in his voice made her feel cheap, like she was a bauble. The crinkle of a five hundred pound note skittered across her mind, and she wasn't caught by his passion anymore. Even for a poor family, it was an embarrassingly small bride price. She shoved him backwards.

"You are my owner," she accused. "You bought me for a pittance! You don't even have my father's bless—"

Atallah stepped closer, easily controlling her attempts to push him away. It was infuriating. *I'm stronger than this,* she thought. He pulled her body against him. Her cheeks heated again. Her skin prickled with a delightful shame everywhere his body touched hers. *I could give in,* she thought. *This was blessed by an Imam, blessed by the haja.* She closed her eyes, willing it all to stop.

"Was this a pittance?" He raised his eyebrows, his hand touching the sapphire necklace she wore. She felt her cheeks go crimson. She couldn't bring herself to say aloud that she was worth far more than his family heirloom.

"I would not marry a slave, Susu," he said gently. "You are my wife. The favorite daughter of a respected family."

His voice was different this time. Gentle and sincere. It caught her off guard. Her body's treachery already had her reeling. His concern just pushed her further off balance. *It's a trick,* she warned herself. *He's just trying to manipulate you.*

She opened her eyes, seeing his face, close, unavoidable. *Those eyes.* She turned her head, trying to look away. He took her chin in his fingers, turning her eyes back to him. He smiled again. There was something charming and disarming about his smile. He waited. She could feel his chest against hers, the calm rise and fall of his lungs, even as she struggled wildly for oxygen, her heart pounding. *This is embarrassing. I'm making a fool of myself. I can't overpower him.*

Slowly, she stopped fighting. She let her body go limp. Taking slow deep breaths, she tried to settle herself. She met his eyes. Her glare was cold, unmoved by his passion. She would attack him with his words, disassemble him with her intellect. *The haja told me I am more cunning than him.* When he was broken, she would go back to her father. *Baba will see this marriage as the sham it is, he'll help me get things set to rights. Perhaps it will mean I can never have another husband….*

"Were you raised to believe you would pick a husband like some

Western movie?"

The question caught her by surprise. It sounded so much like something her father would ask. Her cheeks heated and she looked away again.

"No," Atallah replied for her. "You are a good Muslim woman. You have always known that your father or brother would choose a husband for you."

She felt her strength sapping away with his words. They were true. Yacoob Masoud wanted her to be happy. But he believed his choice would make her happy. A solid, reliable young man, with good prospects would mean long-term happiness for her. Bits of the conversation flashed through her mind: "But you have career prospects. You can provide. That's the important thing." *Is it possible Mahmoud was doing what Baba asked?* She closed her eyes.

She could remember her baba, sitting on the edge of her bed, stroking her hair, promising her a good match when the time came. She didn't want to marry. But he was convinced he knew better. His words from a few days ago, echoed in her mind. "Samira will always bring honor to our family. She will never break her promises, betray a husband or her family."

Isn't that exactly what I'm contemplating? Mahmoud didn't want to marry Esma, but he was faithful to her for years before he strayed. She felt shame heating her face again, vile prickles crawling over her hairline. *I've not even been married an entire day.*

She felt tears coming again as she opened her eyes. Her silent weeping softened Atallah's features.

"I will be a good wife." The words came out lifeless. Driven neither by fear, fight or lust. She just felt empty.

Atallah nodded, still smiling. "You will honor Allah by being an excellent wife."

She felt a little surge of anger at his correction. *Can he not accept what I offered? He has no idea how hard this is for me!*

He pulled the tie on her wedding cloak and it slipped down her body to pool around her feet. Her muscles clenched and she tried to curl into a ball. She stopped herself. *I am Samira Masoud. This will not break me.* She found a measure of calm. Squaring her shoulders, she met his gaze.

She hadn't imagined marriage, but she had imagined sex. In her fantasies, she was confident. Excited. As she looked into her husband's eyes, she felt only a quiet despair.

He put an arm around her waist again, pulling her body against his. His face leaned in and their lips met. She didn't fight. She tried to dig back out that part of her that wanted him, that wanted this — to unearth the fire and fan it into something. She wanted it to burn up the fear and the exhaustion. She wanted to feel like this was not a defeat.

He took her hand, leading her toward the bed.

Baba sat perched on the edge of Samira's bed. Her blanket, pulled up to her chest, was patterned in smiling cartoon cats — an artifact from her 10th birthday she seemed unable to banish. No fifteen-year-old should still have cartoon cat blankets.

"...I don't want to marry anyone," she explained. "I want to run a business, like Dominic Erbach." She saw the little line form between his eyebrows and quickly added, "Like you."

Baba smiled at her, indulgently.

"Your mother died when you were so young," he explained, patiently patronizing. "There is much honor in being a good wife. Pleasing Allah and a husband, raising children...."

She grimaced and he laughed. It was an easy, simple laugh. It always warmed her. His delightful laugh melted away tensions she didn't know she was carrying. If Baba could laugh, it would be alright.

When her mother died, she'd been sure her baba would never laugh again. He looked so broken. She would hear his weeping at night as she lay awake. But slowly, the stern businessman had been reforged in grief. His eyes had turned from silk and ledgers to two little girls. As he doted on them, his smile had returned. He'd brought laughter back into their home.

She did have memories of her mother. Moments, like when her mother would wake her in the morning or the way her mother would straighten her clothes. She had a vague sense of her mother as the center of their universe, her father, brothers, the entire household seeming to move at her whim. The memories that mattered, though, the ones that most shaped who she was today, those were all of her doting father. The whip-smart business man who turned every set back into a victory.

"When the time comes," he continued, "I know you will make me proud. You will bring much honor to our family by being an exceptional wife."

She crinkled her own brow low over her eyes, scrunching her entire face in distaste. He raised his eyebrows at her in expectation. She wanted to argue — the girl who chose the cartoon covers would have. Nearly grown now, she knew better. Slowly she nodded.

"Yes, Baba."

His eyes twinkled in response to her words. He leaned down and kissed her forehead. Rising slowly, his knees creaking, he crossed over to Yasmeen. Samira's sister was asleep. Her chest rose and fell peacefully. Baba bent down, kissing her on the forehead just as he had Samira. He moved to the door.

"I love you, Baba," Samira said.

He gave her a smile and flipped off the light.

Atallah sprawled on the bed, his shirtless torso rising and falling where he emerged from the covers. In sleep he looked utterly at peace.

Samira turned her eyes away, looking out the window. She could see herself reflected in the glass. Even redressed in her abaya, she felt naked. Atallah was peaceful, but she felt only turmoil. *What have I done? How could I let myself come to this place?* In her mind, she knew she was a married woman now, but in her heart she felt dirty. All of this felt like some terrible sin.

The room smelled. It was an unfamiliar scent, the smell of their joining. She shivered.

I've done nothing wrong. Sleeping with her husband wasn't wrong. It didn't matter that she hadn't chosen him. It didn't matter that her baba wasn't at the wedding. Only it did. *It matters to me.*

She looked out the window, more and more people rushed past in the street, one story below her. Did they struggle? Were their lives as complex as hers had become? When she'd awakened this morning, she was innocent, pure. Everything was possible for her. She would be a CEO or a business owner. Now… now she was… a married woman. Her mouth turned down at the thought, the sour expression faintly reflected in the glass seemed disapproving. She had responsibilities that before this moment she had never really considered. What would be expected of her when Atallah woke up?

The conflict in her head found a voice. She could hear the cries of discontent. Like an angry crowd. It was so real to her she would swear it was coming from the streets. The people rushing past were all headed to the center of her pain and frustration. They were rallying to come for her — the wanton woman — the whore. She had defiled Islam and….

She took a deep breath, slowly sighing it out. Her eyes closed and she sought a calm place. Unknotting her fists was a struggle but she relaxed her hands, stretching out her fingers. She was a creature of reason and logic. These fluttery, panicked feelings belonged to someone else. She tried to exhale them away. The voices continued to chant. The cries grew louder and louder.

And who can blame them? She wondered. Lies filled her head. Imaginings of Atallah forcing her, but he hadn't. Oh, he'd held her, kissed her, forced her to look into his eyes. But then, he'd asked. And she'd agreed. It was the agreement she was ashamed of.

She looked back at the sleeping form of her husband. Seeing him at the factory, she'd thought he was creepy. His gaze was too intense. But now, she saw him differently. He *was* intense. He was like a bonfire. Confident, strong and utterly certain. She'd fumbled her way like a child and he'd never batted an eye at her inexperience. Competence was always what she'd most admired in herself. It was what drew her to Dominic Erbach. She appreciated people who knew what they wanted and went after it with intensity. *That's why I hate Mahmoud,* she realized. *For him the business is all obligation.* It shocked her to realize that Atallah wasn't a man like her brother. He was a man like Dominic Erbach. *A man like me,* she thought. That gaze that she'd found so creepy was his intensity, his passion, bubbling out of him.

She felt heat suffusing her cheeks as she thought of their lovemaking and she closed her eyes, trying to blot it out. *It's all a manipulation,* she told herself. *It's part of his game. Getting you to agree, to admire him, that's all part of his sick need to be…* She couldn't find an end to the thought. She didn't know what her evil caricature of Atallah wanted.

The voices continued to condemn her. For the first time, the oddity of it struck her. Her emotions taking on an audibility. Angry voices demanding a reckoning.

"They are protesting."

She started. Atallah stood at her shoulder, looking out the window. He was completely naked. She felt her cheeks heat again. He turned, grinning at her. Delight sparkled in his eyes. It was contagious and it shot through her. She felt something. A connection to him that she didn't feel before. It blossomed in her chest like a fragile flower, a tiny bud of hope.

He rushed for his pants, hopping awkwardly into them. *He looks ridiculous.* Somehow the thought seemed to strengthen the bond she felt with him.

"We will force Assad to reform the government." He stumbled, and then righted himself, buttoning his pants. "Make a better Syria." He hit her full force with that grin again and it warmed her. It disappeared in a flash of shirt pulling over his head, and she missed it. Longed for it. "Come on."

His vision swam in her head. *A reformed Syria.* It was bigger than running her father's silk factory. Important, meaningful — it would change so many lives. Transform her nation. *But is it possible?* Atallah's eyes said it was. *And he's inviting me to do it with him? Not just a wife, a partner in something great.*

The idea was like a balloon in her chest. It filled her to bursting and just kept growing. She was not just some wife. *We're going to change the world.*

He was reaching for her hand, his momentum moving toward the door. She hesitated. Her uncertainty was fading. This was her husband. His smile was warm and charming. They would transform Syria together. Running a business suddenly seemed a very small destiny indeed. *I will exalt you.*

"A change is coming, Susu," his voice was dramatic, wild with passion, "and I will—" She frowned at his 'I.' He stopped himself and looked at her again, his eyes crinkling as his smile grew wider. "*We* will be a part of it."

He leaned over, grabbing her wedding cloak from the floor. Straightening, he threw it around her shoulders. She reached up, situating it onto her head as he pulled her toward the door. She threw her head back, laughing. The hood slipped back and she grabbed it. She was a bride. Her wedding feast would be a freedom march, and her boardroom would be a new Syria.

They crossed through the door into a new world.

five

Mahmoud: Susu's Dead

As he approached the house, Mahmoud felt good. He was strong. He moved with purpose and gravitas. Today, he had defeated his most bitter rival. He'd taken the silk scarf she had ruined and torn it more, adding blood. The process was painful. Every rip seemed to tear at his soul. *It was a work of art.* He told himself that's why it hurt.

He must remove all hope that she would ever return. As far as the family would know, Susu was dead. Struck by a car — no a bus, a large bus! Her body was too mangled to bring home, the sight too gruesome for Yacoob's eyes.

As he stepped through Baba's front door into the hallway, he froze. Something shifted inside him. The narrative he was reciting to himself suddenly had a hollow echo. Words he'd planned to say sounded false in his mind. Steps away from Yacoob Masoud, his imagining of what was about to happen took on a whole new color.

Yacoob would see through this. He would demand answers, details. Heat rose into Mahmoud's face and sweat beaded his brow. Then his perspective shifted again. If he was to fail, if eliminating Samira would not win the attention and affection he craved from his father — and suddenly he was certain it would not — then the price was too high. *What have I done?*

Mahmoud stood in the hallway. From his vantage, he could peek into the living room, but was unlikely to be seen. He needed to enter, but he couldn't. *What am I going to say?*

The sounds of the television babbled in the background. A news program, something about the "Arab spring" as they kept calling it. He frowned. *Freedom is a wild dream,* he thought. It was the dream that led him to sell his sister to a man he hardly knew. *A dowry. I did not sell her.* The anguish that now ripped him from the inside was far greater than he'd imagined. *Soon, these freedom fighters will learn, evil grants no quarter.* The thought was dramatic and melancholy.

He could see Yacoob, his baba, sitting in his usual chair, wrapped in a blanket, looking frail and old. But Yacoob was animated by the pixie in his lap. Somehow the old man was made young by her peculiar magic. It was Yasmeen, his youngest half-sister, of course. However, some trick of the light made her Samira, years ago. Before she was a threat. When Mahmoud still had hope.

"...and that is when we first started making silk. So you, my little Yasmeen, are part of a tradition that stretches back..."

Mahmoud couldn't see the photo album in Yacoob's lap, but he knew it was there. He could tell that story — had told that story to his own sons. He straightened his back. The Masoud family had a history of strength. He would not be weak. He'd made his choice and he would face it, head-on. He took a step forward, and another, and then he was passing through the doorway, moving into the living room.

"Susu?" Yacoob looked up. *Of course, he asks for her,* Mahmoud thought bitterly. When Yacoob saw it was Mahmoud, his smile turned. His brow lowered. *Yes. Your disappointing son is here.*

"Yasmeen," Mahmoud said, "go and play in your room."

She didn't move, of course. She was just like Samira. After a moment, Yacoob ushered her off of his lap.

"Go, my sweet child."

Yacoob followed her out of the room with his eyes, the long silence stretching. The only interruption, the continuous prognostication from the television. Mahmoud struggled to hold himself together. He fought to find the right words. *Susu is gone. Susu is dead. You can't choose her over me anymore. She is gone. You forced me to this.* Mahmoud stepped closer, his hands extending. He held out the scarf. Not news from Tunisia or Libya he realized, the news was reporting local protests. Local violence. *Assad will crush their dreams of freedom,* he thought sadly.

"What is this?" Yacoob snapped. "Is this Samira's?" He looked up at Mahmoud. "Where is she? What have you done?"

Mahmoud closed his eyes. It was a dream to imagine Yacoob would blame some other circumstance for Samira's disappearance. If her stupid German business man had come to the house and taken her away in his jet, Yacoob would have blamed Mahmoud. *But it is my fault,* he thought. *I did this.*

Yacoob could not have missed the blood that stained the scarf or the rips, marring the perfect silk. Destroying the work of art had been painful. It was harder than leaving Samira at the cafe. Each tear forced him to more fully contemplate exactly what he'd done to Samira and to himself. Mahmoud wanted there to be no doubts, no hope that she would return. He turned his head, looking at the television, and Yacoob followed his gaze.

"…were killed tonight as violence broke out in the streets of Latakia…"

Yacoob began to quiver. The photo album dropped from his lap, its photos spraying across the floor.

There. It's done, Mahmoud thought.

"Why were you not with her? You should have been protecting her!" Yacoob sobbed, his words already distorted and mangled by his grief.

I should have been protecting her.

Slowly, Mahmoud laid the scarf across Yacoob's lap. He sank to his knees. He saw his hands, stained crimson. It wasn't her blood. He knew it wasn't. His friend ran a butcher shop. But… there was blood on his hands. *It could be her blood.* He would never see his sister again. He had sold her…

He didn't feel clever. Justifications shredded like paper. But there was no going back. By now, Ata would have defiled her. Her life was changed forever. Mahmoud had changed it.

He bowed his head, unable to look Yacoob in the eyes. A shaky hand found his head, tangling in his hair and then slowly clenched, tighter and tighter until it felt like the old man would tear out Mahmoud's hair. Mahmoud embraced the pain. *I deserve this.* He felt the fingers in his hair and visions of his own hand tearing at Samira's head flashed through his mind.

Yacoob pulled, and Mahmoud's head came back. He looked into his baba's eyes. Tears flowed freely down Yacoob's cheeks. He wasn't animated by grief. His face quivered with rage.

"Why do you only bring me pain and failure?" Mahmoud closed his eyes, but Yacoob jerked his hair again, and Mahmoud met his eyes, tears of his own flowing down his face. It wasn't the physical pain or even the words. He had done this terrible thing for one purpose — so that Yacoob would finally treat him as a son. He was the heir. He worked hard. He fought for his place in this family. Yet, no matter how he succeeded, no matter how he slaved, Yacoob saw only failure. He'd thought, with Samira out of the way, it would be different. But that wasn't true. This was simply another failure to be laid at Mahmoud's feet. Only this one, he richly deserved. It broke him. He wept. They were not wild sobs. Even in grief, he could not allow himself that freedom. Quiet tears tracked down his cheeks, bearing silent witness to a pain deeper than any he could imagine. *What must it be like to lose a child?* Yacoob had made it look easy, casting aside his brothers, but the old man's grief at losing Susu would be bitter. *How does Allah punish someone who steals the child of another?*

Yacoob held the scarf in his fist, shaking it under Mahmoud's nose. "How are we to mourn a scarf?" he demanded.

And he was right. Alive or dead, a good son would have returned with his sister. If he could recover a bloody scarf, he could recover a body. His plan was to eliminate all of Yacoob's hope that she would return. But instead, he'd eliminated all of his own hope that things could be better — that he could have a real father, and Yacoob a real son. So he wept all the harder.

six

Mahmoud: Tala's Wedding

Spring 2013

Mahmoud laughed as he worked his way through the crowd. All around him were friends, neighbors, well-wishers. Everyone was smiling. Loud music trilled through the celebration, and people danced. There was an energy and an explosive joy to the room. Of their own volition, his shoulders moved to the rhythm of the music.

He turned to his friend, Nabil. Friends since the earliest days of their schooling, they'd been through a lot together. Mahmoud was at Nabil's wedding, by his side when he learned he could never have children, and years later, he stood by his friend after Nabil's wife died. Nabil similarly was always a part of Mahmoud's life, even to the point of taking in Mahmoud and his family when they left Latakia to get out from under the thumb of Yacoob Masoud. Mahmoud was incredibly grateful that Allah in his wisdom had granted him such a generous and loyal friend.

Grotesquely fat Nabil licked his lips as a young woman walked past him. *And yet, we are two very different men*, Mahmoud thought. For all of Nabil's flaws, Mahmoud couldn't be angry at the man who was supporting and celebrating Mahmoud and his family.

"You've outdone yourself, my friend," Mahmoud cheered. "Thank you. This is incredible!"

Nabil gestured across the room at Mahmoud's son, Ismaeel. Mahmoud felt a swell of pride. Twenty-six years old, in the prime of health, Ismaeel danced with a beautiful girl in an extravagant bridal cloak. Tala was nineteen. A young woman of character from a good family. Mahmoud smiled.

"You are my closest friend," Nabil said. "I could not deny your oldest son a celebration for his wedding."

But you should never have had to. The move to Aleppo had been difficult. Mahmoud's whole life was in Latakia. There was no job for him here. They lived in Nabil's guest house like beggars. He kept his finger on the pulse of the silk factory — the new manager was a friend. But, after Samira, there was no consoling Yacoob — no path forward for their relationship. Every decision Mahmoud made just enraged the old man. There was nothing for it, Mahmoud had taken his family and moved. The Masoud ring was still on his finger. Yacoob had not disowned him. Someday, the old man would die, and Mahmoud could return home. But those were thoughts for a sad day. *This is a day for celebrating,* he reminded himself.

He clapped Nabil on the shoulder. "You throw a party like no one else, Nabil. Look!" He swept his arms wide, turning his body to take in all the revelers. He even saw his brother, Ali, laughing across the room. *How long since any of us have seen Ali?* "Everyone is happy. For today, there is no war."

Women in bright silks idled together in little bouquets. Smiles and laughter were everywhere.

The usually jovial Nabil's brow crinkled in a frown. It looked comedic on his moon-shaped face. His head turned to take in an older man, keeping to himself in a corner of the room, glowering at the happy young lovers.

"Not everyone is happy, I think."

Mahmoud followed his gaze to Basem. Tala's father was a difficult man. Mahmoud frowned. Working out the bridal contract with Basem had been a painful experience. *But this isn't Nabil's responsibility. He's done enough.* "I'll go talk to him."

Jaber, Mahmoud's middle son, emerged from the crowd. Like Ismaeel and Mahmoud, Jaber was tall and elegantly slim. He had a proud face and a way of watching the room without being a participant.

"How does it feel to have a married brother?" Nabil asked him. "Perhaps you will bed a bride of your own soon."

Mahmoud saw the smile Jaber gave Nabil, wooden and insincere. He worried sometimes about Jaber. It was easy to give offense when you saw yourself as better than everyone else. *Today is not the day to chastise Jaber. Let him celebrate how he sees fit.*

Mahmoud moved toward Basem, steeling himself for the confrontation. The man was prickly.

"Inshallah," he heard Jaber say behind him. He did not think Jaber thought much of Allah's will, nor was the young man hoping for a bride. Jaber's taste ran toward less reputable women. Mahmoud wondered if that was a consequence of living with Nabil. *A problem for another day*, Mahmoud thought, returning his attention to Basem.

"Your daughter looks happy." The girl, indeed, was glowing. White teeth flashed around the room in a contagious grin whenever she could tear her gaze away from her groom.

Basem turned to Mahmoud, his expression grave.

"So it appears," Basem replied, his voice was resigned, dispassionate. *Can he find joy in nothing?* "Tala is rash, and your son is a menace."

Mahmoud's brows lowered and he felt passion boil in his chest. Despite Basem's broad shoulders, Mahmoud was by far the taller. He took a deep breath, drawing himself up and looking down his nose at Basem. Tala's father had a barrel-chested power barely concealed in the weight of middle age. As much as Mahmoud wished to put the man in his place, it would be shameful if their conflict grew physical. He needed to be the bigger man. Squaring his shoulders, Mahmoud forced a smile.

"He will surprise you." Mahmoud's face hurt. He felt the smile was an impressive effort. Esma once told him he could charm anyone when he smiled the right way.

"I think he will do many things," Basem looked at Ismaeel and Tala, frowning. "I don't think I will be surprised by any of them." He turned back to Mahmoud, his expression piercing. "Just remember your promise."

Mahmoud clapped Basem on the shoulder. It was a friendly gesture, though Mahmoud slammed his hand down harder than needed. "Don't worry, old man. Your grandchild will inherit the Masoud silk empire." Mahmoud gestured extravagantly to match his words. "Your daughter is married to my eldest son," he let the garnet on his finger catch the light, "and I am the heir to the family fortune. It is done."

Basem titled his head and made a click sound. Mahmoud felt

another flash of irritation. *Nothing pleases this man!*

"There is no child," Basem pronounced darkly. "It is not done." Mahmoud felt a cold shiver run through him. His joy and enthusiasm was rapidly slipping away.

Why would he say something like that? He did not believe Basem was a djinn pronouncing evil prophecies, but he couldn't shake the finality of Basem's statement. It felt like a curse.

With effort, Mahmoud tried a laugh. "The wedding was just today. You can't expect a child yet," Mahmoud spoke in tones of mock scandal.

"And where is the patriarch of the Masoud clan? Is he not here to bless this marriage?" Basem turned a hawk-like gaze on Mahmoud, who flinched back. It felt like a blow to Mahmoud. *Baba should be here. He should be hosting this celebration!* Instead, Nabil did everything. He wanted to growl and gnash his teeth. He wanted to eject Basem from the party for even mentioning Yacoob Masoud. *I cannot chase the bride's father from her wedding.*

"My father and sister are in Latakia. He…" Mahmoud struggled to find the right words. *He doesn't care. He shames me. He is a hateful old man. I should not have to make excuses for him.* Mahmoud was about to say that the journey was too dangerous when he again saw Ali, who had come from Latakia that morning. "He does not travel."

"Unless it's important?" Basem smiled as he fired his parting shot, and walked away, not awaiting Mahmoud's reply. Mahmoud glared at his back, violent fantasies skipping across his thoughts. He was interrupted by Ahmad, his youngest son. At twenty-two, Ahmad was a man, but it was hard to remember. He was the youngest. He had his mother's soft features and hadn't achieved Mahmoud's height like his brothers.

"I heard Nabil say that Jaber will also be married soon. When will I have a bride, Baba?"

Mahmoud turned. Ahmad was gazing dreamily across the room at Tala, his older brother's wife. The girl was stunning, especially when she smiled. Mahmoud waved a hand, clicking his tongue. If the boy wanted to be taken seriously, he needed to act as a grown man, not moon about like a child.

Mahmoud glared again at Basem, now smiling and chatting with one of Tala's aunts. Basem's grandchild would be the Al-Masoud heir. Mahmoud would keep his promise. But he wished fervently that something dark would befall Basem in the meantime.

Absently, he noted Ahmad was still lingering beside him. Waiting for an answer. Mahmoud glanced at Nabil, who was drooling over a serving woman half his age. The poor girl was struggling to escape him, but Nabil was oblivious to her discomfort. Mahmoud sighed. He couldn't recover his joy now. All he could think of was Basem and Yacoob Masoud. *Am I the only man who cares for the happiness of his children?* "Never listen to anything Uncle Nabil tells you about women, my son."

seven

Samira: Life with Ata

The tea pot's slow rumble drowned out the male voices in the next room. They became little more than a humming. Samira let out a slow sigh. She was exhausted. Closing her eyes, she let her breath come and go, losing herself for a moment in steam, bubbles and humming. She was wary of dreams. Dreams had betrayed her — deceiving her with promises that would never be realized. But she could still close her eyes and float. Not a dream, just a moment of pleasant nothing.

She opened her eyes, catching her reflection in a bit of tarnished silver on the tea pot. Though only a distorted fragment, the image prompted her to look at her worn clothes. Everything was different now. There was no father to spoil her. For a fleeting moment she considered Mahmoud's view of her. She had been pampered, entitled, arrogant.... She bowed her head. Her fist clenched painfully. None of it excused what he had done. The anger slipped away, demanding energy she didn't have to give.

These years had cost her so much. *Our house is always full, why do I feel so alone?*

The tea pot warbled its victory. Water, once cold, was now piping hot. She poured it into a succession of cups on a tray. Some of the tea dribbled from the pot, running down the spout and dripping around the counter and tray. She set it down with another sigh. Everything was a struggle now. Ata worked hard, but there was never enough.

What wisdom would the haja give me? Samira wondered often what the old woman would think of her. *I've joined her list of women who have failed.* Most of Ata's family had been killed as the rebels and the Army tussled over the Salaheddine district of the city.

She mopped up the spilled tea and lifted the heavy tray. Taking a deep breath, she lifted her head, straightened her back, and reminded herself she was Samira Masoud.

"He is dropping bombs on our people in Damascus!" Ata's voice, incensed. He always was when he spoke of Assad. It was personal for him. He blamed Assad for battle that killed his family. His grandmother, his parents, his aunt, those young girls — most of the family she'd met at the wedding she'd never seen again. Neither would he. The passion that first attracted her had grown in intensity as Ata focused more and more on the revolution to overthrow Syria's oppressive leader. Sometimes, Samira found it taxing, but as often she was caught up in it, won by his fire.

She walked into the room with the tea tray. Their apartment was cramped and shabby. The men who filled the living room were young. Precisely trimmed beards and hair warred with threadbare clothing. It wasn't shabby-chic, more the flailing of the desperate. When you could control almost nothing, you took care of the things you could. The war was making life hard everywhere. It was dangerous to travel outside of their small neighborhood. Businesses struggled. Jobs were scarce. You never knew which homes would be destroyed by the explosives. They fell from the sky, flew up from the ground, were blasted out of tanks. So many ways to suddenly die.

Curfews gave the streets to the soldiers and militia men battling for the soul of Syria. Gunfire was normal. The internet, water and electricity came and went seemingly at random. Each day prices climbed higher, while salaries remained the same — if your job still existed and you could reach it. Even food was difficult to come by at times. Plans were vapor. It was hard to keep living when everything was constantly in flux.

At the same time, Samira was proud of how entrepreneurial her people were. The man who lived across the hall had worked at a factory making shoes. It wasn't safe to travel to the factory, so now, each morning, he sold coffee to the neighborhood. She didn't know how he survived, but he wasn't giving up. The black market was thriving. If you had the money and were willing to take the risk, you could get just about anything.

"We cannot stand for it," Ata continued. He sat at the head of their small dining table. Three young men sat around the table with him, two more on the couch, another on a small stool in the corner. There were even two young men standing. Samira scanned their faces. Bashir and Gamal were regulars, devoted to Ata. The others were unfamiliar, but that wasn't uncommon these days. Ata seemed to know everyone, and Samira couldn't keep track of all of his friends. "We will forge a new Caliphate, just as Abu Bakr is teaching."

Samira felt an icy line run down her back. She didn't like the teachings of Abu Bakr Al-Baghdadi. The man didn't want justice, he wanted to slake his hatred in blood. His teachings were poison. Hearing her husband revere them always made her cold. The tea cups clinked as her hands trembled. She quickly put the tray down on the table. Ata reached out, stilling her shaking hand with his own. He looked into her eyes, smiling.

She couldn't help smiling back. His passion for her was also growing, and it lit his eyes. The look warmed her and made her feel a little embarrassed. She blushed and then felt more embarrassed thinking of all the men in the room watching this intimate moment. Ata turned back to his audience withdrawing his hand. She could breathe again. Fear of Abu Bakr need not trouble her. It would be okay. Ata loved her. Everything would be okay. She struggled to control the smile that wanted to erupt from her.

Ata's fist slammed down on the table, making all the tea cups and Samira jump.

"It is wrong to cower in fear of this tyrant!" Everyone in the room was alert, eager to hear what Ata would say next. "Assad." He said the name with contempt. She wished he would speak more quietly. What if the neighbors heard and reported him? It was already illegal to gather like this — for Sunnis. Alawites could still meet together. "We are men, obliged to protect our women and our children. We must show the people they have power over their oppressors!"

There was little room in the tiny apartment, but Samira wanted to hear Ata's speech. He'd been promising something new tonight, teasing her about something he would reveal. She moved to stand in the doorway, near the small kitchen. She liked how passionate he was about seeing her cared for. She knew it came out of his love for her. But some small part of her still burned to run a business, to stand on her own and show she didn't need him or anyone else to give her value. *I am a woman to be reckoned with.* She looked around at the bedraggled apartment, and that voice grew a little more quiet.

It wasn't that Ata didn't include her in his grand plans for Syria. She was invited to every meeting — expected to attend. But her role wasn't to administrate his grand schemes. She was here to make tea and bake cookies. Hospitality was a critical piece of Ata's work, it just wasn't the piece she would have chosen for herself.

The men around the room were nodding, grunting in approval.

"There is a checkpoint near the bus station, where the tyrant's men are always harassing women, demanding their names." Samira knew the spot. Ata had been ranting about it for weeks. It sometimes struck her as odd the lengths to which men would go to prevent humiliation. It wasn't as though women typically didn't have ID cards with their names. Many of the soldiers, though, weren't officials. They were thugs. Street toughs with guns. They would use a woman's name to shame her man and her family. They might even kidnap a girl to show that her husband or father was too impotent to protect her. That sort of shame was enough to destroy a family.

Ata continued, "We will take a stand against them."

The last part was new. Up to that moment, Ata had talked about protests, and fighting Assad's propaganda by spreading the truth. She looked around the room, uncertain what she thought. There was a chorus of affirmations and nodding. The men exchanged smiles and little jabbing punches. *Well, they like the idea. But what does he mean?*

A man standing near Samira, she thought his name was Farid, shouted, "We will kill them all!"

Samira's eyes went wide. She looked at Ata, but from this angle she could only see the back of his head. She was frozen waiting for his reaction. Desperately, she hoped he would calm Farid down. *Tell him to be quiet. Urge them to moderation.*

Another man shouted, "For the Caliphate!" Samira didn't look to see who it was. She only cared what Ata would say. She prayed softly to Allah. *Please, calm them down.* A worm of fear wriggled in her chest that he wouldn't. Perhaps, this was exactly the reaction he was aiming for.

"Assad will pay!" Another faceless shout. Ata's head bobbed. He was nodding. Why wouldn't he stop this? Surely he knew this would bring the authorities to their door. They already lived in constant fear. At any moment Ata or even Samira might be arrested for words they'd spoken. This would make their already difficult life impossible. He needed to stop them. Someone, needed to stop them.

"How?" The word came out of Samira's mouth before she'd thought. Every eye in the room turned to her. The men went silent. Then their eyes went to Ata. She knew what they were thinking: would he let his woman question them? She wanted to be confident in his answer, but she wasn't. Unable to breathe, she waited for his reaction.

He turned to her. His eyes were piercing, and she felt like they bored deep into the heart of her. His lips slowly curved up and he nodded to her. It was an encouragement to continue. She let her breath go, feeling tension evacuate her body in a sudden, heady rush. He wanted her to speak. He would listen. All of them would listen. But she needed to be smart. Even a supportive husband like Ata would not like to be lectured and told what to do by a woman. She needed to play dumb. Ask questions. Guide them to the reality.

"How will you overcome soldiers? Men with training and experience."

She felt more then saw the change her words wrought on the room. Postures hunched and the thrill soured. She wasn't sure if it soured into hostility toward her or into a doused realism about their plan. She hoped it was the latter. *They need to see this for what it is.*

Ata took a breath, and she knew he was going to answer her. He was going to give them hope they could succeed. She couldn't let him.

She stepped quickly forward, putting her hands on his shoulders, lowering her voice. They would still hear, but she needed him to know this was for him, not his friends.

"We could go to Europe. There is safety there. Opportunity. I heard in Germany everyone is free and paid lavishly. There is no war—"

Ata cut her off by placing a hand on hers. She wasn't sure what about the gesture stopped her from speaking, but it did. There was a feeling of command that radiated from him. She feared it, but she also felt in awe of it. *I want so badly to be able to command and be obeyed as he does.* Wordlessly, Ata clicked his tongue several times. The tension in the room solidified. She could feel it, like a weight in the air.

"You are believing lies, Susu," he said. Sadness colored his voice, regret at a broken world. She felt his words knotting in her belly like sickness. "The Westerners hate us. There is no freedom or riches there. Not for us. If we fled to Europe they would leave us in cages, and treat us with contempt." He turned in his chair, looking into her eyes. "If you somehow found a job, they would make you a slave, doing work they don't want to do for wages they would not pay their dogs." The words sunk deeply into her. She knew them. They were Abu Bakr's words. But they still settled on her with a weight that stole away her hope.

Ata turned back to the men, raising his voice. "They hate us because we have truth. We have Allah. His righteous jihad is our salvation."

"Please, Ata," she begged him. "Do not hate—"

"Shhh, Susu." His voice was gentle. He met her eyes and she saw his deep love. Even as she was consumed with fear, his eyes still held a promise of his passion for her. He stood, putting his arms around her. He pulled her face to his chest. "It is not hate." She wanted so badly for that to be true. "It is correction." She swallowed. Correction and justice were the sorts of words Assad used to justify wiping out whole neighborhoods with bombs and tanks. Ata continued, "Like a father, punishing his child for running into the street so he will not be killed." He leaned back, tipping her head to him. "If we let Assad kill and murder our people, we have committed a terrible injustice. There must be a cost."

She nodded. It was reluctant. She didn't want to concede this point. Fear of where this would take them still gripped her, but he was right. If the soldiers continued to kill and murder where would it end? Someone had to stand up to them. She just wished it didn't have to be her husband.

Tears started to blur her vision. She wanted to flee the room, hide in the kitchen. *When did I become this wilting flower?* She hated this part of herself. This girl who wanted to run and hide was a mockery of her self-image.

Ata turned back to the room, one arm still encircling her waist. She couldn't escape while he was holding her. She didn't really want to. She needed the reassurance his arm provided. *Another weakness.* A tear tracked down her face.

"We must take the soldiers by surprise. We need a distraction."

Samira reached up a hand to her face, wiping a tear from her eye. Her raised hand drew Ata's attention. He looked surprised. For a moment he stared at her slack jawed. There was concern in his eyes. Slowly, some thought worked itself out in his mind and then a grin exploded onto his face. He turned to the men, beaming with pride. *What did I do?* Hope filled her. *He saw my tears, my fear.* She couldn't help it. Ata's pride was so evident and contagious. *He will be cautious.*

"Do you see the courage of my bride?" His voice boomed. She felt it in her chest, warm and exciting. "She volunteers to face soldiers for our people!" Suddenly, excitement turned to horror. "She will be our distraction. If she will fight, who are we to turn aside?"

The men erupted in cheers. Samira felt numb. She couldn't tell him he'd misunderstood. Not now. His pride was on the line. In front of all of his friends, she couldn't shame him. She took a shuddering breath. He beamed at her again and she tried to smile back. She felt like her eyes were too wide open. *This has to be a dream,* she thought. *This can't be real.* She swallowed vomit, the burning bile choking her.

"It will be okay," he whispered. "I will keep you safe."

eight
Samira: Checkpoint

Samira tried to keep her cool as she walked down the street, fist clutched to white-knuckles on the small shopping bag she held. The streets were almost empty. On her left, she saw a man furtively pop his head out the door of a shop, and then move quickly away down the street. That was normal now. People moving fearfully at great need. What she was doing, striding down the street with a shopping bag, felt like insanity. Her loose, plain abaya seemed thinner than ever. Scant protection against the giant guns cradled in the arms of the waiting soldiers.

At an intersection one block ahead, a group of armed soldiers paced around concrete barricades. The bus station sat just to the right of the barricades, its cavernous lot like a missing tooth on the smile of the city. As Samira walked forward, a bus pulled into the station. She watched the soldiers, their attention diverted by the arrival of the vehicle. A few people emerged. In earlier times the bus would be full, but now, only the desperate were out and about at all.

She returned her attention to the soldiers. She could remember Ata's instructions.

"Approach the men," he'd told her. "Ask them if they know a place that has fresh mutton today."

It was audacious. Insanely bold. Who would walk up to Assad's goons looking for mutton? *Only someone with nothing to hide. Someone with no fear.* Samira took a deep breath. *I will be that woman. A woman with no fear.*

A man crossed the street from the bus. A hissing sound followed a rumble and the bus pulled away, escaping down the same street Samira traveled but in the opposite direction.

The soldiers stopped the man. He showed them his papers. They shoved him, jostled him about. Samira couldn't hear what was said, but the man's posture screamed weary resignation. The soldiers let him go. A woman followed. She was already hunching, a precious bundle clutched to her chest. She was trying to make herself smaller as she walked wide of the soldiers.

The armed men moved, adjusting their positions to surround her.

"What's your name?" One of the men called in a sweet, friendly voice. They moved like wolves, circling.

Another followed, "Are you married?"

She tried to turn around, go back the way she'd come. Only there was a soldier there as well. He grabbed a hold of her, spinning her around. She was trembling, her eyes closed.

As the man laid hands on other woman, Samira stiffened. Her expression grew grim. She hated what was about to happen. She didn't want to be a part of it. But right in front of her, she was seeing why it had to occur. Ata was right. Someone had to stop this.

"They will demand to see your papers," Ata had told her. "Be slow taking them out. Act as though you can't remember where you put them."

Samira took another step forward. She watched as the woman tried to pull away from the soldier, who gripped her arm. He jerked her back and the bundle she clutched to her chest fell. Samira's heart lurched. She could imagine the baby hitting the rough concrete. Blood. Pain. Screams. Instead there was a puff of white cloud. *Flour,* Samira realized. *Precious enough in these times.*

The leader of the soldiers, the man who spoke first, stepped forward, scooping the ruined flour back into the woman's torn bag and held it out to her. The other soldier released her and she scurried away.

"They will attempt to detain you. Scream. Make as big a scene as you can."

Samira stepped into the crossing street. She froze, terrified as a bus barreled in front of her. She'd been so distracted she hadn't noticed the sound. It passed so close, she could feel the air on her face. On the side of the bus, a giant billboard showed a picture of Dominic Erbach, looking intractable in his power suit. The elegant Arabic script read, *The Power of Different*.

She stood rigid, eyes following the bus that had almost killed her. It rolled into the station and stopped. The doors opened. A few men and women emerged. A strange man, familiar, but no one she knew — or maybe someone she'd met? She couldn't remember. He stepped into the open door of the bus and turned, looking right into her eyes. He smiled, waving for her to come join him on the bus, and then disappeared into the vehicle's dark interior.

She blinked. Her heart was pounding, the misunderstanding with the flour, the near miss with the bus, the specter of the gun-wielding soldiers a few steps away — she was overwhelmed. All she could think about was the previous night. Ata. The memory filled her thoughts.

After Ata had declared the decoy and his friends departed, Samira gathered the empty tea cups and other detritus left in the wake of Ata's meeting. She tried to control her frustration. She felt like a rubber band stretched between being a good wife — doing what her husband expected of her — and being smart and moral. Why did Allah allow such choices?

She sighed, slumping over the table, the tray she was holding thunking onto the wooden surface in a cacophony of rattling porcelain.

Ata looked up from his phone. She could see his worry, his concern for her.

"Ata, I don't..."

In a moment, he was out of his chair, stepping close to her. He touched her jaw with a finger, tipping her face up to him. It was a gesture so familiar... a comfort. He met her eyes. She saw his love and desire for her, burning in his deep brown eyes.

"What is it, Susu?" His tone was light, teasing. "Are you afraid? The fiercest woman I know?"

It wasn't fear. She was afraid. Any intelligent person would be afraid, thinking about attacking armed soldiers with nothing more than a shopping bag and a flimsy story about mutton. That wasn't what was eating away at her insides.

"We shouldn't kill these men."

Ata stroked her cheek tenderly. His touch was a balm to her, melting away the tension in her body. She leaned into his touch, and he pulled their bodies together. They shared a smile.

"It is for them to decide, Susu. You need only ask them for help." That wasn't what she wanted to hear. She turned. He lowered his chin, chasing her eyes as she tried to look away. He was right. She wouldn't be killing anyone. "If they behave with honor," he continued, his tone growing more serious, "no one will harm them."

Her mouth turned down and she pulled away from him, returning to the tray of empty cups. "But they won't," she muttered.

Ata stepped behind her, wrapping his arms around her waist again. He pulled her to him, his breath hot on her neck. She turned in his arms, and he swept the hijab from her head. Her long hair flowed freely down her back. He ran his hands through it, tenderly. A glance into his eyes turned her cheeks red. She couldn't hold back a grin. He kissed her. Passion and fire tangled together like his fingers in her hair.

He pulled back, leaving her breathless. She wasn't ready for the kiss to end. His lips were still achingly close as he spoke. "You must do this for me. For Syria."

Syria. Her eyes grew sad and she slipped from his arms. For a moment, his kiss had swept her away. No war. Just the two of them, in love. With him by her side, she could do anything. She knew she could. *But he doesn't,* she thought. She picked up the tray, walking toward the kitchen.

"I don't just need a wife." His words stopped her. She turned back, looking at him. "I need a partner in the work of Allah."

It was what she wanted, what she most desired: the two of them working together. Squeezing her eyes shut, she nodded to him before taking the tray into the tiny kitchen.

She blinked again, back in the present. The open bus door was like a cavern. Dark. Shrouded in mystery. Samira thought there might be a whole other world through that doorway. A world without war or armed soldiers. A world where she and Ata could just be two people. Happy. In love. Free.

"That bus nearly got you."

The voice was strong, demanding. Samira glanced up. The soldier, the one she presumed to be the leader was looking across the street at her.

She squared her shoulders and raised her chin, pulling in a long breath. "Allah be praised, it did not," she replied, launching out into the street toward the soldiers.

Her confident stride brought an immediate reaction, the men all turning their focus on her, hands shifting on weapons. She could feel them getting ready for… something.

"State your business," the lead soldier's voice was colder now. She was in the middle of the street, closing the distance rapidly and he put a hand up to stop her. She froze in mid-step.

The soldier raised his eyebrows. She struggled to remember what she was to say, to find the words. All those eyes on her, all those weapons…. She opened her mouth but didn't speak.

The soldier began to raise his rifle. A pulse of adrenaline shot through her. *I should run.* It was the only rational action. *Why am I not running away?* The rifle was nearly pointed at her.

She took another breath and met the soldier's eyes. Confident. He pointed the rifle at her chest.

"State your business." He said it more slowly the second time. He sounded wary. He didn't want her moving any closer than she already was. In her loose abaya, she could be wearing a bomb. There could be a weapon concealed in her bag.

She exhaled, smiling. It was a calm smile, intended to ease the tension, but it didn't. These men didn't see confident women smiling at them. That wasn't normal.

"Can you tell me where I can find fresh mutton?"

The soldier shook his head as though he hadn't heard her correctly. The men around him began to look at each other, confused.

She feigned embarrassment and spread her hands in a gesture that both apologized and showed she was unarmed. "It's just that every shop I visit, the meat is half rotted already." She met the soldier's eyes again. "Surely, Assad's brave warriors don't eat rotten mutton?" The flattery felt sour on her tongue.

The leader narrowed his eyes. He wasn't buying her performance. What was she going to do? Her heart pounded in her chest and she kept smiling, trying not to look like a threat. *I am Samira Masoud, I am not afraid.* Her traitorous eyes shot down to the barrel of the gun and she bit her lip. *I am going to die.* She was certain she could see his finger tensing on the trigger. *Safer by far to shoot the crazy woman. Why risk it?*

At that moment, a little girl rushed up to the lead soldier. Everything changed. He lowered the weapon. Sweeping the child into his arms, he spun her in the air over his head.

For a moment, all Samira could see was Yasmeen. Her little sister, in the air, spinning around, laughing. Her jaw fell open. *How can Yasmeen be here? Ata is going to attack. This isn't a safe place for Yasmeen*. She took a step toward the girl and suddenly all the guns were pointed at her.

"Stop!"

She froze, holding up her hands. It wasn't Yasmeen. She could see it wasn't. It was just another girl her age. But her confidence was gone. This wasn't right. She couldn't be a part of Ata's plan.

"I'm sorry," she said, taking a step backwards. "I was mistaken."

"Stop!" another soldier shouted.

She kept backing up. It was a reflex. She couldn't control herself. Her adrenaline was a mad rush and her mind was gibbering at her to run away. Death was coming, she knew. Any minute one of the soldiers was going to shoot her. She needed to stop moving, but she couldn't do it.

The lead soldier put the little girl down, pushing her behind him. He raised his rifle again and he and his men began advancing. Matching their movements to her retreat.

Her phone rang. It was like a talisman, breaking her out of her unconscious mind. She answered.

"What are you doing?" Ata shouted from the phone.

"I…"

"Stop or we shoot!"

Samira froze again. Slowly, she raised her hands, the phone still connected. The little girl peeked out from around the lead soldier's leg. Her expression was all serious concern. Again, Samira saw Yasmeen. Peaking from behind the soldier's leg, her little sister met her eyes. Another soldier appeared beside Samira, weapon at his side. He reached for her arm.

Behind the barricade, she saw Ata. His rifle raised. Her eyes flicked to the little girl again.

"Run!" Samira shouted. And she suited her words to action, running desperately away from the men, away from Ata, toward Dominic Erbach, gazing at her from the side of a bus.

The lead soldier turned, his gun tracking her movements and then the street became chaos. Gun fire erupted, each bullet at an eardrum shattering volume. She could feel the sound in her chest, almost like a slap. She ran. There was screaming and shouting behind her. More gunfire. Another armed man appeared from behind the bus, and she swerved to avoid him, diving forward through the open door.

nine

Mahmoud: Susu was right

Fall 2013

Mahmoud slumped in a dark booth. His body sank into the leather, and he felt the cool of the wood table on his skin. Self-loathing wormed in his chest and belly, twisting in an agonizing way that made him twitch. *I've betrayed everything. I am become the man Susu always saw when she looked at me.*

He reached, his hand scrabbling at the mostly empty bottle on the table. Arak, the cheapest they had. He'd purchased it to punish himself. He could have ordered whiskey or vodka, this bar had everything. But Samira had accused him of soaking in arak. It took several tries for him to get any liquid into his glass. The bottle had a funny weight to it. It didn't tip the way he expected. The glass kept sliding around, too.

No matter how much he drank, he kept having flashes of his last conversation with Ismaeel.

"You say they are liars and terrorist, but they are the only ones telling the truth!" Ismaeel had shouted. Regret rolled through Mahmoud. *I should have argued.*

A shadow fell over the table. Mahmoud blinked. The arak he was pouring splashed onto the table, missing his glass. It was hard enough to see what he was doing with the room swimming, now someone was blocking his light. Mahmoud hazily looked up to see Basem glaring down at him. Short of his own father, he could imagine no one worse to appear at this moment.

I must make an excuse to not speak with him right now. Cordial, but dismissive. Important business. He waved a hand at Basem.

"Go away, old man."

Tala's father's voice was matter of fact, deep and alien. "Your wife told me you were with Nabil."

Mahmoud tipped his head back, the ceiling fan rotating in opposition to the spinning of the room. It was fascinating. *Round and round and round…* He tried, blearily, to follow the thread of the conversation, but he couldn't make sense of it.

"Do not shush me!" Ismaeel had shouted. "I will have my say."

"No one is stopping you." Mahmoud had tried to keep his voice calm, tried to keep his posture erect. It was a struggle. His son was so violently angry. Mahmoud wasn't sure if he wanted to beat the boy senseless or hide in his room and hope this phase would pass.

"What's going on? Why are you shouting?" Esma had appeared in the doorway, looking back and forth between Ismaeel and Mahmoud. *That's where it went wrong. Esma. Why did Allah curse me with such a wife?* He shook his head, once again conscious of the bar around him.

He was startled to see Basem again. *Where did he come from?* Squinting his eyes, Mahmoud asked, "How did you find me?"

Basem smiled, a wicked glint in his eye. Mahmoud flinched. The look was like cold water on his face. "I asked Nabil." Basem spoke slowly, over-pronouncing the words to be sure Mahmoud understood.

The stocky man grabbed a chair from another table and spun it into place. It was an act of coordination that looked both ordinary and incredibly impressive to Mahmoud. *Nabil has betrayed me! I should…* He lost the thread again. Moving his head around caused the room to move in the oddest ways. *I should certainly do… something. About Nabil?* Maybe he would buy Nabil a gift. He smiled. *Nabil is an excellent friend.*

"I am sorry," Basem's words landed like a slap. Those weren't words Basem was supposed to say. Mahmoud squinted at Tala's father. What sort of game was the man playing? Who did he think he was dealing with? Mahmoud wasn't some rube to be taken in by his false sympathy. Basem continued speaking. "I did not like Ismaeel, but I am sad that he is dead."

Those were not thoughts Mahmoud wanted to consider. He shook his head, trying to make the words go away. *Ismaeel is an excellent son.*

The best son. He is dead. Mahmoud lurched at his glass, holding it up and watching the way the light played through the crystalline structure. It was lovely. Pretty. Empty. *That's what I want,* he thought, *lovely. Pretty. Empty.*

Just like that, Mahmoud let his thoughts go, taking him back to those final moments with Ismaeel. He remembered them so clearly.

"Please," he said. "Let no one interrupt Ismaeel. I want to hear what he has to say."

Abdo, the snake, slipped into the room and flopped unceremoniously on the couch. The younger brother of Ata Tareq was a curse. The troublemaker looked gleeful as though he'd come to be entertained. *I should have chased him out.*

"I have found the true Islam," Ismaeel announced grandly. "We were never meant to cower in filth." He swung his arm around, taking in the Persian carpet, the giant flat screen, and the immaculate leather sofa.

Esma cocked an eyebrow, but Mahmoud kept silent. He waited, letting the boy speak.

"The Prophet is angry, Allah is angry, that we — his people — sit in the shadows while the Great Satan and the infidel Jew rule this world." The light in Ismaeel's eyes was feverish.

"The infidels hate us. They tempt our brothers and sisters away from their homelands with promises of wealth and material pleasures, but then make us slaves and servants. They corrupt the hearts of honest Muslims with their haraam movies and pornography. They tell good Muslim girls that they should walk around naked in front of men and dishonor their houses."

The boy was shouting, spit flecking his lips. Mahmoud sighed. The boy was not wrong. A constant barrage of poisonous culture came from the West, infecting the faithful with a dangerous apathy toward Allah.

"Don't scream at us. How dare you?" Esma erupted. "Show your father respec—"

Mahmoud silenced her with a raised hand. He moved to Ismaeel, laying a hand on his shoulder. The boy panted, his face flushed, still overflowing with passion but too keyed up to find the words to express himself.

"And what are we to do about this? Is it not enough to read the Holy Qur'an? To pray five times a day? To visit Mecca?"

"We must cut away the cancer." Ismaeel's voice was a husky whisper.

Mahmoud frowned. "And if that cancer is Nabil's pretty girl? Or your own brother, Jaber?"

Ismaeel looked at Mahmoud, disappointment in his eyes. "I thought of everyone, you would understand. Sometimes even family must be sacrificed so that the faithful may be pure."

The words still burned Mahmoud, as he sat with the bar spinning around him. *I did this. It's my fault.*

"My sister," Mahmoud slurred, "used to tell my father that I came here, drinking." He thunked the glass down on the table. "Arak!" He pointed dramatically to the bottle.

"You don't look like a man who does a lot of drinking," Basem said, roving an eye over Mahmoud's condition.

Mahmoud raised his head, clicking his tongue, and waved his hands back and forth in exaggerated negation. "I never did!" Mahmoud agreed. He looked at Basem, and then jerked his head and clicked very seriously a second time. "Never."

Basem's expression soured. *He finds commiserating with me distasteful. Of course he does,* Mahmoud thought. *I am a horrible, distasteful man. A drunk.* He raised his glass to Basem like a toast and announced, "Susu was right about me."

"I wanted to set you free," Basem began, "from your promise. This war…" The man sighed. Mahmoud felt suddenly cold. He didn't like Basem. Basem was the devil. The man's voice was grating and he couldn't ignore it. "It is costing everyone. I will take Tala home. We will care for her."

Mahmoud felt slapped. It was too much. He'd failed his father, betrayed his sister, and let his oldest son be wooed to his own death by radicals. He wouldn't fail in this. *I promised her child would be the Masoud heir.* Basem was saying he was untrustworthy. He was saying Mahmoud Masoud was not a man of his word. Mahmoud lurched up from the table. The bottle crashing to the floor distracted him. *Why did it do that?* His legs didn't work as he intended, his thighs hitting the table and sending him sprawling back into the leather booth.

"No!" He shouted as he flailed his way back upright. It was a wild effort, the table clattering about and Mahmoud bruising himself against it repeatedly. When he was finally swaying on his feet, he had the attention of everyone in the bar. *I'll show all of them! Mahmoud Masoud is a man of principle!* He raised a pointing finger, swinging it around the room. He loomed awkwardly over Basem, still sitting in his chair, though Basem did put a hand on Mahmoud's elbow to keep him from falling. "An Masoud keeps his word. I will not shame my family."

He tried to make eye contact with the barkeeper, but the man looked away. He wanted them all to know how serious he was. No one wanted to make eye contact with him.

Basem rolled his eyes. Frustration painted the stocky man's face, and his lips curled down in disgust. "You've had too much to drink." He stood. "We can discuss this another time."

Mahmoud lunged across the table, grabbing Basem's arm, and pulling him down. Basem fell onto the table, the two men's faces inches apart.

"I swear," Mahmoud shouted, turning making sure everyone was listening. "I swear before Allah and his holy prophet," he slapped his palm against the table repeatedly, "you will have a Masoud grandchild."

Basem shoved him away, straightening his clothes awkwardly. Tala's father looked horrified. Mahmoud gazed around the room in triumph. They all met his eyes now. Everyone looked at him with wide, startled eyes. They were universally horrified.

Mahmoud slid back into the booth, his muscles liquid. He smiled. *They see now, I am not a man to take lightly.* "She will marry Jaber." He looked into Basem's eyes. It was Tala's father who flinched back this time. "And if he dies too, then she will marry Ahmad. I have more sons."

ten

Samira: Dream Come True

Samira staggered up the metal stairs of the bus, and sprawled. Her foot was hooked on something. Twisting her body, she searched for the obstacle over which she'd tripped. She locked eyes with the bus driver, belly down on the floor in a huddle. His eyes were wide and wild.

Gun fire continued to split the air outside the bus, the deep report shaking the windows. *There was a soldier right behind me.*

She saw the lines of sunlight painting the drivers face. The door was still open.

"Quickly, the door!"

The driver didn't move. He quivered, his terror raw and wild.

She lurched forward, crawling over him. She clawed at the metal handle to shut the door. Reaching it required her head to come above the level of the seats. Above the level of the windows. She would be visible. She closed her eyes, steadied herself and lunged for the handle. She landed heavily on the driver's back. He grunted in pain. She stretched her arm, barely able to lever the door shut.

She rolled off of the man. Panting and gasping, she turned toward the driver, grabbing his face in her hands.

"You have to drive," she yelled, urgently. "Get us out of here."

She tried to shove him toward the driver seat, and then she made a hunched rush up the aisle and slid into a seat. She huddled there, half on the floor. She waited, feeling like the driver looked. Petrified.

Waiting for the next gun shot. But it didn't come. Instead, there was a horrible silence.

She tried to catch her breath, to stop panting like an animal. She was beset with fears. When would the soldiers storm the bus? Was Ata okay? How could she spend her last moments of life like a frightened animal? Where had her strength gone? Ata had to be okay.

She could peek. It should be safe. No one was shooting now. *Maybe they're all just waiting, guns pointed at this window.* She scolded herself, *that's ridiculous.* It didn't feel ridiculous. Forcing herself to raise her head, slowly, she just peeked her eyes over the line of the window. As her eyes crested the frame, she lurched back, diving to the floor. It took a moment for her to realize the terrifying sound was actually the ringing of her cellphone, still clutched in her fingers.

She answered the phone, once again raising her head to the window.

"I'm sorry," she said.

"It's done," Ata replied.

She moved onto the seat, looking out the window. Ata stood on the ground below, just outside her window. He held his phone to his ear. He looked excited. Triumphant.

She bit her lip. "No." It took her a moment, her heart pounding, to understand her own words. They came out of her mouth, but lacked meaning and context. Significance was lost in the rush of adrenaline and fear. "Those men had children."

Ata's voice was calm, gentle. "It's finished, Susu. You're safe."

Am I safe? Can I ever be safe again? She looked into Ata's eyes. *Am I safe with him?*

"You need to come off the bus now." His words were so calm, so measured. Like he was coaxing a frightened child. A child…

She was shaking her head. She could see his cheeks growing red. He was struggling for calm.

"Please," he said. The words were a struggle now. He was conflicted, his calm unraveling. "Do not shame me in front of my men."

His men. Her eyes started taking in the broader picture. There were other armed men standing around the check point, but none of them were soldiers. Faces jumped out at her, men she'd served tea.

"I…" she didn't know what to say. *I should get off the bus. I should go to my husband,* but she didn't want to. She wanted to run to the Ata who had shared her bed last night, but this figure in front of her was different. She spoke like she was in a trance or a fever, her words hollow and disconnected. "The girl…"

"GET OFF THE BUS!" He screamed, jumping up and down, ranting wildly. "YOU ARE A SHAME TO ME! A SHAME TO ALLAH! GET OFF THE BUS NOW!"

Tears tracked down her cheeks. She gathered herself. *I must do as he says. He is my husband. He is trying to protect me and keep me safe. I am a bad wife.* She rose from the seat.

As she stood, she saw more of the picture. Ata was standing over bodies. A man and a little girl. Their blood made a pool around Ata's feet. Her eyes tracked upward, past the smoking barrel of his machine gun, to his red, angry face.

A rumble began in her feet. She glanced away. The driver was in his seat. The bus was starting.

She turned back to Ata.

"You will come home now," he was calm again, but his voice was cold and brutal. The voice of a man standing over the bodies of his slain enemies. "Or you will never come home again."

The words echoed in her mind. It was an odd repetition of the agreement Ata had made with Mahmoud the day she was sold.

Her arm, holding her phone dropped limply to her side and she looked again at the body of the little girl. Her jaw firmed. She met his eyes again and raised her chin. Lowering herself slowly, she resumed her seat.

With a hydraulic hiss, the bus brakes released and it began to move.

She could see Ata, screaming. Without the cell phone connection, his shouts were just muffled noise, indistinguishable under the rumble and groan of the bus. He began running for the door. The bus moved too quickly. Samira watched him get smaller and smaller. Finally he disappeared past the window pane.

She felt her fingers moving of their own accord, almost like they belonged to someone else. Looking down at her hand, she found the old scrap of scarf. All that remained of the beautiful scarf her father had made. The scarf Mahmoud had ripped away. Her finger rubbed it like it was a talisman.

A stranger slipped into the seat beside her. She turned, shocked. Caramel colored skin around eyes twinkling with… something terrifying. He was staring at her.

Deja vu hit her suddenly and she looked around. The bus was empty. She reached for her hijab. It was still there, but she felt completely naked under this stranger's gaze.

She recognized him now. The man who had waved her onto the bus. The man from her vision.

The bus jounced. It shook loose the shock that was holding her together and she felt herself slipping into an endless pit of despair. She flailed wildly looking for something to hold on to and found a rich vein of rage.

"I didn't want a husband!" she spat at the stranger. "I was content as I was, better than content."

He reached a hand out, gently. Like in her vision. She jerked away. She prepared to bat the hand away. He would touch her anyway. She was certain he would. But he did not. Where Ata would have forced his hand on her, touched her until she was calm, the stranger withdrew.

"What kind of God does this?" she demanded. He didn't answer, which only served to increase her anger. "I was content on my own, but now I am…" Her words ran out and she turned and looked out the window. The rage was deserting her. She finished the sentence in a barely intelligible mutter, just short of a sob, "…broken-hearted over love for a child murderer!"

She turned back to the stranger. He just gazed at her with deep, sad eyes. She stared into them, willing herself to believe they were cold and uncaring, but she couldn't. To her, those eyes held understanding, pain to match her own. This man knew suffering. He understood betrayal and he loved still.

She turned away, unable to look at the man's eyes anymore.

"I didn't want to be a wife," she protested softly. "I wanted to be a success… at something. Now I am a failure. I've betrayed my husband, my family… my father." She choked back tears. "What can I do now," she murmured. "I am a used woman. Broken and useless."

"Come to me," the stranger said. "And I will exalt you."

Two days later, Samira stood in an antique shop haggling with a shriveled little Lebanese man. She'd never been to Beirut before. In fact, she'd never left Syria. *But here I am,* she thought. *Samira, betrayer of husbands and shame to the name Masoud. What's one more betrayal?*

She kept her hand on the sapphire necklace, refusing to let the antique dealer take it.

The journey to Lebanon had been uneventful. She'd feared some wild intervention from Ata, but none came. *What could he have done?* The bus stopped for various armed check points, but unless Ata could get to one and fight the armed men there, he could hardly have stopped the bus himself.

"Look closely at the stone, girl," the antique dealer said. His voice was patronizing and exasperated. He looked at her over thin, half-moon spectacles with eyes that had already seen hundreds of refugees. "It's flawed."

She laughed, turning away. "Then I will go elsewhere. I'll not be cheated."

Three agonizing steps toward the door had her confidence disappearing like the tide. *What if he's right? I'll never make it to Germany without money.* She kept her shoulders straight, her head high. She tried to smile, even with her back to him.

"Wait," the dealer said.

She turned back to him. His mouth was twisted and his eyes narrow. She lifted one of her eyebrows.

A few minutes later she was on her way to the Tripoli airport. Wads of Lebanese pounds did little so salve her conscience. The haja was dead, but she'd hocked the woman's necklace — not to feed children, or protect family — so that she could run from the very husband the woman had encouraged her to marry. Samira felt sick.

I'm going to Germany, she coached herself. *There is always hope. The haja told me that.*

The words sounded good, but they did little to relieve the nauseous burbling of betrayal in her stomach.

She'd spent the last several days talking with other refugees, hearing their plans. Everyone agreed. Germany was the place for a bright future. Well, not everyone. She'd met a few people headed to Sweden, but Dominic Erbach wasn't a Swedish businessman. Samira's choice seemed clear enough.

If I'm betraying everything, then I should at least chase my dream.

At the airport, she'd catch a flight to Istanbul. In Turkey, she could bribe someone to take her to Greece. Once she was in the EU, getting to Germany would be easy.

And I'll be in Istanbul in a few hours.

She felt a little thrill of excitement. It felt real. Close. *Maybe dreams aren't always lies.*

Looming darkly into the sky, the wave seemed to hang motionless in the air for a moment before pounding down on the tiny dingy. Samira concentrated on her breathing. Deep inhalation. Slow exhalation. Her chest wanted to tighten, to clamp her lungs until there was no room for air. Another wave began building on the horizon. They were barely visible in the darkness. A slight contrast between the midnight blue sky and the deep blackness of the water. She realized her whole body was quivering with barely contained anxiety.

The flight to Istanbul had been uneventful. The taxi to Izmir was outrageous, but in no way harrowing. Finding the smugglers was remarkably easy. Nothing in the process had prepared her for this moment: crammed into a tiny dinghy, in the darkness, in the middle of the Aegean Sea.

Another wave crashed down. Lurching upward, the boat seemed to be weightless. Then it fell a stomach-lifting forever to smash against the water again. Samira pitched forward, nearly going over the rubber side of the boat. A hand grabbed hold of her orange life vest. She was hauled back into the wet rubber puddle where she sat, crammed into a press of strangers.

The cacophonous sound of the outboard motor sputtered, coughed and went silent. The only sound was the roar of the waves.

"We're out of gas." A male voice, somewhere behind her. There wasn't room to turn and look, not without shoving everyone else around. The exclamation was met with a crackle of human sounds: moans, wails, and inarticulate vocalizations of despair.

Samira scanned the horizon, searching for land or any sort of marker. They needed hope. Something to motivate them all to push forward. If they panicked in this tiny boat, it would capsize. Everyone would drown in the dark Mediterranean waters. Lights dotted the coastline, but the waves and darkness were disorienting. It was hard to tell what was Greece and what was Turkey.

"We're all going to die." For a moment, Samira wondered if it was her own voice. It wasn't.

Another wave hammered the tiny boat. Samira closed her eyes. Beside her, a man fidgeted, the movement of his shoulder and elbow unavoidable in the indecent proximity.

She opened her eyes and saw the whites of his eyes. She could feel him quivering. That was when she realized that her own body had grown still.

"It will be okay," she whispered.

The man continued staring ahead. "You don't understand."

"You're afraid," Samira said, and then thought better. She'd known few men in her life who would react well to a woman telling them they were afraid.

He leaned closer, his weight heavy on her side. His voice was barely audible. "The old woman, did you see them put her on the boat?"

Samira thought back, she remembered a woman being wheeled down the beach in a chair. The wheels stuck in the sand and hung up on rocks. Her friends had struggled to bring her to the boat. If she'd been able to walk even a little bit, she'd have gotten out of the chair.

"She can't swim," the man continued. He nodded his head to his left. A few seats away, a woman huddled with a toddler girl in her lap. "My wife doesn't swim either. And my daughter."

He turned his head, eyes intense as he looked at Samira. "When the boat capsizes, who do I choose? The crippled woman? My wife? My child?" He slowly turned his head away from Samira. "I cannot save them all."

A blinding light rippled over the surface of the water.

"What is that?" Another desperate voice somewhere behind her.

A woman's voice, exultant: "It's a ship! We're saved!"

Eyes finally readjusting to the darkness, Samira could see a ship. She strained her neck trying to get a better view. It was bearing down on them from behind. The ship cut past the small dingy at high speed. It passed so close that the wake nearly swamped the tiny boat, spinning them around. Samira swung her head the other way. The ship swept around for another pass.

"The Greek Coast Guard?" Another woman's voice, questioning, uncertain.

If it was a Greek ship, it would mean they were in Greek waters. A rescue would likely take them to Lesvos, their destination, where they could apply for asylum.

"Turkish," a man's voice said, like a curse. The energy on the dinghy shifted again, despair threatening to become panic.

A Turkish ship would return them to Turkey. The smugglers, who sent them to sea in this death trap, weren't going to give them all a refund. They would have to pay another small fortune for another boat. Another attempt to cross the two kilometer stretch of the Mediterranean required to reach Greece without sufficient fuel, in a boat filled beyond its capacity. Or they would be put in one of the Turkish camps. Samira shuddered. She had no more money for another crossing.

The ship passed a second time, once more setting the boat to spinning. Something smacked into the water nearby. Everyone in the boat flinched. A glimmer of moonlight lit a rope being towed back to the ship.

"What are they—," one of the men behind her started to ask. But Samira cut him off.

"Get the motor running again," she ordered. "Everyone else, paddle." She looked up, sighting the twinkling lights on the horizon furthest from the ship. She flung out a finger. "That way!"

Samira didn't have to look to track the Turkish ship. She could hear it, coming up behind them again. She could also hear the chord on the motor being pulled frantically again and again. The tiny motor sputtered and gasped but never turned over.

The light from the ship landed directly on them, painting the water ahead of them in a harsh, distorted outline of the boat full of refugees. Samira leaned forward, digging desperately at the water with her cupped palms. She felt ridiculous. Praying the tiny boat would move, she continued to paddle furiously. Her hand felt frozen from the icy water.

Something flashed between Samira and the man beside her and suddenly he cried out. She turned, a metal hook was caught in the shoulder of his shirt, the fabric ripped and bloody. The rope tugged and the hook ripped out of the shirt, flying backwards into the crowd.

"They're trying to tow us back into Turkish waters," Samira shouted. "Get that thing out of the boat."

She set to paddling again. She could feel the people scrambling around her, hear their panting breaths, the jostling of bodies. Other hands smacked into the water. In the darkness it was impossible to tell if their boat was moving.

"It's hooked into the rubber," a man shouted.

"There's water coming in," a woman shrieked. Samira could feel it, seeping into the seat of her clothes.

"Get that rope off our dingy!" Samira commanded. "If they pull us back into Turkey, we never reach Europe."

In a sound reminiscent of their struggling hopes, the engine coughed, sputtered and then roared to life again. Samira could smell the diesel fumes choking the dark sky. Sighs of relief and little exclamations of joy pop-corned around the boat. Samira bit her lip. Their tiny motor was no match for the pull of the larger ship. The shadows on the water grew shorter and smaller as they drew closer and closer to the light.

With another rough tearing sound, the hook went flying through the air. It plunked into the water a few feet away. The boat shot forward, its tiny motor driving them wildly ahead into the water. The shadows lengthened, becoming dimmer and less distinct as they escaped the ship.

Samira smiled, turning to the man beside her who sat clutching his bloody arm.

"See?" She said. "We're going to make it."

He frowned. "We're taking on water."

eleven
Mahmoud: War

Winter 2014

Mahmoud sipped coffee on the couch, his friend, Nabil, sitting companionably beside him. Nabil was telling a horror story, one which was becoming too familiar. Since the war started, men were harassing women in the streets.

Across the room, Mahmoud's wife, Esma, sat in fuming silence. Their youngest, Ahmad, sat at her feet. She stroked her hands through his hair. Mahmoud made a sour face. The boy was far too old to be doted on like that. On the television, scenes of war and destruction rode above the Al Jazeera ticker, but Mahmoud knew her anger was for him.

"It is the ultimate test of a man," Nabil continued.

"Why do you say that?" Mahmoud asked idly. Continuing to watch his wife, he wondered how he could make things right between them. She blamed him for the death of the eldest son, Ismaeel. *How does a man ever make that right?*

"A man who lets his wife be harassed by strangers and doesn't seek revenge is not truly a man," Nabil opined. "If my wife was accosted in the street, I would rush to her side and kill the man, with my bare hands if necessary."

"You don't have a wife," Mahmoud smirked. Esma was also angry about Tala's wedding to Jaber — really about Mahmoud's pledge to Basem. She felt that Tala was user merchandise after Ismaeel's death.

Not a fit bride for her precious son.

Nabil raised a chastising finger, "Not all men are blessed with a blissful union like yours, my friend." That got a scowl out of Mahmoud. "But this is about honor and prop—"

At that moment, Abdo burst through the door, drawing the eyes of everyone in the room. Ata's younger brother looked pale. Panting, sweat matted the hair to his brow. His fierce scowl made his tiny, shifty eyes into bare slits. Ragged gasps revealed brown, rotten teeth that explained his terrible breath. Not for the first time, Mahmoud wondered where the older brother had gone, where he'd taken Samira. Ishmaeel's final words still haunted him. *I thought of everyone, you would understand. Sometimes even family must be sacrificed so that the faithful may be pure.*

"What is it?" Nabil demanded. "What has happened?"

Mahmoud felt a flush of shame. This was his home and Nabil was taking charge. There was a proper order to things. Shame became anger and then Mahmoud remembered his circumstances. This was Nabil's home. Mahmoud's home was Nabil's guest house. Anger at Nabil became anger at Yacoob Masoud.

"Where is Jaber?" It was Esma, of course. Her words stabbed at Mahmoud. She was focused on the moment, not trapped in the slights of her past. A crisis involving Abdo when Jaber was not safe at home — Mahmoud could not lose another son. He rose to his feet, grabbing Abdo by the shoulders.

"Quickly. Answer her."

Abdo ignored Esma, glaring through his brows at Mahmoud. "Men stopped us on the street. They demanded to see our papers."

The collective tension in the room increased. Such checkpoints were common place now. They were effective ways to keep people afraid and controlled. But they were also a thinly veiled excuse to throw people in prison or justify murder.

Nabil shifted uncomfortably on the coach. Ahmad took in a sharp breath, pressed back against his mother's legs. Mahmoud saw Esma's fist closed in the boys hair. He felt his own fingers biting into Abdo's shoulders.

The young man shrugged off Mahmoud's hands, rolling his shoulders.

"They took him." Esma made it sound a statement of fact. Abdo nodded.

Mahmoud was frozen. *What can I do?* It was always dangerous to walk the streets. The police were a threat. Rebels were a threat. Daesh was a threat. No one was safe. But he could not lose another son.

"I will go." Mahmoud spoke the words in a near whisper, but Esma was instantly on her feet. Shoving Abdo back, she stood blocking Mahmoud. All the anger and hatred from moments before were gone. She dropped to her knees in front of him, suddenly in frantic tears.

"No. No, my love. You mustn't go. How will our family survive without you? Do you think this toad will continue to care for us when you are not here to listen to his blather?"

Mahmoud gave Nabil an uncomfortable look. His friend looked amused. Mahmoud didn't know what to feel. Some of this was theater. Some fear. Was any of it love?

"You must stay to keep our family safe," she pleaded. *Or is all of it pure self-preservation?*

Mahmoud sighed. He couldn't solve the puzzle of Esma right now. "I cannot wait to find out if my son is dead," he said. "We must know what has become of him."

"If you leave, they will just take you too!"

"She is right," Nabil interjected. "It is foolish for anyone to be on the streets now. Nothing you can do will change Jaber's fate. It is in Allah's hands."

Mahmoud clicked his tongue, giving his head a little jerk. He couldn't do nothing. Ismaeel was dead. His precious first born was taken from him forever. Somehow, he would find a way to rescue Jaber.

"Last week, Saleem's son was taken in the streets. They asked for his papers and took him to the police station." Mahmoud gave Nabil a pointed look.

The fat man shrugged. "They have not heard anything."

"How long should we wait?" Mahmoud demanded of his wife. "How long until we decide he is dead, or we go out looking for him?"

Mahmoud looked at Ahmad. The boy wouldn't meet his eyes. He understood. Mahmoud felt a gnawing terror of what he knew must be done. He feared to face it alone, but it would be wrong to risk his son. Still, there would have been comfort in sharing the danger with someone.

"Send him!" Esma practically spat, pointing and clawing at Abdo. The boy's eyes grew wide. "It's his fault anyway. If something happened to my Jaber it is because of this monster. You, go and find my son!"

Abdo backed up against the wall, shaking his head. "Kill me if you must. I will not go out there again tonight."

Mahmoud took a step toward him, carefully stepping around the still kneeling Esma.

The boy's hands went up defensively.

"How many nights have you slept on my couch, whispering your poison to my sons, Abdo?" He stepped close, as the boy pressed himself nearly flat against the wall. "Kill you?" He was close enough to smell the boy's terrible breath. "Do not tempt me."

The boy slid to the ground, huddling beneath his arms. Mahmoud wanted to kick him. Then shame pooled in his belly. *I am not a violent man,* he reminded himself.

Mahmoud turned. "That coward cannot help Jaber. He is good only for trouble. I am going. If you must beg," he said to Esma, "beg Allah that I will bring our son home tonight."

"Ahmad, fetch me my jacket." The boy leapt off the couch and fled into the hallway, apparently grateful to leave the room.

Passage through the streets of Aleppo was perilous. Bands of armed men in black clothes haunted the streets, especially at this time of night. Mahmoud didn't know if it was his wife's prayers, Allah's mercy, or the look of murder in his eyes, but they all left him alone.

Arriving at the police station without incident, Mahmoud felt a surge of hope. Perhaps, Allah was with him. Perhaps, he would find his son and return him home.

The entry hall of the station was dimly lit. An old stone building, once grand, now was an oppressive tomb of cobwebs. The stone itself seemed to be yellowing like old paper.

It is long after curfew, Mahmoud thought. He tried to look confident.

"*As-salam Alaikum* " Mahmoud said to the heavyset man, slumped over the counter.

"*Wa Alaikum As-salam,*" the man replied robotically.

Mahmoud licked his lips. "A few hours ago, a policeman invited my son here to answer some questions…" Mahmoud paused watching the other man, his fat bunched on the counter. There was no reaction. The other man didn't even look up. "I've come to take him home."

"Name?"

"His name is Jaber. Jaber Masou—"

"Your name?"

"Mahmoud—"

"Here!" The man cut him off. He pinned a form to the counter with a heavy finger and slid it toward Mahmoud. Mahmoud looked around for a pen. *Am I to lose my son because I don't have a pen?* Desperation shook him. His eyes were too wide, his breathing too fast. *I must be calm. Where am I to find a pen at this hour?* There was a wire on the counter that cut off. He was sure it had once held a pen. Working saliva into his mouth, Mahmoud firmed his resolve.

"I need a pen."

For the first time, the other man looked up. His eyes were hard. They bit into Mahmoud, who flinched back. At Mahmoud's flinch, the man laughed and waved a hand toward a shadowy corner across the room.

Turning, Mahmoud saw there was another pen anchored to a small table. He'd missed it in the dim light.

Moving to the table, Mahmoud took the pen and began to fill in all of the details required. There were many questions, most of them useless and inapplicable, but he put everything he could down on the paper. He worried about the details he was sharing. *Am I calling attention to my family? Am I putting Esma, Ahmad and Nabil in danger?* But what choice did he have? He wanted Jaber back, and he only saw one path forward.

It was hard to concentrate. The lights made a humming sound which seemed to grow louder and louder, occasionally punctuated by the creaking of the fat man's chair.

"There." Mahmoud laid the paper on the counter. The policeman ignored it. Mahmoud waited. The fat man was staring at his cell phone. His thumb swiped. There was a pause. His thumb swiped again. "Now, I would like to see my son."

Without a word, the man turned from the desk and walked away. He left the paper. Mahmoud felt impotent. He stood there. Alone. Uncertain what to do.

He waited. Perhaps ten minutes passed. The phone rang several times, but no one answered.

Finally, the fat policeman returned with another man, taller thinner. The new policeman's eyes were even harder. "Come with me."

The paper still sat on the counter, unread. Mahmoud reached for it and paused looking at the two men. They watched him impassively. He left the form and moved toward the tall man. Walking around the desk, he stepped awkwardly passed the fat man's bulk. The taller policeman turned and Mahmoud followed him into the bowels of the police station. They walked narrow hallways, lit with flickering green fluorescents. Finally, they arrived at a room with a frosted glass door. The tall stranger opened the door. He gestured Mahmoud inside. Mahmoud froze in the doorway. Jaber was not in the room. It had no other exits. It was a tiny concrete box with a table. A ring sat in the middle of the table. *To hold shackles,* Mahmoud realized. He'd seen interrogation rooms on television. It was different in real life. More terrifying.

The policeman gave Mahmoud a little push. Mahmoud stumbled a few steps forward and stopped again.

"I thought you were taking me to my son."

Closing the door behind them, the tall man shoved Mahmoud toward a chair.

"Now, I'll need to see your papers."

It took hours. Mahmoud tried to be polite, but his emotions were in turmoil. He knew this man held his life by a thread. Any reaction might lead to his death, or might just lead to another question, or being let go. Mahmoud struggled to answer properly, to behave with decorum. No matter what happened, he hoped to bring honor to his family.

Finally, the questions ground to a halt. The detective just perched, half on the table, staring down at Mahmoud. He was smoking a cigarette. Of course, he had not offered one to Mahmoud. *I don't even smoke,* Mahmoud thought. *Still, what happened to basic hospitality?*

The detective blew a slow streamer of smoke, and then rose, opening the door.

"Get out," he said.

Mahmoud rose, he took two steps toward the door and then stopped.

"What about my son?"

The man blinked. He had just offered Mahmoud a way out, an escape. Mahmoud hadn't taken it. What would happen now?

The man took another drag on his cigarette. Slowly, he exhaled and ground the butt out on the table. There was no ashtray. He flicked the remains at Mahmoud and walked away, leaving Mahmoud alone in the room with the door open.

It took thirty minutes for Mahmoud to find his way back to the lobby. Thirty terrifying minutes wondering if his son was behind one of these doors, or if he would pass someone in the hallway and they would drag him away.

When he emerged into the lobby, the same fat man sat on a high stool, belly flopping out onto the counter. The man was still swiping at his phone, his thumb moving like the second hand on a clock. The form Mahmoud had filled out lay discarded on the floor.

I must demand to see my son. He stood frozen in the lobby. *I must....* Fear and terror took hold. Emotions he'd tried to hold in check for hours overwhelmed him. The sheer weight of terror from the previous hours all hit him at once. *Perhaps the same thing happened to Jaber,* he justified. He fled out the door and into the night.

The angry purpose that had carried him to the station had deserted him. He darted into the night like a terrified rodent. Shame burned him. *At every opportunity I have failed.* His eyes darted every direction. Half searching for Jaber and half terrified he would run into more trouble, he ran from shadow to shadow and flinched at every sound.

He navigated the streets. Some had lights, others had none. He traversed a few streets by the flickering light of a car on fire. In the distance he could hear shouts and screams and gun fire. But the streets seemed deserted.

He scurried quickly, trying to take the fastest route to Nabil's house. Feeling he had used up every ounce of luck and goodwill Allah had for him in the last several hours, he believed his best chance of survival was to get back home before Allah noticed.

He rounded a corner onto a wide avenue. There were people far down the street, silhouetted in a street light. They were walking away from him, but moving in the same direction he was. He walked cautiously after them.

A chance flicker of light illuminating a hijab confirmed what height and walk already implied. The furthest silhouette was a woman. Nothing about her was familiar, but Mahmoud thought she moved like a young woman. Light, tiny, uncertain. He couldn't imagine what she was doing on these streets alone. She carried a bag — probably groceries. So he didn't need to imagine at all. *Black market food for her family.*

It took longer to identify the other figure... the man. It was so unbelievable. Even after Mahmoud recognized him, he kept second-guessing himself. *What are the chances?* The more he followed, the more certain Mahmoud became that it was Jaber. He tried walking faster, but he was already struggling to keep up. The woman was moving quickly and the man, Jaber, he thought, was pursuing her.

What is he doing? Mahmoud thought. *A beautiful wife waits for him at home and he stalks some woman in the street?*

Between the cacophonous sounds of war, the night was eerily quiet. An explosion would echo, and then it would be just their footsteps on the stone streets.

"What's your name?" He heard the man shouting at the woman as she moved faster trying to get away. Mahmoud was almost running, but barely making up any ground on them. The sky burst alight and another thunderous sound echoed off the walls, the ground shaking beneath Mahmoud's feet. He stumbled and nearly fell to the ground.

Why? Jaber had always been a scoundrel where women were concerned, but the behavior still mystified Mahmoud. *You just escaped the police....*

The man caught up to the woman, grabbed her arm. "Where do you live?"

"Leave me alone." She pulled her arm free, trying to escape, but he grabbed her again.

Another burst of machine gun fire erupted. Closer. Louder. Mahmoud tried to walk faster, but he'd rolled his ankle. Every step was painful.

"You are beautiful. I know how to make a woman smile." It was Jaber's voice. Mahmoud still couldn't see his face, but he was certain.

"My husband will come. You don't want to meet him." She tried again to pull away, but Jaber's grip was strong now. He pulled her closer, putting his face close to hers.

"I don't think you have a husband. Perhaps tonight, I can be your husband.

She slapped him, dropping the grocery bag and running away as fast as she could. He took off after her. Mahmoud tried to run as well, but he got three steps and his ankle gave way again tumbling him to the pavement. When he managed to rise, he saw Jaber had caught the girl and was manhandling her.

Why? Tala was beautiful. He had often caught himself admiring her when he thought no one would see. She was a prize. A jewel he'd intended for his sons. A beautiful woman of good breeding — nothing like the harridan he'd been forced to wed. *Esma.* The thought of facing her again made him want to throw up. All to please Yacoob — *a man who will never be pleased with anything.*

But he saw they were no longer alone. Another man, a much larger man was emerging from an alleyway behind Jaber.

"Run!" Mahmoud shouted.

Jaber turned, confused. First, looking for Mahmoud, Jaber shoved his neck forward and squinted into the night. Disbelief painted his face as he recognized his father. Then a flash of movement drew his eyes to the other man. Mahmoud saw the sudden widening of Jaber's eyes.

"Let go of my wife!" Roaring, the stranger lunging at Jaber. Something sliver flashed around the man's fist as it plunged into Jaber's throat. The young man crumpled to the pavement, the larger man standing over him. Mahmoud heard the husband spit. He lifted the bag of groceries, tenderly putting the spilled contents away, and then went to the woman. She clung to him and he escorted her swiftly away.

Moving as quickly as his ankle would allow, Mahmoud hobbled and crawled forward. He could hear a terrible bubbling sound in the eerie stretch of quiet between gunfire, explosions and now the rumble of armored vehicles. It was a terrible night to be out.

Jaber coughed. His lungs sounded wet. His entire body convulsed. Mahmoud ran forward and fell again. Crawling a few steps before pushing back to his feet, hopping forward. The boy was still shaking. And then he stopped.

Finally, Mahmoud made it to his son's side. It was Jaber. Or it had been. A ragged hole had been punched in the boys throat. In some distant, logical part of Mahmoud's mind, he connected the silvery flash and the hole he saw in his son's throat and identified it with a screw driver.

Mahmoud looked up at the sky, looking directly into the moon as though it were the eye of Allah looking down on him.

"Why?" He whispered. And then he screamed. "Why?"

The eye gazed back. Mahmoud felt certain his son was not dead because an angry husband had killed him. His son was dead because the Almighty looked upon his boy with disgust. He could not imagine why Allah would let so many evil men roam the streets, but put both of his boys in the ground. Mahmoud slumped his shoulders. *Men cannot understand the ways of Allah.*

For a time, he knelt beside Jaber's body, as the cold crept over his son and into Mahmoud's very bones. He was oblivious to the sounds of war growing ever closer, or to the increasing danger that he faced. His pain was so deep, so keen that it left him numb. He felt the tears tracking down his cheeks distantly, and heard his own ragged sobs as though they belonged to another man.

Tenderly, he pulled his son into his arms. Cradling the boy to his chest, he rose painfully to his feet. He began to walk home. Each step sent an agonizing jolt of pain up his leg. He didn't care anymore. He was numb to everything.

At one point a group of men, dressed all in black rushed around a corner. Each held an AK-47 machine gun. They looked at Mahmoud and took a few steps in his direction. When he met their eyes, they turned away and rushed off in a different direction.

The sky was a deep blue, the color just before dawn when Mahmoud arrived back at Nabil's estate. He rounded the main house, continuing toward the guest house.

Fat Nabil, came running, — jiggling. His eyes were wide and white, his mouth hanging slack as he panted. When he saw Mahmoud, he froze, saying nothing. Lowering his eyes to Jaber, Nabil matched his stride to Mahmoud and walked beside his friend toward the house.

It was Ahmad who opened the door, but Esma shoved the boy aside. Filling the doorway, she blocked Mahmoud from entering. She looked at Jaber's corpse cradled in his arms, looked at Mahmoud and at Nabil, looked back into the house at Ahmad, and then closed her eyes.

For a moment they all just stood there in silence, no one said a word. No one wept. No one moved. Mahmoud's arms were shaking with strain, his ankle burned like fire, but none of it could compare with the black nothingness that had consumed his heart.

Finally, Esma opened her eyes, her posture collapsing. She stepped back from the doorway, looking up into Mahmoud's eyes.

"You did this," she whispered. "I told you if you left there would be tragedy. His death is your fault."

For a long moment there was no sound. No gunfire or explosions. Nabil and Ahmad looked between Mahmoud and Esma, uncertainty painting their features. Mahmoud ignored them. He just stood, his gaze locked on Esma.

Finally, Mahmoud nodded. "I am guilty," he agreed quietly.

twelve

Samira: Europe

Low and orange, the sun painted the horizon. Light rippled over the waves. They looked harmless. Beautiful. A stark contrast to the existential threat of the night. Samira was struck thinking about how frequently beautiful things were dangerous.

Ahead, the beach was a dream. Their motor was dead again. The boat was low and heavy with water. Most of the refugees around her sat numb, letting the tide wash them slowly toward shore. They were too exhausted to paddle. Physically and emotionally they had nothing left. She could see several cars pulling out onto the sand of the beach. People in vests pointed at them, coming closer. They splashed out into the water, shouting and gesturing.

Samira's eyes drifted shut, her head dipping forward and then lurching upright again. The boat was near the beach now, and there were men all around pulling it in to shore. She tried to shake herself awake, tried to make sense of what she was seeing. The boat dragged up onto the beach with a soft grinding of sand. Suddenly, all around her people were scrambling out of the dinghy. The men and women on the beach threw shiny blankets around them and offered bottles of water.

For a long time, Samira sat watching, unmoving. She reveled in the freedom of not having bodies pressed against hers. Tears tracked down her face. She was disbelieving. She had spent the entire night certain they would die — she would never leave this boat. And now… now they were in Greece. She was still grieving, still trapped in the melancholy of certain death, unable to process this new information.

"Puncture the boat," a man shouted in English. She looked up. He was standing nearby, logoed as being with the U.N.H.C.R.. She didn't know what the letters stood for, only that they were the United Nations. "If it's seaworthy, we have to send them back."

Closer, a man stood over the edge of the dingy, a wicked knife poised in his hand. "Uhhh," he looked up at the U.N. official. "It's already wrecked. It's a miracle they made it to the beach."

Samira blinked as a hand reached out to her. They wanted to help her from the boat. She followed the hand to an arm, reaching her own hand out to grasp the one extended to her. Then she saw the face. The man smiled at her, gently. The stranger from the bus, from the cafe, and from her vision. She slapped his hand violently away, anger giving her the boost she needed. With some struggle, she stood in the slopping wet boat. She stepped over the side and onto the beach.

A woman offered her a water bottle and another smile. "You have to climb up that way," the woman pointed with an apologetic shrug of her shoulders. It was a steep road up a rocky incline, but it was on dry land. Samira smiled. "It's about half a mile. There's an aid station there."

A woman with a baby asked, "Could you drive us in your car?" The aid workers all studied their shoes.

"I'm afraid it's against the law."

"To give us a ride?"

Samira's hadn't spoken English in years, but she could follow. Yacoob had insisted his children learn English. It was good for business. She looked down at her wet, filthy abaya and nodded to the aid worker. Samira thought the accent sounded American. It sounded like television.

"They'll get you some fresh clothes and a bus to the camp," the American woman added.

Samira took the water bottle and nodded appreciatively. "Thank... you." The words came out a rough sort of stammer. She blamed the difficult night and the time since she'd last spoken English. The American woman beamed at her.

Looking ahead, Samira started after the line of refugees wending their way up the rocky slope. She kept putting one foot ahead of the other. For a full minute, she just closed her eyes, and felt each step sink into the soft sand. She felt the breeze blowing across her face, chilling her in her wet clothes, and the rising sun on her back. She'd made it to

Europe.

Shocks creaking, the bus bobbed along a barren stretch of highway. Umber-colored dust rose in faded clouds obscuring the landscape. Everything felt dream-like and alien again. Samira stared out the window. This was not Latakia, Syria. She was somewhere else. Everything felt wrong.

The bus hit another bump. The sound of the shocks reinforced her sense of deja vu as she was flung sideways. Samira nearly hit her head on the glass. That's when she saw him. Reaching toward her, to touch her hair. She jerked away. She realized her hijab was missing. She looked around quickly. Everyone was staring. As before, his hand touched her head, and suddenly she was covered again. No one was watching.

She wasn't surprised. It was happening just as before. *Why be surprised?*

Withering, taciturn, she glared at him. Just as before, he smiled. Gentle. Kind.

"Come to me," he repeated, "and I will exalt you."

Samira's eyes snapped open. She whipped her head around. Her eyes confirmed what the jouncing and rattling suggested. She was on a bus. Surrounded by other refugees, her hand shot up to her hair — her hijab. It was there. The woman sitting next to her was not the stranger.

She let out the breath she'd been holding. Another lurch of shocks bounced her in the seat.

Given the choice between a t-shirt and shorts and her ruined abaya, Samira's modesty had insisted on the abaya. The abaya was still cool, and rough with dried salt. The air was hot. The smell of fear, exhaustion and inadequate hygiene was pungent.

"I don't feel very exalted," she muttered.

The woman next to her turned expectantly. Samira smiled roughly and the woman looked away.

A hydraulic squeal brought the bus to a sudden halt and everyone lurched forward. Everyone was staring out the windows. *What now?*

The bus door slid open. No one moved. When she saw that everyone was afraid to move, Samira stood and made her way off the bus. She was followed by a flood of other refugees. They pooled together in shared uncertainty. A trio of aid workers in orange vests faced them.

To the right, a man with a slight German accent smiled, "Welcome to Greece!"

But all eyes drifted to the woman in the middle. She was tall and elegantly thin. Corded muscles and a razor-sharp jawline made her look anything but soft. The effect was accented by a shock of straw-colored hair across her brow, and the boy-short hair covering the rest of her head.

Samira couldn't imagine. The woman was in her early 20s, beautiful, but icy. Terrifying. Western to an alien degree.

"Okay!" The icy-blond barked the words like a drill instructor. "I need any single men to move over to Martin." She gestured and the smiling German who had welcomed them waved his hand.

A few men peeling away to cluster around Martin. Others looked around confused. The refugees started to mutter to one another.

A woman leaned toward Samira, whispering in Arabic. "What language is she speaking?"

"English," Samira replied.

"You understand?"

Samira nodded.

"Families with children, head over there," the blond pointed at a smiling woman in a long black dress with an odd white head covering. It was not a hijab. Samira thought it looked like something from a cowboy movie. It was still alien, but… somehow more familiar. *Not a Muslim,* Samira thought. "That's Dorcas." The woman with her head covered gave a wave.

"She said you should take your children and go with the modest woman," Samira told the Syrian woman who had been whispering to her. She watched the woman sigh in relief as she gathered two boys who looked shocked and listless.

"The rest of you," the terrifying blond woman continued, "I'm Suzi. I'm here representing Eurescue Syria. Follow me."

Suzi immediately turned and set off into the camp, utterly confident her orders would be followed.

A few people followed her, but several just looked at one another uncertain what to do.

"Follow the scary one," Samira translated before she began walking in the direction Suzi had gone.

The camp itself was terrifying. The tall fencing wore razor wire and encircled low stone buildings. It looked more like a prison than a place of shelter. But it was alive. Everywhere Samira looked, she saw people. Mothers. Children. Young men. They huddled together in clusters, laughing, talking, sharing tea. She saw Syrians, Iraqis, Afghanis and Africans. The clusters tended to be monocultural, but as she walked she heard many languages she didn't recognize and strains of an Arabic dialect she could barely make out.

As she caught up to Suzi, the woman turned, walking backward. "If you need fresh clothes," she pointed a finger at a large tent, one side rolled up. Folding tables filled the tent, stacked with clothing items as a couple of orange vested workers moved things from one pile to another. "You can't be too picky, but we'll get you warm and dry."

Samira sighed. *More immodest Western clothes.*

Suzi turned back around, still talking. "Very important: you'll need to get registered," she gestured toward one of the stone buildings, a seemingly endless line of people snaking around it. "No one leaves the camp or moves on to anywhere else in the EU until they're registered and they've completed their paperwork."

Turning again, she walked backwards through an open gate. A wide road divided the camp from an olive grove packed with tents. Many of them were alike: large, thick canvas tents, off-white and stenciled with the UNHCR logo. Samira also saw smaller tents in blues and greens, thin translucent material like one might see on a camping trip.

"You'll share a tent," Suzi continued, "with 26 other ladies. We'll have bread for you twice a day."

Suzi halted in front of one of the larger tents.

"Any questions?"

One of the younger women raised a hand. When Suzi nodded, the young girl spoke.

"What's over there?" She gestured up the hill where the tents grew more haphazard.

"That's the single men's camp," Suzi replied. "Don't go over there."

Suzi turned her head, looking at the other camp, her mouth turning down. Her posture changed, something vital going out of her. When her head turned back, she didn't make eye contact like before.

"If you see a single man in this camp..." Her no-nonsense tone faltered for the first time Samira could remember. "Hide. Or run."

thirteen

Mahmoud: The Butcher

Winter 2014

Mahmoud's finger pressed the doorbell. He heard it playing chimes inside the small apartment. It wasn't that Mahmoud didn't experience the sensations, it was that they meant nothing. Each was a disconnected stimuli, washing over him. They left no mark.

He heard the footsteps approaching the door. Slow. Inexorable. *I should feel dread,* he thought. Instead, he felt nothing. Empty.

"We should not be here. She isn't our people." Esma's voice was harsh in his ear.

"Mother," Ahmad retorted, "don't be cruel. She lost Jaber, too."

A dizzy wave spun Mahmoud's head as the words passed through him. He didn't think about them. They didn't mean anything. But they stole his equilibrium none-the-less. He gripped the door frame to steady himself. The wood released a vindictive splinter into his palm. He pressed his weight against it. It was good to feel something. *I deserve this pain.*

"Who is it? Jaber?" Tala's voice was hoarse, scared.

"It's okay, Tala," Ahmad was quick to respond. "It's your family."

Her family? Mahmoud wasn't sure. *Is she still my daughter-in-law with two husbands in the ground?* The thought skittered over his mind, but he didn't touch it. It went away.

She opened the door. He tried to look at her but he couldn't focus. His eyes floated around, lighting on nothing, barely seeing anything.

"*Ya Allah!* What has happened?" Tala sounded panicked.

Mahmoud struggled to respond, to find words. Finally, he focused his eyes. He saw Tala, her angelic face, the hints of her body as she moved in the abaya. He licked his lips. *What are you doing, you old fool!*

His own depravity shocked him back to life. Pain hit him like a tidal wave. It rolled over him and obliterated him. There was no Mahmoud Masoud, only this empty shell.

"Jaber," he said, his voice a harsh croak. His throat felt sore, and his mouth tasted of bile.

"I seek refuge in Allah from the cursed Satan," the rote words rolled from her mouth. She sounded as empty and desperate as Mahmoud felt.

"He is…" Mahmoud closed his eyes.

"Jaber is dead." Ahmad's voice was too eager. He didn't sound happy, not exactly. There was hope there, though. It stood out to Mahmoud. Like the smell of a midden, Ahmad's hope was impossible to miss.

Tala shook herself. "Come in."

She moved back from the doorway, letting them into the apartment.

Mahmoud, Esma and Ahmad crowded in. Mahmoud moved with a woodenness, an awkward robotic gait. Esma looked down her nose, evaluating every detail of the home and finding it wanting. Ahmad saw everything with a sort of boyish wonder.

Mahmoud stumbled up to a shelf, where he picked up a photo. The wood felt harsh, the texture gritty to his fingers. Jaber looked aloof in his wedding suit. Too good for the smiling Tala. *Too good for this terrible world.*

"I should get coffee," Tala said the words, but she didn't move.

"Let me," Ahmad jumped in, rushing off in search of the kitchen.

Tala moved slowly into the room. Her eyes followed the boy as he moved into her kitchen. "What am I… Where will I…" She swallowed, her eyes wide and vulnerable. She bit her lip. She looked at Mahmoud. "Am I to marry Ahmad now?"

The girl looked vulnerable and confused. Who could blame her? This pledge he'd made before Allah, the commitment to Basem… It was insane.

"He is very young," Mahmoud answered. She nodded gratefully. He couldn't contemplate it. He found himself staring into her eyes. They were beautiful. She was looking to him for wisdom, comfort, protection. Somehow that was filling the void in him. Making him feel strong. He grimaced. Those eyes would drink away his soul. *As they drank away the souls of my sons.* "We can discuss it when he is older."

Tala looked confused by the answer. Ahmad was older than her.

Esma turned on Mahmoud. "I will not see another of my children sacrificed to Basem's whore!"

Tala dropped onto the couch, more falling than sitting. If the two women had not been across the room from one another, Mahmoud would have thought his wife hit his daughter-in-law.

Tala was looking at him again, those eyes asking questions. Would he defend her? Did he also think she was a whore? Those eyes reminded him: Ismaeel was killed by his infatuation with Daesh. Jaber didn't die at home in her bed. He died betraying her. Those were the eyes of a victim, the same eyes that greeted him each morning in his mirror.

She started to sob. He knew the sound of her breaths. Even her weeping was familiar. He knew her entirely now. The grief, the words, it was all part of a terrible, unthinkable deja vu.

He didn't know the answers. *What are any of us to do?* He continued digging in the rubble of his soul. The smoking ruin of his life was choking him. He wished a bomb would fall from the sky and kill them all. It happened. Everyday, it happened. *Why not to me? Why not now?*

He glanced at Esma and saw in her eyes the same desperation for death. For him it fed a sucking emptiness, for her it transmuted into rage. But it was the same. *Perhaps we are more alike now than ever before,* he thought.

"Where am I to live?" Tala's words drew him back to her. Her voice was small. He wasn't even sure she was asking him.

Rage tore through him, hatred for her grief. *Who is she to grieve? Twice wedded to my sons, twice a widow.* She was a curse on the Masoud line. Marriage to her was like a killing disease.

He glared at her and she met his eyes. "Please, Baba." She slipped off to the couch, kneeling at his feet. "Help me."

Mahmoud had forgotten the photo frame in his hand. It fell from his limp fingers, the wood splintering and the glass shattering as it hit the tile floor.

Mahmoud turned looking past Tala, weeping on her knees. Ahmad watched him from the doorway. He held a tray of steaming coffee cups.

Ahmed. *She'll want to kill him next.* He saw Ahmad's eyes cut to Tala, the desire there, the lust. Mahmoud's lip curled. *He would be only too willing to walk into her web.*

He looked at Esma. Finally, they were seeing eye-to-eye. His hatred for Tala was now a match for hers. He'd thought she was just jealous. A beautiful woman replacing her in the hearts of her boys, but he saw it now. A cancer was murdering their family. She must be cut away.

"I am not your father, Tala. And I have no more sons for you to marry."

He ignored the shocked look Tala and Ahmed exchanged. *Had they already worked it out between them?* He slapped his chest, extending his hand toward her dramatically. Rage was building in him. It was good to feel something.

Tala is poison.

"Go. Find your own people," he told her, sweeping his arm… away.

Ahmad rushed to Tala, who buried her face in her hands.

"Get away from her!" Esma snapped. She began tugging their son, trying to pull him away from the kneeling girl.

Mahmoud just walked out through the still open door.

Weeks later, rage and grief continued to stalk him. Mostly he felt empty. Then, like a gun shot, or a screwdriver to the throat, rage would take him. He would lash out at Esma, at Nabil, at Ahmad… whoever was near to hand. Sometimes he wept. He preferred to weep alone; it was unmasculine. But he could barely bring himself to care who saw. More and more, he found himself taking risks. Some necessary, some not. He didn't know if that was why he was out at night again.

The streets of Aleppo were dark. An unnatural quiet smothered the city. Mahmoud moved furtively, his eyes darting defensively. He was terrified of the soldiers he was sure would be just around the next corner. His foot had never healed properly after he'd carried Jaber's body home. Limping along added to his distraction.

It was strange, to long for death one moment, and feel terror for his life in another. Terror was good, though. It reminded him he was alive — and that being alive was good.

Tripping on broken concrete, he barely avoided a fall into the bricks that fanned across the narrow street. The war ruined everything. *This city used to be beautiful.* With a heavy sigh, he ducked into an alleyway. Flickering light from a streetlamp lit the far end of the passage in short, orange strobes. Each flash revealed the hulking shadow of the man Mahmoud was meeting. *The butcher.*

Mahmoud's pulse pounded heavy in his ears. He could feel his sweat, beading on his forehead. He moved closer to the man.

"You have it?" Mahmoud hissed.

The bulky shadow dipped its head. *A nod?* Mahmoud hoped it was a nod. He pulled out a wad of bills, extending them toward the shadow. Another move, this time a shake of the head. Mahmoud grimaced. *This is extortion,* he thought. Digging in his pockets he added more bills to the handful.

Money was nearly worthless now. The most trivial items cost a fortune. Snatching the bills, the shadow offered a heavy plastic bag. Mahmoud took it, quickly and tried to peer inside. It was meat. He hoped it was meat. Some sort of meat. In the dark it was impossible to tell.

Mahmoud turned and took a few steps away before uncertainty stopped him. He had crossed so many lines, broken so many vows. Still….

"This is halal?" he asked, concerned the meat might violate Islamic law.

The butcher just laughed, his shadow growing larger as he moved closer to the light. He rounded the corner, and there was only Mahmoud, standing in the dark, staring into the blinding streetlamp holding a bag which probably contained illicit pork.

I drink in bars. I roam the streets after curfew. Allah has taken my sons. What does pork matter?

He sighed again, steeling himself to dart back to Nabil's home. Turning away from the light the darkness of the alley came alive, grabbing him and knocking him to the ground. He felt his head. There was pain where he'd struck the stones. *No blood. Too convenient I should just die.* He looked up, and saw a horrible vision.

"Where is she?" Flashes of light showed him a bald man, face twisted with rage shoving a machine gun in Mahmoud's face. "Where are you hiding her?"

There was so much to understand. Too much information coupled with a blow to the head. He tried to work through it methodically. The gunmen looked ready to shoot, menacing with his AK-47. He was panting in his rage, eyes wild. Those eyes… Mahmoud knew him.

"Ata? *Ya elahi!* What are you—?"

Ata lurched forward, poking his rifle at Mahmoud, who scrambled backwards on the filthy stones.

"Where is my wife, Mahmoud?"

His wife? What is he talking about?

"I will find her. You cannot hide her from me," Ata insisted.

And then, the truth struck Mahmoud harder than the stones. *Samira!* If she wasn't with Ata.... Suddenly all Mahmoud could feel was fear.

"She's back?" It came out as a strangled gasp. "You promised me she wouldn't come back."

Please, Allah, I have suffered so much. Don't let this shame come to light.

Ata's expression changed, weakened. His shoulder's sagged.

"You haven't seen her," he said hopelessly, the barrel of his rifle dipping.

Mahmoud grabbed the end of the weapon and pulled, dragging Ata forward while levering himself to his feet. His ankle screamed as it took his weight, but Mahmoud ignored it. Pain was his life now. The older man grabbed a hold of Ata's shirt in his clenched fists, spittle exploding from his lips.

"We had an agreement! Honor—"

Ata shoved him back against the wall, clearly the stronger and the more violent. Mahmoud's head struck the stone wall, ringing again. It hurt. He blinked his eyes. Shocking pain tried to overwhelm him. He shook it off. Samira would ruin him. He had so little left. All he had to live for was the belief that his remaining son would someday inherit Yacoob's business empire. There would be no inheritance if Yacoob knew what had happened.

"Don't lecture me about honor," Ata hissed, his lips inches from Mahmoud's throat. "Where is your wife tonight, Mahmoud Masoud?"

"My wife?" *Surely, she is home. Isn't she home?* He could remember her expression when he'd left. She'd been cold. Numb. But she'd been that way for months. Since the death of Jaber. Like him, she experienced bouts of rage, followed by long stretches of nothing. She'd told him goodbye as he walked out the door. No anger. No nagging. In Mahmoud's mind that goodbye suddenly seemed more final.

"She walks the streets, begging for death," Ata continued.

Mahmoud surged forward, his fist colliding with Ata's head with all of the force of his pent-up passions. Ata staggered back into the opposite wall. Mahmoud moved to strike him again, but Ata was too quick, raising his rifle.

"Think of your family, Mahmoud."

That's all I can *think of.* Gasping for breath, rage still painting his cheeks red, Mahmoud raised his hands in surrender.

"If you see Susu, tell her I will find her. I have not forgotten the promise we made before Allah."

Ata turned and left the alley. His shadow disappearing into the darkness.

He could be waiting for me around the corner. Another ambush. Mahmoud shook his head. *It doesn't matter. I have to find my wife,* Mahmoud thought, rushing frantically into the night, his bag of meat forgotten on the stones behind him.

fourteen

Samira: Moria

Samira sat up suddenly, breathing hard. Around her, other women tossed and snored. Scattered around her tent, the women were wrapped in thin blankets, pressing together for warmth. She tried to control her lungs. Over the course of a week in the camp, the weather had turned from boiling hot to miserable and wet. Day after day, the dream kept coming. "Come to me and I will exalt you." *Can I not rest one night?* She thought.

Rain and dripping water drummed endlessly against the canvas ceiling. Pulling her blanket around her shoulders, Samira rubbed at her arms. She struggled to get her blood flowing.

Closing her eyes, she slowed her breathing. *It was just a dream.* There was no prophet dogging her steps. Exhaustion and stress were more than enough explanation for her seeing the dream prophet in the cafe, on the bus, and at the boat.

Beside her, a young girl twitched and moaned in her sleep. Samira reached over, laying a gentle hand on the girl's shoulder. The girl quieted, her breathing becoming more even. Smiling sadly, Samira thought of Yasmeen. She'd seen visions of Yasmeen, too. She thought of Ata standing over the body of that little girl. *How could he do that?* She still couldn't rectify the husband she'd adored with that man at the bus stop. Ata was always a radical. *But a murderer?* A chill ran through her. She wouldn't be able to go back to sleep now.

It was time to get started on the day.

Gathering her blanket around her like a sort of poncho, she moved toward the tent flap. She stepped carefully over the other women. At the flap, she peered out at the water sluicing from the sky. Reluctantly, she pulled the blanket from her shoulders. *I'll want a dry blanket tonight when I sleep.* She tossed it back where she'd been sleeping. She rubbed the goosebumps from her arms again and moved out through the tent flap into the cold morning.

Rain pelted her and snatches of wind conspired to make it feel like ice. A few steps into the wet, muddy camp and she was drenched. She passed few people. Those that had to be about, moved in a chilly, hunched shuffle. Some held shirts or other garments over their heads to try to block the rain. They looked just as wet.

The early hour and the quiet of the rainy camp gave her hope, but the registration line still wrapped around the building. She joined the crowd, shifting foot to foot — anything to keep warm. It was maddening. Yesterday she'd stood in this line for half the day, only for the office to close before she could register.

Hours passed. The rain stopped. The sun reached its apex in the sky, its pale light giving false hope against the wind and wet clothing. The line had doubled in length, but forward movement was slow. Samira began to wonder if she would wait the entire day. The sun began its descent. She felt like it was a race. Would the sun get to the horizon before she reached the head of the line?

She was tired, wet, and devoid of hope and purpose. *Where is Allah?* How could he continue to mock her with visions promising she would be exalted while she rotted in this muddy prison? She'd been a good Muslim. Said her prayers, gone to the mosque, listened to her father and brothers even when they were fools. She didn't deserve this. She'd been an obedient wife. *I followed the dictates of a husband who was a psychopath!* She sighed, the fight going out of her. Love was a confusing business. She hadn't sought it with Ata, but love had claimed her none-the-less. She saw him again in her mind, screaming at her in the midst of a massacre he instigated.

Time lost meaning. She shuffled forward when the person before her in line moved. It all became a fog. *Does any of it matter?*

Eventually, she reached the front of the line. She was ushered into an austere little office. A small, officious-looking man, gazed at her over his spectacles.

"Your name?" He turned his attention to a laptop on his desk. She looked around the room. There was another woman at a table in the corner. She sat with a clipboard and a pen. Samira blinked. The stranger sat across from the other woman. He wasn't speaking, but he was totally focused on the other woman as she filled in her form. *The hallucinations are getting worse.*

The official cleared his throat. She shook her head. Turning back, she found the little man staring at her, his eyebrows pointedly raised.

"My name," Samira said. He nodded. "Samira Maso…" She ground to a halt, blinking. She could almost hear her father, the memory was so clear. "Samira will always bring honor to our family." It landed like a blow. "She will never break her promises, betray a husband or her family."

She looked down, unable now even to meet the eyes of the official. It didn't matter that he was a foreigner. Surely, he could see her shame. *I can't claim the Masoud name now. What can I say?* She glanced over at the stranger. He was watching Samira with expectation, waiting for her answer. *Who am I, now? No longer a daughter or a wife.* He seemed to see the answer on her face. His eyes grew sad, and he shook his head before she spoke.

"My name is Samira Mohammed." It was a good name. The name of the Prophet. But also the name of Ata's father.

The official didn't look up. "Spell that for me."

She looked at the stranger again. It was almost a compulsion. She didn't want to see him. He wasn't even real, but she needed to see his face. His eyes met hers and the words seemed to echo through her entire being, though his lips never moved.

"Come to me."

"Did you speak?" Samira's question was urgent. His lips hadn't moved but it was his voice, like the visions and the bus.

"Yes," the official responded with annoyance. "I asked you to spell your name."

Samira forced herself to turn away from the hallucination. She looked at the man who was real. He looked small and pinched, like the weight of bureaucracy had compressed him.

"How long will this take?" Samira asked.

"A very long time if you don't answer my questions," the official replied.

Samira pursed her lips in annoyance. "I answer your questions, you write my answers on your form, or put them into your computer… then what?"

She could feel the people outside, the pressure of the line. *Every moment I am here, someone else is waiting.* And yet, it had taken so long to get into this room, she needed to know.

"We have to determine whether or not you are a refugee."

She blinked, trying to understand what that meant. "Everyone in this camp is a refugee."

The official shook his head. "Some of them are just looking for a better life."

"All of us," she fired back, "are looking for a better life."

The official grimaced. "Not all of you needed to look here. Please spell your name."

As Samira spelled her name, she felt overwhelmed by all of the desperate people. Ata's words haunted her. "The Westerners hate us." She didn't see hate in the official's eyes. He just looked brittle, like a man too often disappointed. He had many more questions. She struggled to answer them.

She staggered from the temporary building back out into the cold evening. The line seemed to stretch forever. The people looked sad, miserable. The hope that animated them when they arrived was being ground away by endless lines, mud, cold, wind.

"If we fled to Europe they would leave us in cages…" Ata's words floated through her mind again. She looked up at the fencing and razor wire. This miserable camp wasn't built to torment refugees. No one thought razor wire would be needed for managing a humanitarian crisis. But someone had decided, somewhere that the appropriate place to house and process refugees was an abandoned prison. "…and treat us with contempt." She sighed. She didn't want Ata to be right.

fifteen

Mahmoud and Samira: Shame

Spring 2014

Moving like a zombie, Mahmoud allowed Nabil to drag him into the house. His eyes glazed over the rich trappings of Nabil's success. Nabil's living room looked much like the guest house, where Mahmoud lived. Both were show pieces. Both were designed to maximize comfort while making a lavish declaration of wealth. Nabil's aesthetic was often gaudy, but Mahmoud made no judgments. There was no teasing, no friendly banter. He simply responded to Nabil, incessantly tugging at his arm, until he was able to flop onto an overstuffed couch.

"Mahmoud is here," Nabil shouted. "Please, bring strong coffee."

The oddity stood out in Mahmoud's wandering thoughts. Nabil hired serving girls whom he treated as near slaves. Yet he said please when calling for coffee.

The fat man lowered himself to the couch beside Mahmoud. He reached out a companionable hand, as though to pat Mahmoud on the shoulder, but then stopped. Nabil broke eye-contact. The hand returned to his lap. Mahmoud just stared at his friend. He watched as Nabil repeatedly took a breath, opening his mouth to speak, only to close it again without saying a word.

After a while, the serving girl appeared. She was young enough to be Nabil's daughter. Properly covered, only her face emerged from the oval opening in her hijab. As ever with Nabil's servant girls, she was attractive and stylishly made up. *How much money must Nabil be paying,* Mahmoud wondered. *A girl this beautiful could easily attract a husband, yet she is here serving Nabil.*

The girl set a tray down on the coffee table. The smell of cardamom filled the air. Mahmoud didn't need to look to know the spice was floating in the steaming coffee pot. He'd introduced Nabil to the practice when they were in University. Mahmoud's friend leaned over the tray and inhaled deeply, savoring the smell. He smiled at the serving girl and gave her a nod. She turned and left the room without a word.

Mahmoud's eyes followed her all the way out. He could imagine the motions of the body hidden under her abaya. *She's too young, too much like Tala.* The drifting thought stabbed at him, and he retreated again into numbness.

With practiced efficiency, Nabil poured two cups. He offered one to the unresponsive Mahmoud. After a moment, Nabil returned the cup to the tray and brought the other to his lips, slurping loudly. He froze suddenly, cutting his eyes to Mahmoud who continued to stare vacantly.

It's not as though Mahmoud hadn't seen Nabil drink coffee before. They had coffee in this room almost every day. His world was an endless, empty spiral.

Nabil returned his coffee cup to the tray looking sheepish. He studied Mahmoud, took another deep breath and finally spoke.

"I'm sorry, my friend. She was…" Nabil searched but couldn't find the word he was looking for.

Mahmoud just stared at Nabil, watching his friend shift uncomfortably. Emotions flared inside Mahmoud, like the shroud lifting on a lantern. He felt suddenly wild. Angry. Pain was exhausting. He wanted to hurt someone. Nabil's eyes grew wider and he leaned away from Mahmoud. Just as quickly the feeling leaked out of Mahmoud with an apathetic sigh.

"She was a tyrant," Mahmoud finished Nabil's thought.

The tension broke out of Nabil in a harsh cackle. Mahmoud looked down at this finger, turning the elegant ring Yacoob had given him.

"I only married her to please my father."

Nabil's gaiety faded. His hand fluttered uncertainly toward Mahmoud again. "Nothing you do will ever please that man."

Mahmoud let go of the ring, nodding. He should throw it away. Or trade it for something he wanted. Swap his inheritance for… *something that doesn't hurt.*

"She was with me for twenty-seven years."

This time, Nabil's hand made it all the way to Mahmoud's shoulder. His fingers tightened. The contact was a strange comfort. Mahmoud felt better and he wanted to sob like a child. Two sons dead, and then the wife he'd despised… just disappeared. Walked out into the street never to be seen again. And… he missed her. He missed the battle. The stability of her in his life.

She could still return. Even in his mind, the words sounded empty. Esma hadn't gone to a friend or relative. People had seen her wandering the most dangerous streets, courting death. And then… no one had seen her. Somewhere, another corpse lay severed from its identity. Mahmoud and his last remaining son, Ahmad, were left to mourn with no closure and no body. *Like Baba and Samira.*

"You need someone young," Nabil said, his voice low and salacious. "Someone to remind you that you are alive."

Mahmoud waved a dismissive hand. He was not Nabil. Then he thought of the servant girl. Perhaps this was Nabil speaking from experience. He found it hard to believe such an attractive girl would let a disgusting creature like Nabil touch her. For a moment, Mahmoud gazed at his friend's rolls of fat. He eyed Nabil's sagging cheeks. Mahmoud frowned, discarding the thought. It was not Nabil's fat that made the idea repugnant. It was his age. *And I am not any younger.*

"I'm not ready for a new wife."

Nabil smiled, his shoulders rising in a way that reminded Mahmoud of a tricky negotiation. "Nothing so permanent," Nabil's tone was mincing, a hushed dance of words. "A temporary wife. Just a girl to help you forget… everything, for a night or two."

Mahmoud should have been outraged at the suggestion. He knew men who made such bargains. He had always seen them as lesser. However, his spirit was too broken for moral outrage. Lust bubbled in him, a far more pleasant emotion than pain or desperation. He looked up at Nabil and nodded slowly. It would be lovely to forget.

* * *

Summer 2013

Samira rocketed awake again, breathing hard. It took her a moment to remember where she was. The ground was a hard reminder. Around her, women tossed and turned. She closed her eyes a moment, trying to imagine something pleasant, something other than the endless dream that plagued her sleeping mind.

The words came to her unbidden: "Come to—"

She jumped up from her blankets, launching out of the tent. She would find a distraction.

The day was bright, warm and blessedly dry. *There is much for which to be grateful,* she coached herself. Sadly, no amount of sun could make the camp less dreary. People shuffled past her, weary and hopeless. It didn't matter where they'd come from, what they were fleeing, or where they dreamed of going. Every day, a few people would inexplicably leave. Some joyously proclaimed they were on their way to the mainland. Others simply vanished without a word. But they were few. And every day more people crowded into this prison. More tents appeared in the olive grove.

Samira made her way to the end of another line. The lines were a part of the endless cycle of the camp. There was a line for everything. As the weeks passed, the lines began to blur together. Samira closed her eyes.

"He is coming," a man whispered behind her.

"We can only hope," another replied.

Hope was a bitter pill in the camp. Each day, new refugees would arrive. They were full of hope. They'd finally arrived in Europe! The long ordeal was over… so they thought. A few days in the camp turned hope to horror.

"When he arrives, he will punish the Westerners and we will be set free."

Samira sighed. She didn't know who the men were talking about, but she'd heard the sentiment before. As the people despaired of leaving the camp, sometimes they began to hate this place they'd fought so hard to reach. They bought into the propaganda from Daesh that this was all a trap made by the Westerners. That was what Abu Bakr Al-Baghdadi taught. *What my husband believed.*

It was hard to understand why people would carry those teachings with them even as they fled the carnage the teachings encouraged. But the situation here was terrible. Despair was a tricky business. *Who am I to judge?* Samira wondered.

From the little Samira was able to glean, it seemed the European

Union was paying the Greek Government to stop the flow of refugees into Europe. The conditions of the camp were an acceptable side effect. Maybe it was true. She didn't really know.

"Abu Anas Al-laziky can't come soon enough."

Samira's head whipped around at the name. The two men behind her flinched back. Then they glared at her. They didn't like being startled by a woman.

"I'm sorry," Samira said, dropping her head and raising her hands in surrender.

The men grumbled and she turned back to her place in line.

Samira understood how the men of Daesh — the ISIS terrorists — got their names. She could decode this one easily enough. Abu because he was a first born son. Anas for Anas bin Malik, the servant of the Prophet Mohammed. Al-laziky because he was from Latakia, her home town.

Latakia was a large city. Samira certainly didn't know everyone. Yet some terrible premonition made her certain this Abu Anas Al-laziky was someone she knew. She prayed it was not her nephew, Ismaeel, or her brother, Ali. Ismaeel was passionate and desperate to enact justice as he saw it. He was like Ata in that way. She didn't know Ali well, but her brother had proven he was capable of murder. *He's brought enough shame on Baba already.*

This line moved quickly. After a half an hour, she faced Suzi's icy blue eyes. There was an unspoken challenge there. Samira didn't feel she could measure up to the blond woman's expectations. The German extended a small round of bread. Samira took it and walked away, the conversation of the men in line forgotten as she recriminated herself for withering before Suzi's stare.

As she passed those waiting in line, she saw him again. The stranger. He stood beside a small child. The two were playing a game, smiling and laughing together.

Samira raised her chin, narrowing her eyes in rage. *How dare he? He promised to exalt me, and now he plays while I take bread like a beggar!* The stranger and the little boy turned to her offering a smile and wave. Samira just stomped past them, her fingers crunching through the hard crust of the bread.

Huddling on the ground against the outside wall of a tent, Samira tried to block out the screams. Clamping her hands over her ears would not make the sounds stop. Samira gave up, her hands falling to her sides. She could hear the footsteps of the woman running. They were soft, haphazard and desperate. Punctuated with gasping breaths. The sounds of her pursuers were different. Their tread sounded heavier. Laughter and catcalls came from many voices.

"Hey pretty girl," one man called. "Come out. We are lonely and the night is cold."

I should do something, she thought. She couldn't talk herself into action, though. She felt naked under the open stars. Samira shivered, but not from the cold. She squeezed her eyes shut. She wanted it to be over, but she knew what that would mean. The men wouldn't leave until they got what they wanted.

When the woman suddenly broke from cover, Samira knew the end was written. The sounds were too frantic. They ended quickly in another cry and the sound of a body hitting the ground, air suddenly and harshly vacating lungs.

"Tell me your name," another man's voice. Harsher. Filled with malicious relish. *Is it not enough to abuse her? They must shame her family?*

The woman was weeping and stammering. Begging to be released.

"What's your name?" Another man, taunting.

"Yasmeen," the girl croaked weakly between sobs.

Samira's eyes shot open and she scrambled to see around the tent. The woman was a few feet away, sprawled on her back. Her hijab was half unraveled, strands of hair clinging to her face and dragging across the muddy soil. The girl's eyes were already red and puffy. Snot ran from her nose and tears from her eyes. The men were invisible, a pattern of shadows across her terrified face.

On the verge of rushing out, Samira got a good look at the girl's face. *That isn't my Yasmeen.*

There was no hallucination. No vision replacing the woman with Samira's little sister. *Does that matter?* Samira slowly slipped back into her hiding place. She felt herself shrivel inside. The ugly feeling of self-loathing whipping her with every gasp and cry from the girl as the men went about their evil business. Samira hid. She was safe while the other woman was violated. She covered her ears again, clamped her eyes shut, and tried to pretend she could do nothing.

Like the smoke and the darkness, the flashing lights were designed to conceal and distract. *You aren't supposed to notice how old the men at these tables are,* Mahmoud thought. He placed his hands on his cheeks, pulling downward. He wanted to believe that this place was too depraved even for Nabil, but it was wishful thinking. It was Nabil who told him to come. Mahmoud stared through the smoke at another table. A man sat alone, middle sixties, tailored suit, not a hair out of place. Everything about him oozed power except the lust lighting his eyes. The successful man nearly drooled up at the girl dancing on his table. Mahmoud wouldn't let himself look at her.

This is rock bottom, he told himself. The slamming bass shook his chest. *What am I doing here?* He didn't need to see the girl's face to know what she looked like. They were all the same. A mask of makeup and paint aimed to conceal, just like the smoke and darkness. The owners of the club didn't want you to notice how awkwardly the girls danced, their lack of curves.

Mahmoud looked down into his drink. More alcohol. He was probably drunker than he intended. *Not nearly drunk enough for this club.*

Nabil had partially explained the situation to Mahmoud. Women made desperate by the way, women without husbands or fathers to care for them, came here to earn money. Usually they were here with a female relative, an older woman who could negotiate on their behalf. "It is a way to provide for women in need," Nabil had suggested. *He never mentioned they would be children.*

"Nabil," he muttered, "you are a fool."

Enough. I'm leaving. Mahmoud planted both hands on the table, ready to lever himself to his feet. A woman, who looked even older than the successful man at the other table, slid into the seat across from Mahmoud.

He waved a hand at the woman. "I'm not interested."

"Please, you haven't heard my offer, sir."

Mahmoud looked into her eyes. She was younger than he'd thought. Perhaps forty. Hard living had aged her too fast. He saw how thinly she hid her desperation under enticing.

Mahmoud spoke firmly, "I am not like them." He waved at the rest of the room and got his butt about three inches off the chair before she responded.

"Of course." Her words came faster as he continued rising. "I have a special woman for a man who is not like the others."

He ignored her pitch, turning away from the table. Usually hidden behind a heavy curtain, the exit was visible. The curtain was held by a young man with twinkling eyes. A shaft of light from the doorway, cut across the floor, landing squarely on Mahmoud. Mahmoud didn't think he'd seen the man before, but they locked eyes. The stranger looked at Mahmoud like they were dear friends. He was holding the curtain for Mahmoud, making a way out of this terrible place.

The haggard woman lurched over the table. Grabbing Mahmoud's arm, she spun him around.

"Please," she begged, all pretense gone. "We haven't eaten in three days."

Mahmoud's eyes latched onto a figure over the woman's shoulder. Across the room, a beautiful woman walked through the crowd. Mahmoud moved his head, trying to get a clear view through the crowd. There was something about her. Something desperate within him seized on her. She was not another underaged dancing girl. She was a woman grown — still young enough to be Mahmoud's child — but old enough to be married. *Old enough to know a man.* The thought was oily and alien. It thrilled through Mahmoud.

"My Haniya will be whatever you desire…" The old woman still clutched Mahmoud's arm, flying through her rehearsed sales pitch.

Mahmoud continued to crane his neck, trying to see more of the mysterious woman. She was dressed more conservatively than the dancers. Her dress was indecent, clinging to her curves. It was a dress a woman might wear alone with her husband. But it was expensive. The neckline less plunging, the skirt slightly longer. *The other girls are wearing a sluttish parody of this dress,* Mahmoud thought.

The light was still on Mahmoud. He could see his shadow stretched long across the floor. It seemed to speak to him, reminding him there was a way out. *The door is open. I'll go,* he told himself without moving. *I need to go.* The door was waiting, held open for him. He continued to watch the beautiful woman as she moved through the crowd. She was so different than the pathetic girls. Curiosity held him in place.

"Which one is your Haniya?" Mahmoud asked, desperately hoping it was the woman he followed with his eyes.

The light across the floor disappeared and the old woman smiled.

She shifted, tugging Mahmoud's arm to turn him toward one of the platforms. The girl she indicated might have been 13. She danced uncertainly, her eye makeup increasing the startled look on her face. One of her dark red lips was trapped between her teeth as she worried it.

Mahmoud slashed a hand across his chest. "I don't want her." He pointed. "I want that woman."

The haggard woman slumped. "I cannot negotiate for her."

A flash of light caught Mahmoud's ring — Yacoob's ring. Mahmoud ripped it from his finger and thrust it at the woman. She jumped back, scared. Then she saw the fine silver and the garnet. It pulled her back to him.

"This is my family ring," Mahmoud explained. "Take it to that woman. Make the arrangements and I promise you and your daughter will eat tonight."

sixteen

Samira: Taking Control

Taking another nervous step forward, Samira coached herself: *I can do this.* The revelation was more than a week old. She'd been procrastinating. In line again, Samira stood a few people from the front. At the head of the line was an open-sided tent. A volunteer, who Samira thought was called Jenny or Gemmi, was greeting each woman that approached. The tent itself was filled with battered folding tables, each one adorned with donated clothing. Jenny would help the women in the line try to find clothing that fit.

"I'm sorry," Gemmi was saying. "It's all we have." The woman at the front of the line was holding up a thin t-shirt. Samira didn't know the woman. From this angle, Samira couldn't see her face, but she knew the expression.

It was a constant problem. Almost all of the women in the camp were Muslim. Some wouldn't have minded wearing more Western clothes in a different context, but the clothes were immodest. The last thing any woman in the camp wanted was more attention from the men. Some men saw Western clothes as an invitation or a wrong to be punished.

The woman reluctantly took the t-shirt and walked away. Samira stepped into her place.

"Hi there," Jenny bubbled. *It's Gemmi. Isn't it?* Samira needed to be better with their names. Many of the volunteers were only in the camp for a few weeks. Then they were replaced with a new crop with new names. "What size do you wear?"

Samira steeled herself to speak. Her eyes flicked over Gemmi's shoulder. A woman was folding clothes further back in the tent. *Suzi.* Something inside Samira froze. She always felt a little jolt of terror when she saw the cold-eyed German woman. Everything about her, from the short cropped hair to her sharp commands and unsmiling expression made Samira feel rejected. *It's like something about me offends her.*

Gemmi—She was almost certain it was Gemmi—opened her eyes expectantly. She was still waiting for Samira to respond. Letting go of a shuddering breath, Samira lifted her chin, clicking her tongue. She gave the woman her best reassuring smile. *I can do this. It is a small thing.*

"Can I," Samira said cautiously, "help?"

The idea was simple enough. Samira was tired of floating along, being a victim. She needed to take control. If she could begin helping in the camp, then she had a purpose. She wasn't sitting in limbo waiting for some unknown bureaucrat to move her on. She wasn't a beggar subsisting on handouts. She was a volunteer and she was here for a reason. It made a lot of sense in her head. It seemed straightforward. Even elegant. She hoped it would be enough to shake off the visions. *It's something else to focus on at least.* But standing there, she was uncomfortably aware that she hadn't seen a single refugee volunteer in all her months in camp.

Jenny — it was Jenny — looked surprised and turned to Suzi. The German woman met Samira's eyes. Samira felt her stomach knot. Suzi gave a curt nod. Tension melted into elation as Samira stepped around the table. She began folding clothes beside Suzi, grinning. Suzi didn't say a word.

"Thank you, Gemmi," Samira said.

"Jeanie," the girl replied with a grin before greeting the next person in line: "Hello! What size for you?"

A month later, Samira wiped the sweat from her forehead, trying to catch it before it rolled into her eyes. She should be delighted at the change of seasons. The cold that cut through the tents and the rain that made everything sodden were both gone. However, the sun was brutal — a relentless, malevolent ball smothering the camp in hot, muggy despair. She was exhausted. Restless nights colluded with the heat. She returned her attention to the box in front of her. It was filled with tennis shoes. They were all worn. Used. Donations from North America and other parts of Europe. She lifted out a pair of high-tops that looked brand new. The few scuffs could easily have come from sharing the box. Checking the size, she placed them with the other ladies size 10s on the table. The next pair out of the box had a hole in the toe, grass stains, and smelled like a locker room. In Syria, Samira would have tossed them in the garbage. Here, someone would need them.

"Um," Samira looked up to see a blond girl in an orange vest. "Pardon me, miss....?"

The constant cycle of volunteers was such that Samira had played out this ritual many times.

"Sammie," she replied. It was easier. They knew that name. None of them managed to say Samira properly.

"Miss Sammie, I think both of these are left shoes." The girl's spoke English in an accent that reminded Samira of a cowboy movie. The American held up two identical shoes. With a quick scan of the table, Samira was able to find another identical set. As she handed them to the girl she said, "Just Sammie, or Susu if you must."

They loved nicknames. One volunteer had tried calling her Siri, after the automated assistant. After all, Samira was the only volunteer from "Siri-Ah." Samira hadn't thought it particularly clever.

Quickly pairing the shoes correctly, the girl returned to her work at another table. Samira looked up as Suzi walked swiftly past. The German woman had her phone to her ear and was looking distraught.

"No! That isn't—Look, can I just talk to..." That was all Samira heard as the other woman passed. *So she's human after all.* It was an uncharitable thought. Samira had seen so little emotion from the other woman, it was a relief to see her upset. It meant there was something she cared about. Samira had hoped volunteering would bridge the gap between them. She would get to know Suzi. Her fear of the other woman would pass as she saw her good qualities. Despite spending more time together, the woman still seemed like an alien creature. Cold. Aloof. Hostile.

"They say she's trapped," said the American.

Samira felt the word on her skin. That terrible moment in the cafe when Mahmoud had shoved her back into the chair flashed through her mind. She had tried to resist but he was stronger — the moment when she had realized she could not escape him still terrified her. *Trapped.* She glanced up from the pair of shoes she was holding. She'd been searching for a size. She couldn't remember which size, now. Turning, she looked at the blond girl at the next table.

"Like she's a prisoner?" It was crazy to imagine. Samira felt like a prisoner. All the refugees did. But Suzi was a volunteer. She could leave anytime she wanted. She had a passport to go back to Germany.

"Like she did something," a wicked twinkle lit the girl's eyes, "and now she's afraid to go back to her normal life. Can you imagine?"

The girl smirked and continued sorting shoes. It was idle gossip to her. The words shuddered though Samira's soul. "She did something and now she's afraid to go back to her normal life." *I* can *imagine.*

She found the scrap of scarf in her hand, her fingers stroking it. She wanted so badly to call her father. Many of the women in camp had offered her their phones for that very purpose. "Call your family. Tell them you are safe." But what could she say?

I left my husband. I broke my vow. But it's okay, I'm safe. She squeezed her eyes shut, shoved the scarf back into a pocket and resumed sorting shoes. She could never go home. She would never see her father or her sister again. No one else in camp could understand. To them, it seemed she was being childish. You have a family. You can call home. Suddenly she saw the connection. *Suzi has a passport, she can go home.* Samira raised her chin making a click with her tongue. For the first time, she felt a connection to the German woman. *Suzi is human, and not nearly so different as I thought.*

Winter 2014

The weather was growing cooler again. Wind gently rustled the branches of the olive trees. Longer sleeves were making a comeback in the desperate utilitarianism of camp fashion.

Samira swung her hammer. She missed the tent peg and barely missed her hand. *Isn't there a man to do this?* It was a thought born of frustration and she immediately regretted it. She was perfectly capable of securing a tent.

The rope holding the tent to the peg was badly frayed. As she hammered the peg into the ground, it snapped. The side of the tent partially collapsed.

Samira let out a slow frustrated growl. Throwing the hammer on the ground, she rubbed tired eyes. The dreams hadn't stopped. She did have a purpose now. She loved helping. She was a leader now, someone the volunteers looked to and respected. She knew the camp and its residents. Now she knew the people and organizations involved in the relief efforts. As a sort of liaison, she was often able to help the workers be more effective by resolving cultural conflicts which neither side saw at the outset. But, no matter how much she helped or how valuable she became, she still had the visions. She still felt she'd failed her family and missed her purpose.

That wasn't all that disturbed her dreams. The tensions in the camp continued to rise. Rumors of Abu Anas Al-laziky continued to grow and with them the belief that the police, the islanders and the relief workers needed to be punished. Each day, more and more refugees arrived and fewer left the island. The former prison had never been designed to hold so many.

I just want to quit, she thought. *To run back to my tent, bury my head under my smelly, threadbare blanket, and hibernate until the whole world is a different place.* This constant, never-ending limbo was too much for anyone to endure. The camp was restless with nagging uncertainty. There were fights and talk of revolution. Many of the Greek islanders were angry. The refugee crisis had ruined the tourist industry that kept the island solvent. Refugees required far more food and water resources than the island was capable of supporting. None of that was the fault of the refugees, but someone had to take the blame. Relations between the two communities grew more and more tense.

"Still not exalted," she muttered. She started pulling the canvas around looking for the broken piece of rope. Pulling it back to a point where she could try retying it proved to be no small undertaking. She quickly discovered she needed four hands.

"Abu Anas Al-laziky should come do something useful and hold my tent peg," she muttered.

The sound of footsteps filled her with hope. She looked up expectantly. Not that she expected a terrorist to come and help her, but perhaps it was another relief worker. She held back a sigh of disappointment at what she saw.

A young mother, holding a baby, was engaged in an intense discussion with Suzi. The German woman looked dazed, like she wasn't really tracking what the other woman was telling her. For her part, the mother looked angry. She was unloading a tirade on Suzi.

Samira didn't know if it was deserved, but she doubted it. Many of the refugees just needed a focus for their feelings. Anyone would do.

"Uh, hey Sammie." Samira was caught by surprise as two other volunteers approached her. She knew them by sight and was fairly certain their names were Amy and Kelsey. Amy was the one who had spoken. She was a large-boned, tall woman from the U.S., while Kelsey was petite and from Canada, Samira thought. Somehow they'd come with the same group.

"We finished with the blankets."

"Great," Samira said. "Hold this."

Amy grabbed the rope and Samira pulled up the connecting line. In a moment, the two pieces were tied together.

"Thank you," Samira said. "You're looking for something else to do?"

Amy nodded. At that moment, Suzi looked over. Samira tried to catch her eye, but the woman rolled her eyes and marched away. The woman with the baby was gone, presumably inside the tent across the way.

"Good," Samira smiled. "Can one of you go and check on Yara?"

Kelsey looked confused, "Who is Yara?"

Suzi reappeared carrying a sleeping bag. It was rolled up, but stuffed full of baby items. The roll was so packed, things were slowly working their way out of the folds.

"Is Yara the older lady," Amy asked, "with the limp?"

Suzi looked over at Samira again. The glare was ugly on her face. She tripped. Samira watched like it was slow motion, the sleeping bag seemed to unravel in the air, baby items flying every which way as Suzi dropped into the dirt.

"Yes," Samira explained, "She's having trouble getting up and moving around. Make sure she got something to eat today."

"On it," Amy replied with a smile.

She and Kelsey turned together to walk away. Samira reached out, catching Kelsey's arm. She glanced past the volunteer to see Suzi back on her feet, dusting herself off.

"Perhaps Suzi has a different task for you," Samira suggested.

Kelsey looked taken aback. "Suzi?" She turned her head and looked at the other woman trying to reroll the sleeping bag. "Why would—"

Suzi didn't bother to look up from her work. "I'm fine. Go help your friend."

Kelsey smiled and trotted off in the direction Amy had gone.

Suzi glared at Samira shaking her head.

"I'm not one of your charity cases."

Samira nodded. "I'm sorry. I didn't mean to offend you."

Suzi began shoving the toys and baby items back into the sleeping bag with excessive force. She didn't seem to notice the stranger kneeling beside her, holding the bag so it wouldn't all unravel again. Samira blinked. *I'm never going to escape him, am I?* Eventually, she was going to have to so something about him. Samira was snapped from her reverie by Suzi's voice.

"What do you think?" She said, jamming a rattle deep into the bag. "Somehow if you do enough here, someone will give you a visa? They'll let you out?"

"No," Samira said, giving Suzi a sad smile. Then she turned back to her tent peg and lifted her hammer.

"I left people." She slammed the hammer down onto the peg with all the force she could muster. "I can't help them." She slammed the hammer down again. She looked up at Suzi. There was a moment of understanding and then Suzi grimaced and looked away.

"Helping these people won't wash away what you've done."

Samira slammed her hammer down again. The words cut deeply because she knew they were true. *There is no absolution for what I've done. I can't be forgiven.*

She heard a long sigh from Suzi. Almost too quietly to make out, the German woman said, "Trust me."

seventeen

Mahmoud and Samira: Mut'a

Sitting forward in his chair, Mahmoud rubbed intently at his naked finger. For years, Nabil's living room had been a refuge for Mahmoud. It was a place he could escape his shrewish wife and foolish children. But he could find no peace here today. He looked up at Nabil, whose bulk was folded deeply into the sofa.

"What am I to do?" Mahmoud carped. He should have left it there, but he couldn't. The weight of his shame was too much. He needed somewhere else to put it. "Why did you get me into this?"

Nabil raised both eyebrows. He didn't laugh. Barely. "Why did you give her the ring?"

Mahmoud sighed, throwing his hands up and flopping backward in the chair. This time, Nabil laughed.

"This isn't funny!" Mahmoud slumped forward, dramatically burying his face in his hands. "What am I to do?"

Nabil opened his mouth, but Mahmoud looked up at him, pulling his cheeks downward with his hands. "The girl has disappeared."

Nabil nodded sagely. "Maybe I can help you search. What was her name?"

Mahmoud slumped even lower. Nabil worked hard to keep his features still, but Mahmoud could see the judgment in his eyes. There was an etiquette to *Mut'a* — temporary wives. It was still a marriage, just one with a predetermined expiration date. What sort of man didn't even bother to learn a wife's name? *What game am I playing?* Mahmoud cursed himself. *I don't even believe in temporary marriage.*

"What did she look like?"

Mahmoud felt his cheeks heating. He turned his head away, panicked. If he told Nabil — *If anyone will understand this, it will be Nabil.* He took a deep breath. It was all so repulsive. Mahmoud was a good man. He didn't drink in bars, or run around with loose women. *Well, I didn't used to.* He sighed, his shoulders slumping even lower than before.

"Just describe her. Maybe… did she resemble someone you know?"

Mahmoud's eyes shot open. *Does Nabil know?* Mahmoud's mouth hung open. Nabil couldn't know. How would he? Mahmoud shifted awkwardly in his seat.

A dark grin spread over Nabil's face. He spoke in a scandalized whisper. "Oh," he said. "She did. Who? Who did she look like?"

Mahmoud lowered his head even further. He felt a deep and ugly shame growing, boxing him in.

"Tala!" Both men swung their heads to the doorway, where Ahmad suddenly burst in. Mahmoud flinched at his son's exclamation. Nabil looked back and forth between the two Masoud's in confusion.

"Basem is throwing her out of the house. We must help her, Baba." Ahmad rushed to his father, dropping to his knees in pleading supplication.

Mahmoud felt a spike of terror seize him. His lungs locked up. He couldn't breathe or speak. He couldn't even look at his son.

"Why?" Nabil asked. "What has she done?"

Ahmad turned to Nabil, his expression darkening. His words were livid. "He says…" the boy sputtered. Clearly he found Basem's claim so ridiculous he could barely give it voice. "He says she's pregnant!"

Mahmoud swallowed hard. *It can't be,* he thought. *It must be a coincidence.* Mahmoud dropped his head into his hands again. He prayed silently to Allah that his son and friend would think the shame reflected in Mahmoud's face and posture was purely a response to Tala's indiscretion. *Please don't let them see what I have done.*

Ahmad lurched to his feet, pacing like a caged animal. He was ringing his hands, his body quivering. Mahmoud could feel the manic energy rolling off of his son in waves.

"Basem is many kinds of fool," Nabil said, eliciting a nod of agreement from Ahmad. Mahmoud knew Nabil too well. The tone told him where his friend was headed. Mahmoud's dread increased all the more. "But he isn't stupid. He would not accuse his own child of pregnancy when she is not. It heaps shame on his household."

Mahmoud peeked up at his son. The boy was frozen, his stiff back to Mahmoud. Ahmad still quivered — every muscle in his body was taut. Like a flipped switch, he whirled around and Mahmoud flinched back into his chair.

"She could not provide a child to either of my brothers, but now she gets pregnant whoring?" Spittle flew from the boy's lips.

Mahmoud closed his eyes. Ahmad had long carried a torch for Tala. Love slid so quickly into hate. He could imagine the boy's feelings of betrayal. It was easy to imagine that hate turning on Mahmoud.

"I would have married her," Ahmad ranted, "but Allah has protected me." He stopped, dropping to his knees by Mahmoud's side again. "You protected me. You were right about her, Baba."

Mahmoud felt the blood leave his face. He couldn't meet his son's eyes. He started to quiver himself. Between gasping breaths, he tried to mitigate the damage.

"We should withhold judgment," Mahmoud began. Ahmad looked shocked and Nabil intrigued. Mahmoud felt a wash of disgust. The unimaginable perversity he'd tangled himself in would be an easy guess for dissolute Nabil. "She has been through a lot. Two husbands dead. Maybe…" Mahmoud sighed. *Please let it be so.* "Maybe there is an explanation—"

"What possible explanation could there be?" Ahmad demanded, springing to his feet again. He pounded a fist into his other palm, screeching his words through gritted teeth, "She has dishonored our family."

"She is a young girl," Mahmoud's voice was steadying, slipping into a hollow coolness. He felt nothing. Fear burned away to emptiness. "She won't survive on the streets. They will—"

"Good!" Ahmad shouted. "She deserves worse! She has betrayed everything!" Mahmoud could hear what the boy really meant. She had betrayed him. Ahmad turned suddenly to Mahmoud. "Would you go to a brothel?"

Mahmod flinched back, his eyes shockingly wide.

"Of course not!" Ahmad answered for him. "You are a righteous man, a man of honor. You uphold the dignity of your dead wife and your dead sons. You represent our community and our values."

Every word felt like a blow. Mahmoud wanted to disappear into his chair. The more Ahmad expounded on Mahmoud's virtues, the more horrible it all became. The emptiness of moments ago was lost again in a sea of shame and self-loathing.

As Ahmad continued his tirade, Nabil's too young servant girl slipped into the room. She bowed to Nabil. Somehow, she ignored Ahmad's screaming and the layers of tension in the room.

"Tala bint Basem," her eyes cut to Mahmoud as she said the name, "is at the door."

Ahmad fell silent, his face almost purple with rage. Nabil rose from the couch and slipped silently from the room, following the servant girl.

Ahmad paced. Mahmoud was silent. *The truth will come out now. There is no hiding it,* he thought. He lifted his head. *I am Mahmoud Masoud,* he reminded himself. *I am not so easily defeated. Nabil will do as I ask. No one but Nabil will suspect anything. Ahmad is right. If we just turn the girl away, our problems disappear.* It was a dark, horrible thought. Yet it felt a warm comfort to Mahmoud. *For all I know, it is a coincidence. There is no proof to connect the girl to me.*

"I can't believe Nabil is even speaking to her," Ahmad muttered. He turned sharply to Mahmoud, his voice crescendoing into an accusation. "Does he care nothing for your friendship?"

Mahmoud didn't answer. Nabil cared deeply for their friendship. He would cast the girl out to be raped and murdered if Mahmoud asked it.

Nabil appeared in the doorway behind the overwrought Ahmad. He waited until he had Mahmoud's eyes before holding up the Masoud family ring. Mahmoud felt cold. *Not a coincidence. It* was *Tala. Oh, what have I done?*

Sickness fluttered in his middle. The paper thin justifications barely held. *She was in a brothel! Anyone could be the father.*

Ahmad looked at his father and then spun, following Mahmoud's gaze. Nabil made the ring disappear before Ahmad could see it. It was an impressive piece of sleight-of-hand.

"I will send her away," Nabil said. He made it a statement, but his eyes asked Mahmoud.

He turned in the doorway and Mahmoud watched. Out of the corner of his eye, he could see Ahmad nodding in approval.

"Hey pretty girl." The man's voice was coy and sinister. "Where are you hiding?"

Samira ran. Her breath was labored and her heart pounding.

There was a terrible sound of ripping fabric. Samira stopped. She looked into the eyes of the would-be rapist. Samira planted her feet on either side of a girl lying prone on the ground. The girl's abaya was ripped apart.

"Look," the man said, a wicked glint of moonlight flickering in his eye. "Another one." He moved in a stalking circle around Samira. "Maybe I like her better."

There were chuckles and catcalls from half a dozen other men all moving to encircle Samira. She tried to hide her fear. In moments there would be two women being gang-raped. Her attempt at rescue would be less than meaningless.

"Does your wife know where you are tonight?" She challenged the leader.

He stepped forward his hand flashing, an open palm dismissively blasted at her face. She stopped the strike with her forearm, knocking the blow away. It hurt terribly, but she refused to show the pain on her face. She swung back, staggering him with a slap he never saw coming.

"We are not defenseless," she said. Fear quivered through her. She would be punished for this in ways she couldn't fully imagine. It didn't matter. She couldn't sit quietly for another night listening while more women were abused. She couldn't do nothing. Not anymore.

She waited, watching the leader recover, watching him wipe blood from his lower lip. His eyes burned with anger. They promised terrible retribution. She wanted nothing more than to back away, to turn and run for all she was worth. But she locked her knees, raised her chin and met his eyes. She would bite and claw and make these men pay in every way she could manage. She felt something wild in her, a raw animal rage. In a flash, she couldn't even see the would-be rapist, she just saw Mahmoud. The hatred that burned in her for her brother boiled away all of her fear. She would destroy him utterly.

One by one, the men began stepping backward, moving away. Samira was disbelieving. She can't really have intimidated them that much. As the rage slipped away and her brain began to process again. The tunnel vision lifted. She realized she wasn't alone anymore. A crowd of women stood around her.

Relief nearly robbed her legs of their strength. It was all she could do to remain standing.

The leader gave her one last look of hate. "I will not forget." He turned and walked away.

"I won't either," Samira answered quietly. She meant it for him, but also for Mahmoud.

"When Abu Anas Al-laziky comes, traitors like you will be punished." She didn't see the man who said it. She wondered, *would Ismaeel hurt me? The boy I played with as a child?* She didn't think her brother Ali would even know her. It didn't matter. She'd faced these men. She'd face Abu Anas Al-laziky or Mahmoud or whatever monster showed up next.

She turned to kneel beside the woman lying on the ground, but the stranger is already there. He held the woman in his lap, covering her modestly with a blanket. Samira looked at the stranger, weeping for this injured woman. *No,* she realized. *He's weeping* with *her.*

The scene didn't make sense to Samira. A man she often thought of as a hallucination held a woman who'd narrowly avoided being raped — a woman who doubtless didn't know him. *Yet somehow he shares her pain.* Samira couldn't grasp that. She felt anger. Hate. This brokenness in the camp needed justice. Someone needed to pay!

Samira felt a hand on her shoulder, patting her gently.

"You saved us," the woman said.

Samira looked at the stranger again. Her anger disappeared like a snuffed candle. She turned away, her cheeks burning. She suddenly felt horribly ashamed.

Spring 2015

Mahmoud approached Nabil's house furtively. Gunfire echoed in the distance. The rebels were being driven from this part of the city. Soon, it would be even more dangerous to be a Sunni in Aleppo. As he rushed to the door, an explosion erupted in the distance behind him. He flung himself to the ground.

For several minutes, he just lay there. He heard nothing over the sound of his pulse beating in his ears and his ragged breathing. *Is it safe? Can I move? No,* he reasoned, *quiet is never safe.* After a long time the gun fire came back. It was more distant now.

He put his hands on the cement walk, preparing to push himself back to his feet. His eyes caught a flicker of light against Nabil's drawn curtains. It was very faint. No outside lights were on. The blackout curtains were drawn. Still, a soft blue flicker nagged at the corner of the living room window. Mahmoud smiled. Nabil was at home watching TV.

Getting to his feet, Mahmoud approached the door. He tapped three times. They were quiet taps, but they echoed in the still night.

Mahmoud waited a long time. He heard no sound from the house beyond the soft chatter of the television. He raised his fist to knock again. He waited, nothing. He wrapped his knuckles against the wood three more times. Adrenaline drove him to knock more forcefully.

Still no sound from inside.

"Nabil?" Mahmoud hissed. "Are you there?"

"Coming." He heard the sigh of relief in Nabil's voice. The man had been terrified that someone was knocking at his door. "Just a moment."

The locks ticked over one by one and Nabil pulled the door open. Mahmoud took in his bare feet and the pillow on the floor by the couch.

"Syria is in flames and you are having your feet rubbed?" Mahmoud teased.

"It is a stressful time." Nabil shrugged. "Anyway, you are insane. Why are you on the streets tonight?"

Mahmoud grabbed Nabil's shoulders, looking his friend deep in the eyes. "I'm leaving Syria. It isn't safe here. My family and I..." Nabil was avoiding his eyes, and Mahmoud ground to a halt.

The two men said nothing, Mahmoud waiting for Nabil to look at him. When Nabil continued to look away, Mahmoud finally spoke again.

"I'm sorry." He'd been avoiding Nabil — avoiding everyone really — for nearly a year. "You've done so much for me." Hiding out seemed the only solution to the shame. Yacoob had surely disinherited him. Ahmad would be the heir now or possibly Yameen. *But the heir of what? What will be left when this war is over?* "After things with Tala...."

Nabil waved for Mahmoud to say nothing more. It was the sort of friend he was. No shame was too great and no thanks were needed.

"You should come with us."

A bitter smile curled Nabil's lips. Finally, he looked at Mahmoud.

"I'm not built for that journey."

Mahmoud wanted to argue. A thousand protests flashed through his mind, but they withered on his lips. He couldn't deny it. Nabil was grotesquely fat. He rarely left his home for anything he could have a servant bring. He was so out of shape even a walk to the market left him panting. Mahmoud dropped his head.

"Thank you, Nabil. You are a good friend to me."

Nabil gave Mahmoud a shy smile, a hint of mischief dancing in his eyes. "With you gone, who will remind me of the words of the prophet?"

"And who will prompt me to disregard them?"

Nabil looked as though he wanted to laugh, but he kept it in.

"You remember that coffee shop just outside the university?"

Mahmoud choked out a laugh. "You begged her to marry you for months."

Nabil nodded, a slight flush lighting his cheeks. "I was thinking about the day when we snuck into the upstairs…"

"…and dropped bags of water on the customers as they left the shop," Mahmoud finished for him. They laughed and it was as though no time had passed since they were last together.

"And the bald man with the limp. You used to lecture him about 'the rights of the customer,'" Nabil mimicked Mahmoud's patronizing tone.

"So you could steal falafel from his truck."

They both smiled but couldn't meet one another's eyes. For a moment, they were silent. Gunfire popped in the distance and a chill breeze prickled the hair on Mahmoud's arms.

"You will be missed, Mahmoud Masoud."

Mahmoud wanted to throw his arms around his old friend, curling his tall, skinny body, to the other man's roundness. But men didn't do that sort of thing. Mahmoud turned to go.

"You will not stay for a last coffee? I've grown used to your company."

Mahmoud turned back with a smile.

"It's a long journey to Latakia."

"Latakia?" Nabil looked shocked. Then his face darkened. "Yacoob won't go with you."

Mahmoud shrugged. "I must try," he said. "If not my father, perhaps I can help my sister and my son."

Nabil looked concerned, but he nodded his head. Mahmoud knew the things Nabil wanted to say. *Ahmad will not see me, and Yasmeen will do nothing without Baba.* Yet, Nabil understood how much Ahmad's leaving had hurt Mahmoud. He understood how desperate Mahmoud was for some sort of reconciliation. Reluctantly, Nabil placed a hand on Mahmoud's shoulder.

"Peace on your journey."

Mahmoud nodded back. Tears stung his eyes as he gave Nabil a last smile. Over his friend's shoulder, he saw the serving girl peeking out, worried who was at the door. He'd kept his friend standing in the dangerous night too long. He turned and walked back up the road with more confidence than he felt. Looking back, he saw the door was closed again, but he could see a small slit in the curtain. He gave Nabil one final wave.

eighteen
Samira: Come to Me

Summer 2014

Samira walked up the street of the tiny Greek village. Less than a kilometer from the camp, she wasn't the only refugee on the street. Many of the locals smiled and greeted her. Others glared or looked at her with concern.

Seeing her reflection in the window of a cafe, she adjusted her hijab. Inside, the Australian girl behind the counter gave a friendly wave. Samira smiled and waved back before continuing down the street. After more than a year in the camp, she knew many people in the small town of Panagiouda.

Nearly a block up, she stopped at a storefront. One of the aid organizations rented space for meetings there. Samira paused, wanting to go in, but unsure. She knew the workers would try to answer her questions, but she was afraid. In the tight community surrounding the camp, everything was fodder for gossip. The other women in the camp might ostracize her if they heard her questions.

She raised her chin. *This is the right way forward.* Pushing open the door, she walked confidently into the office. *I can ask questions without shame. Curiosity is not controversy.* As soon as she was through, her resolve faltered.

All of the aid workers were sitting in a circle around a table with their eyes closed. Heads bowed. It looked nothing like prayer at the mosque, but she recognized what they were doing.

A young girl looked up from the circle. Samira recognized her. *Kelsey,* the girl had extended her time, her original group long gone. Kelsey slipped quietly from the table and approached Samira.

"Sammie, it's good to see you."

Samira nodded. "I don't mean to interrupt."

"Let's step over here," Kelsey said, leading Samira to a ratty couch several feet from the table where the others prayed.

As Samira sat down, Kelsey asked, "Can I get you something? A coffee?"

"It's not needed," Samira replied. She wanted to leave. Her heart fluttered. She'd sat down on the couch. It would be rude to jump up and rush out.

Kelsey looked confused, she bit her lip and looked toward the small kitchenette in the back of the room.

Working with the volunteers, Samira had learned to read them. Kelsey was worried that Samira was rejecting her hospitality.

"I understand your culture is different," Samira explained. "I value your time."

Kelsey's face broke into a broad grin. "Let me get you a coffee."

Samira smiled back and watched Kelsey move toward the kitchenette. This was a strange world. Greek, American, German, Canadian, Afghan, African and Syrian cultures crashing into each other. Samira tried to understand and make small gestures to acknowledge the cultures of the people she interacted with. It was a pleasure to have someone respond in kind.

Kelsey returned with two mugs of coffee and took a seat beside Samira. For a moment, the two women sat in companionable silence. They savored the human connection even steeped in the aroma and flavor of burned coffee. It was comforting and beautiful.

In a matter of moments, Samira felt her purpose nagging at her. She felt nervous. Shifting on the couch, she set down her mug and rubbed damp palms on her thighs. Then she fussing with her worn abaya.

Kelsey looked over the rim of her mug. "What can I do for you?"

American's get to the point quickly, Samira reminded herself. *It isn't rudeness.* Samira nodded, looked away from the woman and took a long breath.

"I… keep having dreams."

Kelsey just listened. She appeared calm. Mildly curious to hear what Samira had to say. *We all have dreams,* Samira thought, *get to the point. Don't make the impatient American girl wait.*

"I see Je—" she stopped herself. Kelsey raised an eyebrow. Now, her interest was piqued. "I see a man. He… speaks to me. He wants me to come to him."

Samira looked up and saw him, the stranger. He was sitting in Kelsey's place at the prayer table. He was watching her, smiling. Turning back to Kelsey, she tried not to look wild-eyed.

"'Come to me,'" Kelsey quoted, smiling, "'all you who are weary and burdened, and I will give you rest.'"

Samira felt her body stiffen. Her lungs suddenly felt too small. This woman had seen right through her.

"Those are Jesus' words in the Bible," Kelsey finished, picking up a heavy black book from a low table. "Let me show you."

Samira shifted again on the couch. She felt stiff and uncomfortable. This was what she feared. As Kelsey began thumbing through the book, Samira laid a hand over the pages, stopping Kelsey. There wasn't any point in continuing. The best thing was to put a stop to the whole conversation.

"There can be no rest for me," she said. *I am wicked. I have broken my vows, betrayed my family.* "I should go."

"You think you aren't worthy?" Kelsey asked and Samira flinched. This woman could read her mind. "You haven't earned it?"

Samira shook her head, seizing on the semantics. "I know I am not worthy. I…" *Am I really going to say it out loud?* "I betrayed my family." Saying it felt like lifting a car. She knew it wasn't enough. She had to finish, to get it all out. She needed Kelsey to understand. "I abandoned my husband. There is no forgiving the things I have done."

Suddenly, she couldn't even look at Kelsey anymore. She was too afraid to see her shame reflected in the girl's eyes. Burying her head in her hands, she tried to hide the tears running down her face. Kelsey didn't say anything. The silence stretched and Samira knew the girl was judging her. *She thinks I am a harlot. She's right. I should run from this room and pray to Allah that I never see this girl again. She will leave soon, as they all do. I should run.*

"I understand," Kelsey spoke softly, but with an iron determination in her voice. Samira looked up into the girl's eyes. Kelsey leaned forward intently. She spoke in a whispered confession. "I'm not worthy either." Samira blinked in surprise. *She can't really understand me. Maybe there was a problem with my English. Maybe I explained things badly.*

There was a bustling behind them. Samira glanced over her

shoulder and saw the prayer circle breaking up into little knots of conversation. The stranger remained seated, head bowed in prayer.

Kelsey continued, "But Jesus died for me anyway."

Samira's head whipped back around. She was familiar with this lie. "He did not die!" This was part of the Christian corruption of the truth. "He was taken up to heaven."

Kelsey nodded agreement. Samira was surprised. *Why is she agreeing with me?* "He was," the girl said. "But first, he took all of my sins, all of the ways I have rejected and dishonored God — and all of the ways I will in the future, and he accepted the full punishment for all of them."

Samira's mind went wild. She wanted to argue. To point out how ridiculous that claim was on its face: that a single man could take the punishment for all of the people who ever lived or ever would live. But the thoughts were swamped in the emotional weight of her own failures. She didn't have to struggle to tie her behavior to a consequence. She'd seen the ISIS videos and the footage from Iran and Saudi Arabia. She knew what happened to a woman who betrayed her husband. It was a death penalty. A painful, brutal death.

Kelsey reached out, placing a hand over Samira's.

"I don't have to live under God's judgment," the girl said, her voice gentle and joyous. "My debt was paid. Jesus paid it."

Samira felt a little thrill of hope run through her. It ran against everything she believed and everything that made any sense, but she couldn't control it. She desperately hoped she knew what Kelsey would say next — desperately hoped it would be true.

"And he paid your debt, too," Kelsey finished. She offered Samira a radiant smile.

Samira wanted to smile back, to celebrate. But she couldn't. Instead, she lifted her head, clicking her tongue, tears rolling down her cheeks. *My debt can't be paid. My failure is too great. I can never do enough to offset the damage I have done.* She realized at that moment that all of her work in the camp wasn't just about taking control of her life, it was also about trying to balance the scales. She was hoping to buy off Allah by doing good.

"You can't stand worthy before God on your own merits." Kelsey spoke with a soft intensity. "But, if you let him, Jesus can step between you and God. And then, when God looks at you, he will see Jesus."

As Kelsey was speaking, a shadow blocked the window. Samira glanced up and saw the stranger. He was looking at her, outlined in the sun streaming through the window. He looked angelic. Glorious.

Samira gazed into his eyes. Suddenly, she felt it wasn't Kelsey she was talking to at all.

"What must I do?"

"Give him everything," Kelsey continued to speak, but Samira only saw the stranger. "All your plans, your hopes, your dreams. All of it. Let it go and trust him."

"I do," Samira said.

The stranger's face split in a giant, eye-twinkling grin of pure joy. Samira felt a nervous little thrill, almost as though it was her wedding. Not the rough, forced affair she'd had with Ata. This was the wedding of which she'd never dreamed. She found herself blushing, crying and smiling uncontrollably.

"It won't be easy," Kelsey's voice was a lecture now. "He'll ask you to forgive people who have hurt and wronged you."

The words rolled over Samira, registering but not taking on meaning. She was too caught up in this joy. She would agree to anything. Nothing mattered. Tears streamed from her eyes, washing her pain away.

"I do," she repeated. "I forgive them all."

The stranger moved to the kitchenette and Samira followed him with her eyes.

Kelsey wasn't done. "The bad feelings—"

"They're gone," Samira interrupted.

A little crease appeared between Kelsey's brows. "Eventually, you'll take them back."

Samira couldn't understand the girl. *This is the most joyous moment of my life. Why does she seem so mournful? Why isn't she celebrating?*

"Never," Samira said, shaking her head. "Why would I want them?"

That brought an involuntary laugh from Kelsey who raised her eyebrows, utterly perplexed.

"I feel… free," Samira said.

"Well," Kelsey paused, her face looking for all the world like a parent — delighted with their child's joy, but worried about whether they really understood what was going on. Samira could remember that look on Yacoob's face when, as a girl, she'd first started taking an interest in the business. She grew so excited about all of the details. She'd ignored his protests that a woman could never take over.

"If you do," Kelsey continued, "you'll need to give them to him again. Let them go."

Samira threw her arms around Kelsey, eyes still sparkling with joyful tears.

"I will," she proclaimed, "I promise I will. Thank you!"

nineteen

Mahmoud and Samira: The Hope of Europe

Summer 2015

The rumble and bounce was the only way to sense they were moving. Squeezed together in utter darkness, Mahmoud couldn't see the people around him. He could feel their bodies pressing in on all sides. Another lurch, another little hop, and Mahmoud's head struck the ceiling. Again. He'd lost count of how many times that had happened. In the same way, he'd stopped noticing the smell of urine and excrement. Some of the people around him were unable to hold it for the many long hours they'd been trapped.

There was a clank. Another lurch. Everyone was shifted forward and then jerked back the other way. Mahmoud would have fallen, but for the press of bodies. He wasn't able to balance, but he couldn't fall either. The engine idled. Mahmoud thought they were no longer moving. He hoped they'd reached their destination. He couldn't check the time. His phone was trapped in his pocket.

For what seemed the thousandth time, Mahmoud undertook the methodical clenching and releasing of each muscle in his body, trying to keep his blood flowing. Claustrophobia had never been a problem for him. He wondered if he would ever be able to face a dark enclosed space again after this journey.

Soon, he promised himself, *soon you'll be in Europe. A job. Safety. A fresh start.* He didn't really believe that in Germany the government simply handed everyone wads of Euros. Nor did he accept the promise that people no longer cared how you behaved. He was looking forward to a life where no one would know the shames and failures of his past.

Mahmoud wondered how much time had elapsed. Had the truck been stopped for hours? Mere moments? He gulped in stale, over-breathed air, and hoped the doors would open soon.

Please, Allah, let the doors open soon.

For a fleeting moment, he hoped that his prayer would open the door. Then hope left him. Mahmoud was uncertain if Allah really listened to prayers, let alone answered them. It would have been uncharacteristically generous had the door suddenly opened.

Outside, he heard a door slam — the truck door, he imagined. Footsteps were moving around. Two voices began speaking in rapid-fire Turkish. Mahmoud didn't speak Turkish, but surely their conversation meant the doors would open soon.

In a few more minutes, there was a fiddling at the latch. Mahmoud could barely breathe. All around him, he felt bodies strain toward the door. The sense of excitement was palpable.

Mahmoud was positioned with his back to the door. He couldn't see the sun as the doors opened. Bright lines of light — almost too bright to endure — painted the interior of the truck. He saw the ragged people around him, squinting and leaning into the light. He felt the cool breeze, and tasted the sea.

The Turkish voices were animated now. They gave instructions no one understood.

"Quickly, you must get out and go to the boats," a voice called in thickly accented Arabic.

At first, Mahmoud was pulled backwards. He struggled to keep his feet. A desperate fear gripped him. He imagined being trampled by people yearning to escape the truck. The pressure finally loosened enough that Mahmoud could turn around. The daylight was even more blinding. The air was gloriously fresh. He could identify the scent of human waste again. He smiled, squinting, and jumped out of the truck.

The drop was longer than he remembered. He twisted his weak ankle when he hit the ground. It didn't matter. He sucked in real air again. He could move his body.

Turning back, he reached to help the next person down. It was a boy, perhaps ten years old. Mahmoud lowered him to the ground and looked down the gentle slope to the water. Several rubber dinghies were lined up along the beach. Heavy outboard motors grumbled a promising of freedom. Men stood on the sand with life jackets, haggling with the arrivals.

Mahmoud smiled. The sea air whispered assurances of a bright future.

He reached up and helped the next passenger out of the truck.

Fall 2014

Sliding her thumb back and forth over the fabric, Samira stared at her scrap of scarf. The scarf had been a masterpiece. The colors were faded some, but the silk was still tightly woven. She felt empty. Hopeless. *I shouldn't feel this way anymore.* The scarf was the promise she'd held. It represented who she could have been. Like her future, it had been torn to shreds. She closed her eyes, holding the silk to her nose.

With a slow inhalation, she pulled in Syria: tobacco, coffee, the smell of the Masoud home, Yasmeen's shampoo… hope. She held it all, her chest tight to bursting. Then she slowly let it exhale out, away… so far away.

"Next," a voice called from inside the building.

Samira returned to the moment. She was in a line. Baking in the sun outside one of the temporary steel buildings of the camp. She looked around for the stranger. *Not a stranger anymore. Jesus. My… other husband?* The relationship was confusing. She didn't see him. Didn't feel a sense of his presence. *I saw more of him when he* was *a stranger.*

Pushing aside resentment, she moved toward the door. She squeezed sideways so a young man could exit, his brows low and bristling with hostility. *Bad news,* she thought. *It's nothing but bad news.*

Stepping into the UNHCR office, she looked at the official. He blinked at her through his round glasses. His movements were efficient, perfunctory. She could feel his annoyance. She glanced to the corner, looking again for Jesus, but she didn't see him.

"I'm Samira Mohammed. Is there any—"

The official cut her off with a raised hand and tapped at his keyboard. Little clacking sounds seemed to prick and mock her. She swallowed. *Calm. Peace. It's okay.*

After a moment, he turned back to her and she raised her eyebrows expectantly. He continued to turn past her and began digging through the papers on his desk. Each page turn required he lick his thumb. She could hear the little sounds his spit made, and soft grinding of paper on paper.

It isn't his fault, she coached herself, *he's just doing his job.*

She shifted on her feet, frustration bubbling through her. Surely, they'd been able to confirm her story by now. *How hard can it possibly be to prove there was a massacre by a bus station in which a little girl died?*

The official dropped his pile of papers and returned his attention to her.

"Spell Zah-mee-rah for me?"

She gritted her teeth. "S-A-M-I-R-A." It was an effort to spell her name using Roman characters in the way a Westerner might write it. She kept on, spelling out "Mohammed" for him as well. Fingers clicked away at his keyboard again.

"Nothing," he announced. "We'll let you know when something changes."

Don't come back, she heard the unspoken words. *You're no different than all the others. Just wait your turn. The system is overwhelmed. We rather like keeping the brown people locked in an old prison.*

She stopped herself. The official continued to look at her. His eyes looked too big. *I don't know his heart,* she reminded herself.

"Thank you," she said. It didn't sound grateful to her ears, but it was the best she could muster. She could feel her own brows lowered, her own bristling bitterness. She turned to leave the room.

"Next."

twenty
Samira: Dreams

The rain sheeted down in wild, chaotic bursts. It churned the road to a collection of mud and tiny lakes, each one deeper than the last.

Samira danced through them with a practiced wariness. There was little about camp life she found desirable. Squelching around with a wet shoe managed to top her list of indignities. A few of the men had built small camp fires where one might dry a wet shoe. She found it difficult to put herself in such a vulnerable position with the men — being stranded with only one shoe. The rain was sufficient to have doused their campfires in any case. Besides, if she had to hear about Abu Anas Al-laziky coming to rescue them one more time she was going to scream.

She moved quickly across the road in front of the gates, dashing for the small collection of food trucks which had taken up permanent residence outside the camp. A warren of translucent plastic sheeting stood before the trucks. Inside, a few folding tables made a sort of dining room. It allowed a moment of peace from the rain while people ate.

Ducking through the sheeting, Samira sluiced the water off her clothes. Then she took a moment to drip before she ordered her tea. At home, this would have been a daily ritual — the tea, not the dripping. Here she was lucky to afford it once a week. It was a comfort, though. A reminder of times past. A hope that times would be better again.

Ordering her tea, Samira surveyed the tiny dining area. Approaching the plastic shelter, she hadn't seen anyone. A muffled snuffling sound drew her eyes to the only other customer. Suzi was slumped over a steaming cup of coffee. Lines of eye makeup told a story on her cheeks, and a glistening line ran from one nostril to her quivering upper lip. Samira was confident an extra salty flavor would be present in Suzi's coffee.

Really, Lord? A thousand women in this camp and she's the only one here?

Thanking the man for her tea, Samira made her way to Suzi's table.

"Can I join you?" She wanted to sound casual, but she and Suzi had never really connected. For most of the first year, Samira was terrified of the German woman. She seemed ruthless and cold. Some of that, Samira learned, was simply the German culture's complete lack of artifice. As one aid worker had explained it, "Why would I smile at you if I don't feel happy? Do you want me to lie?" The rest, Samira attributed to optics. Eyes the color of ice, porcelain skin, a jawline so sharp it could cut you… Add the punk hairdo and it was hard to imagine Suzi as warm and fuzzy.

As Samira was given more and more responsibility in camp, Suzi's stock plummeted. Again, Samira didn't see the two as related. Suzi was becoming more distracted and less reliable. Whatever personal drama she was experiencing consumed the efficient, powerful woman Samira first met. The brittle shell that remained was frequently more liability than asset to the aid workers.

Samira's little flutter of fear as she approached Suzi made no sense. She'd faced far greater dangers than Suzi's bad opinion. However, braving gunfire and rape gangs didn't make her more comfortable getting yelled at.

Suzi slowly raised her head and glared at Samira. Suzi shook her head with an annoyed reluctance. The denial just put Samira's back up. She was trying to be friendly. Who was Suzi to drive her back out into the rain?

She pointedly took a seat across the table and immediately felt bad. *I'm clearly intruding.* Forcing her way into Suzi's personal space wasn't likely to make them friends.

"Tea, huh?" Suzi asked. Her voice sounded hoarse, dead. Words were coming out of her mouth, but they didn't mean anything. They were just noise. Distraction. "Not coffee?"

Samira didn't care about Suzi's tone. This was an invitation. A chance to connect. She smiled, trying to be vulnerable. "I don't think they make it right here. Not like home."

Suzi gave her a flat look. "It must be exhausting," she snarked, "being perfect all of the time."

Samira should have been offended. Clearly the woman was trying to goad her. All she could think of was her dream. The words, "I will exalt you," floated through her mind. Here she was, in a grubby, plastic shanty. Her shoes were covered in mud. Every part of her was soaked to the skin. *Exalted? Perfect?* She laughed.

"I had a dream once…" she mused. Suzi flinched, like Samira had slapped her. Samira paused, but Suzi didn't speak. There was no explanation.

Samira started again. "I dreamed that I would rule over all of the people who mattered in my life." She could picture it. It felt tangible, the memory of being so smug and self-assured. She'd shamelessly lied about Mahmoud, trying to force her father to turn the company over to her instead. It was her birthright. A prophet had promised it to her in a dream. She'd been so convinced. She lowered her eyes, feeling the shame of it.

"I was so pleased with myself," she continued. "I never considered their feelings — my family's, I mean. Now, I sleep on the ground in a cold wet tent. Not exactly what I imagined."

She smiled at Suzi again. The other woman looked pale — well more pale — and a bit green. Suzi shifted in her chair, struggling to swallow. She didn't look angry anymore. She looked like she had nothing left.

"Um, yeah," Suzi commiserated, "my hotel is a total dive."

Samira ignored the imbalance. "Why do you stay?"

Suzi dropped her eyes, staring into her coffee like she might be able to scry an answer. She swirled the cup, watching the ripples move across the surface.

Samira just waited. She didn't know what was happening. But something was. They were talking. This wasn't like any previous interaction. Suzi had heard something, some piece of Samira's story, and it had shifted things. Samira didn't know what would come next. She didn't want to ruin it with empty chatter.

Finally, Suzi spoke, not looking up from her coffee. "You've heard of Dominic Erbach?"

Samira felt an electric thrill run through her. Dominic Erbach was her personal hero, her business idol. *Have I* heard *of him? Is that a joke?* She tried to control the sudden giddy energy running through her. Whatever Suzi wanted to share, it didn't seem like bubbly exuberance was a proper reaction, but… *Dominic Erbach?!?*

"He wants to be sure the money he sends to the camp," Suzi sighed, never looking up from her coffee, seemingly oblivious to Samira's reaction, "is being spent… efficiently." Suzi over-pronounced the word. Then she shrugged. "I guess."

Samira's mind whirled. *Suzi works for Dominic Erbach? Not the point. But— Focus, Susu.* She could tell Suzi was on the edge of a cliff. So far, nothing in the story seemed extraordinary — except Suzi's proximity to one of Samira's heroes.

"You've been here a long time," Samira said, "to do a checkup."

Suzi stood up, trying to wipe away tears that were tracking down her face again. Her fingers smeared the streaks of dark eye makeup. "I've got to go," she muttered.

Samira reached out, grabbing the other woman's arm. Suzi froze, her body going stiff. She looked at Samira's hand like Samira had crossed some terrible personal boundary.

"I'm sorry," Samira said. "But…" *How do I tell her she needs to wipe her face?*

Suzi's posture softened and she slowly sank back into her chair. Her eyes roamed the tiny space, tracking over everything in the room, but never alighting on Samira.

Samira just waited. She was desperate to hear this story now. She could tell that some part of Suzi needed to tell it. But for Samira the appeal was mostly Erbach. She'd read all of his books. Most of them in both Arabic and English. She'd watched his TED Talk a hundred times, and studied all the speeches that were on YouTube. She tried to care about Suzi and her feelings. She succeeded to an extent. She didn't like to see the German woman suffering, but deep in her heart, she was fascinated by the sudden connection.

"A few months back," Suzi spoke in a low mutter, barely articulating the words. It was a struggle for Samira to make them out. "He called me."

"Mr. Erba—" The question exploded out of Samira in a desperate whisper.

"Dominic," Suzi corrected. Her eyes caught Samira's flashing annoyance. "There was an… error in one of my expense reports." The pause spoke volumes. Suzi broke eye contact. Her cheeks flushed. "Well, several of my reports. He was," she sighed, "really angry."

Samira listened, her mind spinning. Was Suzi saying she'd stolen money?

"I tried calling some friends at the office," Suzi exhaled sharply.

"Nobody knows what he's thinking. He hasn't called again. I haven't called him." She looked up at Samira suddenly. "I don't want to lose my job. I can't go back and…" Tears started leaking from her eyes again, and her words grew thick.

Samira squeezed where her hand rested on Suzi's arm. Suzi sucked in a couple of ragged breaths and composed herself.

"I keep having this dream," she confessed. "I don't know why I'm telling you. It's stupid. But you mentioned your dream and — I can't get it out of my head. I'm a child, lying in the mud. I'm crying and screaming for help. I'm reaching my hands out, but no one comes to take me. I just lay there. I cry and I cry. Finally, my father comes. He lifts me out of the mud — and then I'm me again. Grown up me. And everything is fine. I'm clean — no mud. And it's such a relief. I'm so thrilled to have everything be okay," she paused, working her mouth, her hands turning into claws. "But then I wake up and I'm still in my dingy little hotel room. Dominic hasn't called. Nothing changed. And it all feels worse, because of that moment in the dream where everything was right. I keep having to remind myself that it was just a dream that this," she spread her arms wildly, her eyes big and hopeless, "is my real life."

Her arms flopped down to the table with an audible thunk. She shook her head and started wiping at her eyes again.

"But," Samira objected, "you can leave anytime you want. You don't have to stay here."

Suzi looked up, her eyes flat and cold again. "Can I?"

An uncomfortable silence stretched between them. Slowly, Samira realized what Suzi was saying — or at least what she thought Suzi was saying. She had a passport and permission to leave, but her shame trapped her. She could no more face Dominic Erbach than Samira could face her father. *Our actions — no, our failures — make returning home impossible.* Samira began to nod her head.

"Sometimes," she said, the truth of her words only really striking her as she said them, "Jesus tells me what dreams mean."

Suzi snorted, rolling her eyes. A genuine smile battled its way onto her face. "You've been drinking the Kool-Aid haven't you?"

Samira heard the sound of the plastic parting as someone entered. She glanced up. It was Jesus, come to order coffee. She glanced back at Suzi, who didn't even look at him. *Is he a hallucination,* she wondered. *Can other people see him?* She shook her head.

Suzi raised her hands in mock surrender. "Okay then," Suzi's voice was patronizing. "What does my dream mean?"

"You're the little girl," Samira began.

"I said that," Suzi pointed out flatly.

"You're reaching out, hoping you'll be put back where you were before," Samira continued.

"Oh," Suzi replied. "You're a real pro. Are you sure you don't need to feel my palm while you do this?"

Samira kept talking, gesturing around them. "The mud is what you've done."

Suzi suddenly looked away, her cheeks heating. She bit her lip hard. Samira could see the skin going white under her teeth.

"The hand is Mr. Erbach."

"Wow," Suzi deadpanned, "just wow."

Samira tightened her grip on Suzi's arm, squeezing hard. She locked eyes with the other woman. "He's going to come. To give you your job back. To take you back. And all the mud will be gone."

Suzi blinked. Samira's sudden intensity cut through the wall of her cynicism. She looked hopeful. Desperate for it to be true. But then Suzi erected the wall again. Her eyes grew cold and the wonder on her face became something hard and ugly.

"Jesus, huh?" She cocked an eyebrow. "Shouldn't it be Mohammed?"

Samira ignored the jibe. She wasn't wholly certain what had just happened. On the surface, Suzi's dream was obvious. She wanted things to go back the way they were. Hiding here, avoiding her life and the consequences of her actions was childish — like a crying baby. *Anyone could have explained it,* Samira thought. Embarrassment lit her cheeks. *But most would have felt fools saying the words.* She shook her head, but… it had been like a compulsion had seized her. She knew, knew with absolute conviction that she was right. It wasn't a dream. It was a prophesy. Dominic Erbach *was* coming to get Suzi.

"Please," Samira said, suddenly taken with the full realization of what Suzi's restoration could mean. "When you get your job back, please, get me out of here."

Suzi jerked her arm out of Samira's grasp. She glared, shaking her head.

"I should have known," she said.

She rose from the table and stormed out into the rain. Samira slumped on the table. *What did I expect?* She thought. She stared at Suzi's cold coffee still sitting untouched on the table.

twenty-one

Samira and Mahmoud: False Arrival

Spring 2015

Time marched forward, with little change to mark it except the passing of one season into another. Samira saw Suzi a few more times and then she disappeared. Samira was confident Erbach had taken the woman back, but there'd been no thank you. No farewell. Certainly no rescue for Samira.

Green leaves swayed and idled on a warm breeze. The air made a gentle shushing sound, adding a cool caress to the sun-drenched day. Samira watched Lina, a little girl of eight, from the other side of an olive tree. Slowly, Lina counted, her eyes screwed tightly shut.

"Nine. Ten!" the girl shouted snapping her eyes open. Samira quickly pulled her head back, trying to stand very straight and very still so the bole of the tree hid her from view. Lina was a soft hush of movement through the underbrush. There was a loud crack as Lina stepped on a stick. Samira whipped her head around to grin as Lina grabbed her.

"Got you!"

They laughed and Samira quickly covered her eyes.

"One," she began, listening to the little girl scamper away amid the cloud of giggles and excited gasps.

At the count of ten, Samira opened her eyes and immediately spied

Lina peaking around another tree a few feet away. Methodically, Samira hunted. She was careful to make a wide circuit around Lina's hiding place.

"Where did you go?" she called, eliciting giggles. "I can't find you anywhere."

When she'd sufficiently built the drama, Samira turned suddenly, grabbing the girl, and sweeping Lina into her arms.

"I got you," Samira said, spinning the girl in the air amid a torrent of laughter.

She set Lina down. Looking up, Samira saw the approach of Basma, a tired looking woman in her late thirties.

"You're very good with her," Lina's mother said as the girl ran off in search of a new hiding space.

Samira watched the girl, smiling. "She reminds me of my sister."

Samira turned back in time to see Basma's nod. The woman didn't say anything. A moment of awkward silence stretched between them. *Of course,* she thought, *I'm here alone.*

"She's alive," Samira announced. She could hear how defensive it sounded. "I think."

Basma looked away.

"In Latakia," Samira finished.

Basma curved her lips, eyes brimming with pity. Samira turned away.

"You could call," the mother said. She even held out her phone.

The war began again, just as it always did. *She means well,* Samira tried to reason with herself. Logic didn't matter. She felt a wave of rage. *Who is she to tell me how to manage my family affairs?* She closed her eyes. *She's trying to care. Butting in. Telling me to do it her way. Ignorant of my family situation… but trying to help.* It was a kind gesture, but Samira had her own phone. *Yacoob Masoud will never accept his ruined daughter.* She gave Basma a sad smile, unable to meet the woman's eyes.

"Sometimes what a father can't hear can be said to a mother," Basma said gently.

Samira traced the lines of Basma's abaya. It was worn and ragged, but utterly shapeless. A marked contrast to the jeans Samira now wore. They were the baggiest she could get, and she wore them with men's shirts that hung down and covered her hips like a skirt. But she still felt scandalous looking at the other woman. She was all too conscious of her own shame. She still couldn't imagine talking to Baba. She couldn't explain where she was or how she got here. She couldn't imagine trying to explain to him who she was. *Not a virgin. Not a good wife. Not modest. Not even a good Muslim anymore. My father would not know me.*

What might it be like to have a mother to talk to?

Basma was still holding out her phone. Samira jerked her head up with a click of her tongue and then bit her lip. The pain pricked at her eyes. Her vision blurred. Basma relented, withdrawing the phone. It was a mercy that the tears made it impossible to see Basma's sympathy.

She dashed the tears from her eyes and gave the older woman a level look. *I am in control.* Behind Basma, the distant camp sprawled along the base of the valley below them. Samira could see a bus making its way through the trees toward the camp. Seeing the bus drove her thoughts back to Yasmeen. She smiled, wistfully.

"I meet the busses sometimes," Samira confessed. "I keep hoping she'll step out of one of them."

Basma glared in the direction of the tents. "I would not wish this on anyone I love."

Samira's smile faded. The remark felt like a slap. Her jaw firmed and her brow lowered. "If she were here, I would protect her."

Basma nodded politely, but her posture said she didn't agree. She was wishing Lina were far away. It was written all over her face.

Samira sighed. Yasmeen was with their father. *Please, let them both be okay.*

The landscape was dark. The craggy rocks were little more than jagged black cutouts against the deep blue of the predawn. The motor of Mahmoud's boat sputtered and choked, but they'd arrived. With elation, he jumped from the dinghy, into the icy water. It came to his armpits. Jolting with cold, it licked up, spraying his tongue with salt. Pushing through the shock, he and another man tried to haul the boat, loaded down with forty other passengers, up onto the beach.

The water would wash the boat forward faster than they expected and then pull it suddenly back, dragging them with it. At one point, it swept Mahmoud completely off his feet and he went under. He sputtered back to the surface and tried to get a grip on the slick rubber side of the boat. He thought there were handholds but he couldn't find them in the dark. Gauging their progress was nearly impossible. Another man jumped out to help them. The boat was swept backwards again. The shore was so close they could taste it.

Eventually, they managed it. The boat secured, Mahmoud ran up the beach. He barely noticed the stabs of pain from his weak ankle, or the awkward hobble of his gait. He'd seen a shape, an outline moving in the darkness. It was a man — at least, he thought it was.

"Wait!" he cried, breathless. Wet clothes dragged at him, allied with his weariness. He pushed on, rushing into the darkness. Running for the place he thought he'd seen a shadow. Uncertain if it was real. "Please."

Panting, Mahmoud bent nearly in half as he arrived before a rough, male silhouette. The man's posture was stiff. Mahmoud didn't know if he was frightened, affronted or some combination of the two.

"Thank you," he panted, struggling along in broken English. *Do most people in Greece speak English?* He hoped so. He knew they wouldn't speak Arabic. "Sorry."

It was a struggle to get his breathing under control. His heart was pounding wildly, and he felt both lightheaded and suddenly sick. The man wasn't answering. *Is it the language? My accent? The soggy, gasping old man?*

"Did we make it?" he gasped. "Is this *Yunan*?"

The shadow shimmered and shook, bursting into a wild laughter. *That was wrong. Yunan is the Turkish word. They say Greece. Don't they?*

"You are in Turkey," The shadow said, shaking his head. Mahmoud wanted it to be a joke or a lie. The accent was unpleasantly familiar. "But don't worry. I'm sure the smugglers will be happy to take your money a second time."

Mahmoud fell to his knees, his chin dropping onto his chest. His stomach boiled and acid burned up his throat. He couldn't imagine spending all of that money a second time. Worse was contemplating the ride in the truck and a terrifying night at sea. *What choice do I have?* The camps in Turkey were a nightmare. Prisons where Syrians were treated worse than dogs. Slowly, he struggled to his feet again, the Turkish man long departed. Someone had to break the news to the others.

twenty-two
Samira: Following

"He started reading with me!"

Samira smiled at Mariam, a twenty-year-old who had only been married six days when she and her husband fled Syria. Six ladies sat together in a small circle on the ground. Each of them had found the truth here: Jesus is not merely a prophet. The Word of God. The savior of the world. They met each week to study the Bible and to encourage one another as they shared the truth with friends and family in camp.

Mariam's husband is reading the Bible with her, Samira thought. *An incredible victory*! A few days ago, he'd been livid, demanding she stop attending these meetings. Now, he was curious. He wanted to know. To understand. *Mariam is changing, and he sees it.* For a moment, Samira was lost in her thoughts. *Would father see a difference in me? Does mother?* She imagined her mother watching her from heaven. *But my mother never gave her life to Jesus....* Samira frowned, a sense of hopeless longing running through her.

I'm supposed to be leading these women. I have to focus. She smiled at Mariam, the yawning despair ebbing away as she focused on the other woman.

"That's wonderful, Mariam." Samira turned to a woman in her early forties. "Fatima, what about you?"

The older woman grimaced. "My husband read Matthew 25 last night, about the sheep and goats?"

Several of the women around the circle nodded. They knew the passage.

Samira wished she had family to share with. She wished she could tell Yacoob and Yasmeen — or even Mahmoud the truth. A little shudder of fear ran through her, thinking how her father might react. She was not ashamed to talk about Jesus to ladies in the camp, but she still couldn't bring herself to call home.

"He wanted to know," Fatima continued, "if these are the words of Jesus, why do his followers leave us locked up in this camp?"

Fatima's husband often spoke of Abu Anas Al-laziky. Samira prayed Abu Anas would never arrive.

"They are feeding us," Samira responded. It was hard. Conditions were horrible. There were many in the camp who wanted to assign blame. Responsibility for the terrible conditions did lay with someone, but… Samira had the impression no one in charge was actually seeing the conditions they were creating. The camp was someone's utopian vision. On paper, they were providing food, shelter, restroom facilities… They were helping. Sort of.

"I know," Fatima answered, "but…" The woman seemed to collapse a little. "Where are all of the Christians?"

Samira clicked her tongue, lifting her head. "Many of the relief workers—"

Past the gates, behind Fatima, a bus arrived. Samira could see the doors clearly. She could see the new arrivals stepping off the bus. As always when she watched people being shuffled into groups by volunteers in vests, she longed to see Yasmeen.

"But they are so few," Fatima protested. "Are there really so few in the West who believe Jesus's words?"

The new arrivals were so close. Samira could see their fear and confusion. She could see their faces. They were close enough that she could recognize a face she knew well.

"Maybe following Jesus is not so different from Islam," Mariam said. "Many claim to follow, but for most it's only a show."

Staggering awkwardly to her feet, Samira continued to stare.

"Susu," Samira barely registered Fatima's question. "Are you okay?"

All she could do is stare at a figure in the crowd. He wasn't alone. There were others with him. Following him. Samira couldn't breathe. She should say something. Tell the ladies she needed to go. Make an excuse. Something. She turned and ran as fast as she could.

She ran through the camp like the devil himself was on her heels. People watched her in shock. She kept running, nearly colliding with a man holding the hand of a toddler and then moments later, with a startled female in a volunteer vest. Heedless, she ran on. She would run them down if necessary.

She dodged and turned. Winding her way through the camp, she tried to throw off pursuit. *Do I really think I can hide in this camp?*

Finally, she flung herself between the flaps of her tent, rolling across the floor in a heap of panting, sweating terror.

Samira scurried back into a corner, pulling her jean-sheathed knees up to her chest. Some of her hair had come loose from her hijab, dragging in straggled locks over her face.

She continued gasping. The sound of her breath was terrifying. She tried to calm herself. Tried to keep quiet. But the panic had her. Her emotions were a train, plowing off the rails, demolishing her control.

He's here. My husband *is here.* She didn't know what he would do. If he learned she'd become a follower of Jesus, he might kill her. He might kill her simply for running away. She could still see him, standing over all of those bodies — over that little girl's body. The image was burned into her. *He* will *kill me*. She was certain. Hiding was her only option. How many days could she huddle here in her tent? How long before someone in the camp mentioned her in front of him? *Maybe I can run away,* she thought. *Hide on the other side of the island?* She bit her lip. *What would I eat? How would I live?* She was utterly dependent on the camp.

A hand grasped the edge of the tent flap and pulled it open. Light spilled in, blinding Samira.

"You've changed."

Her heart thudded heavily in her chest. It was a woman's voice. Samira blinked and struggled, first making out an outline and then resolving it into Suzi. She, too, had changed. A designer suit hugged her curves in a way Samira found even more lascivious than the skin-tight jeans worn by the volunteers. The high heels were utterly impractical for the rough dirt terrain that made up the camp. Her hair looked as though a stylist had just finished with it. The shock of long hair hanging onto the woman's face arced in graceful perfection. This, Samira realized, was Suzi in her natural state. Not the tired, sweaty, hopeless woman Samira had known. This confident, immaculate person made so much more sense with Suzi's eyes and face.

"Aren't you going to invite me in?"

Samira blinked, her panic beginning to recede. It left her feeling empty. Exhausted. Jealousy burned in her. This version of Suzi was exactly what Samira always dreamed of being. Not the skintight clothing, of course. It was the precision and power that Samira envied. *She looks like a harlot.*

Hospitality was an instinct. A comfortable pair of shoes Samira could slip into. It seemed the only refuge from the envious, debilitated judgmentalism clawing her heart.

She glanced around the tent. It was a mess of scattered blankets and sleeping bags. A clothesline bisected the tent with someone's laundry pinned to it. The space was chaos in the best of times. Samira had just crashed through it all, churning the mess even more. Of course, Suzi had been in the camp every day for most of a year. None of this should surprise the woman. Seeing her, though, looking like a model in a magazine.... Samira sighed and waved a hand at the mess.

Suzi took it as invitation and came the rest of the way into the tent. Her mouth turned down distastefully and she pointedly did not sit. Though, Samira wondered, if it would even be possible to sit in a skirt that tight. Suzi squatted on her heels.

I should offer her a cup of tea.

Samira saw Suzi looking at her clothes. "The donations," she tried to explain, "are almost all Western clothing. There aren't enough Arabic clothes to go around." It sounded defensive in Samira's ears.

Suzi nodded. "You're doing community service."

Samira grimaced. *She's mocking me. Is that why she's back? To rub my nose in her restoration? Has she forgotten I predicted it?*

"I care less how I'm dressed," Samira snapped. She meant it as an indictment of Suzi.

"Good," Suzi smiled. "I was worried about you needing everything to be perfect. I want you to meet someone. Follow me."

Samira opened her mouth to object. She needed Suzi to understand, she couldn't leave the tent. Her life might depend on it. Suzi didn't wait to hear Samira's objections. She just turned and walked out of the tent with absolute confidence Samira would follow. *And I'm going to,* she realized. She didn't want to plumb her reasoning. Hope was a fragile, often painful thing. But Suzi returning gave her a little flutter of hope.

"Jesus," she whispered, "please protect me."

She scrambled out of the tent, trying to tuck her stray hairs back into her hijab. She fussed at her rumpled t-shirt as she pursued Suzi.

It's hopeless, she reasoned. *Suzi didn't know which tent was mine. She asked. Ata will just ask.*

"I don't..." She called after Suzi, who somehow walked faster in heels on the uneven terrain than Samira could manage in her tennis shoes. "I can't!" Samira huffed. "Please slow down!"

Suzi continued mercilessly, leading Samira to the back gate. Blessedly, it was far away from the busses. As they stepped out onto the road, Samira saw the car. A sleek, black Mercedes.

"He wants to meet you," Suzi said.

Samira froze. Her voice was wooden, disbelieving. She looked down at her clothes. Looking back at the car, even with the layer of road dust she could see herself reflected in the paint. "Dressed like this?"

Her secondhand t-shirt was stained. Her hijab askew. She was covered in sweat, her face streaked with dried tears. Suzi wanted her to meet Dominic Erbach.

Suzi shrugged, walked to the car, and pulled open the rear door on the passenger side. She smiled at Samira, gesturing for her to get in the car. Samira could just see the toe of a glossy wing-tip shoe, and the precise cuff of a pair of navy-blue trousers.

She took a deep breath and looked at Suzi. The German woman smiled at her. There was only the tiniest hint of malice in her eyes.

twenty-three
Samira: Powerful Men

As she slipped into the dark car, Samira's stomach fluttered. Dominic Erbach was looking at her. *Dominic Erbach!* Glacial eyes seemed to catalog every flaw from her disheveled hijab to her baggy, ragged clothing. He was sitting behind the empty driver's seat. Only the half-sized middle seat separated them.

Samira had often imagined this moment. Chiefly, she feared being awed by celebrity. Some people turned into chattering ninnies when they met their heroes. Samira didn't want to be like that. She wanted to project strength, power, and equality. She was someone to collaborate with, not someone to step over.

The reality was nothing like she imagined. She might have felt a touch of awe at his celebrity. She certainly didn't feel strong or powerful. Their proximity felt incredibly intimate to her. Yacoob would never have approved her being in such tight confines with a strange man. Ata would have a melt-down.

Ata. He's here. She tried not to shudder. She still needed to slide closer, to make room for Suzi. Suzi's presence wouldn't solve the fundamental spatial dilemma, but it would reduce her shame. It meant there was another witness to say nothing untoward had happened in the black Mercedes. She turned to look at Suzi. She wanted to gauge the German woman's size, hoping she wouldn't have to scoot too close to Erbach. She just managed to catch Suzi's smile as the woman slammed the door in her face.

Samira swallowed. *This is… the worst scenario I can imagine. Now I have to tell him, I'm so small minded — I can't even sit in a car and talk.*

"I, ummm," she stuttered, feeling nauseous. "I really shouldn't be alone with you like this."

She met Erbach's eyes. They were narrowed, weighing and evaluating. She couldn't face them. Turning away, she reached for the handle. *I don't have to explain myself.* She would simply get out of the car. *If he wants to speak to me, we can do it somewhere proper. Somewhere with other people.*

As she moved, she spotted Ata through the front windshield. She froze. Ata was prowling around, searching. He would grab someone, jostle them, demanding. Then, dissatisfaction etching his features, he'd grab someone else and begin the cycle again. She didn't need to hear him to know the question. *He knows I'm here.*

"Suzi tells me," Erbach began, his voice low and elegant, "you are good with dreams."

Samira took a deep breath. She'd forgotten he was in the car. *What am I supposed to do?* Propriety demanded she get out of the car. She should not be sitting alone with a strange man. But as soon as she left the car, Ata would see her. He would find her. She opened her mouth, intending to explain. If he could just ask Suzi to get into the car with them… As she turned and looked at him, her heart sank. A powerful Westerner like Erbach would never understand. She clicked her jaw shut.

"I've been having nightmares." His voice was calm, devoid of emotion. It sounded like "I've been doing yoga" or "I had a milkshake with my lunch." She was shocked to see indecision flicker across his face. It barely registered and then he was calm again. Commanding. "I want you to make them stop," he finished.

Samira blinked. *He wants me to control his dreams?* She made an inarticulate sound. Closed her mouth, took another breath and tried again. "Sometimes," she explained, "I *have* dreams and…" Her face flushed. She felt so awkward. She was in an indecent situation with a man who was her hero, and she was about to start talking about visions from Jesus. *He's going to think I'm some religious nut.* She closed her eyes, drew in all the composure she could muster and continued, "Jesus tells me th—"

"Spare me," Erbach waved a hand. His dismissive look said he did, in fact, think she was a religious nut. "There is no Jesus, no Allah, no almighty higher power pulling the strings of man's destiny."

The look he gave her was hard. He was daring her to challenge him.

She felt tiny and utterly overwhelmed.

"I just need," he emphasized the word, speaking slowly, "the dreams to stop." He spoke like she was mentally deficient. As though, if he just made the request simple enough, she'd comprehend and acquiesce.

Samira let her breath go in a long slow sigh. She looked out the window again. *I've dreamed of meeting this man my whole life. Now, I'm trapped in a car with him by my psychotic husband.*

Ata continued his hunt. *How long before he looks through the windshield of the car?* She squeezed her lips. *And now I'm going to blow this meeting.* She turned back to Erbach, shaking her head.

"What you believe," she said firmly, "is entirely immaterial, Mr. Erbach. You're asking for my help. *I* can do nothing apart from God."

She struggled not to quiver. *Slow breath in.* Some deep part of her, some unbroken fragment of the girl she had been, was desperate for this man's approval. *And exhale.* She knew he wouldn't get it. Slapping him down like she had was the worst thing she could imagine doing, but… she couldn't pretend that what happened with Suzi was her doing.

He turned his head away from her. Disapproval deepened the lines on his face and made his eyes even harder. *He hates me.* The silence between them went on and on. *What have I done?* Samira nodded. *It's over.* She reached for the door handle.

"It's always the same," he said. His voice sounded distant. "They're all around me. Hundreds," he said the word slowly, boldly. "Maybe thousands—I don't know." The phrase sounded unfamiliar on his lips. "Children. Desperate, hungry." That made him angry. She couldn't tell whether he was angry at the children or at their hunger. "I'm giving them food," he spread his palms, "with my own hands."

He looked down, seeing his spread fingers as though they were deeply significant to what he was saying.

"There is gunfire and shouting in the distance." Samira's eyes jumped to Ata involuntarily. He took two steps toward a woman, shouting, and she turned, running away. He spun away from her, angrily trudging in the direction of the Mercedes.

"But it's growing closer." Samira shuddered as Erbach continued to speak. "It… feels like a conversation," Erbach was struggling to explain the dream, to make sense of the way dreams twisted logic. "But only one person is talking. There is never a response."

He looked at her suddenly, locking eyes. "I try to turn away," he explained, "to leave but I can't. The children... they're distorting, aging. They grow desperate and angry — terrified. Some are still children, but now some are..." his breath seemed to collapse out of him, "grown." He looked away from her. "Sinister. Sneering."

He swallowed. It was the most discomfited she'd seen him. He shook it off, his features firming. "That's when the explosion comes. Everything is screaming and fire. I'm thrown to the ground and then there's nothing. Silence. I get to my feet and everywhere I look," he met her eyes intently, "there are bodies."

She flinched, momentarily seeing the checkpoint near the bus station. Once more, she felt a burst of that terror — of the revulsion of seeing Ata, his gun smoking, over the bodies and the blood. She was gasping for air, she realized. She tried to control her breathing, to calm the panic. She needed to focus on Erbach and his dream. But Ata — the real Ata — was steps from the car.

Raggedly, she asked, "The children?"

He shook his head, looking out the front windshield.

"Grown-ups. My people. Subordinates... Friends."

Samira felt something slick in her palm. Glancing down, she saw her thumb sliding on her tiny scrap of silk. She had nothing. There was no sudden clarity. Jesus seemed completely absent. She felt fear. Horror. Painfully cutting embarrassment.

Erbach said nothing. He just stared out the window. Samira watched her thumb on her scarf running back and forth, back and forth. She was afraid to look up. Ata was probably waiting at her window. She was terrified of the judgment she was sure she would find in Erbach's eyes.

"I've wasted your time," Erbach sounded angry. Samira had the distinct impression that he meant the opposite. He turned suddenly, meeting her eyes. The look was worse than she'd feared. "Please go."

Samira quivered with shame. Tears burned at the edges of her eyes. *I've just utterly failed Dominic Erbach.* She looked back down at her scarf. *I've lost so much. How can this still hurt?* But it did.

Calm hit her like a train. Overwhelming peace swept away all of the paralyzing feelings and words just started to flow from her.

"They are inevitable," she said, looking up at him. It wasn't quite right. She tried again. "*We* are inevitable. Everyone here," she smiled, "all they talk about is getting to Germany."

Erbach grimaced. "You're saying I can't stop it."

She just met his eyes. Being powerless was a feeling she understood well.

"This is what?" Erbach spat, "Justice?"

Samira looked out the window. She felt no need to meet him in his anger, to give it a stage. Through the glass she saw a little girl running, playing some game. The girl laughed. She didn't see Ata.

"The violence," Samira continued, "comes because no one answers it. You said it yourself. It's a conversation."

She turned back to Erbach in time to see him blink, taken aback.

"But I'm there," he sputtered. He let out a sigh. "I'm giving food to starving children. Is that not an answer?"

Samira watched the little girl stumble, lurching forward. The girl shoved out her hands, trying to catch herself but she landed heavily. She began to cry, wanting everyone to see her scraped hands and knees.

"Would it be enough for you," Samira asked, genuinely curious. "Living on handouts?"

Erbach's face darkened. "What's your answer then? Everyone gets a private jet?"

Samira turned back to the little girl. Jesus approached her.

"Here in the camp," Samira explained, her voice still calm and even. "We're given everything. Clothes. Food. A place to sleep." She looked at Erbach, trying to see if he understood. "We have no choices and no pride. We don't need a handout. We need a chance. Jobs. Housing…."

She looked back out the window. Jesus met her eyes and she felt suddenly ashamed. *I promised God's answer and I'm trying to give him my own.* He knelt, kissing the girl's scrapes and helping her to her feet.

"…Education," the word dribbled limply out of Samira's mouth on the momentum alone. *I can't leave it there.* She nodded to herself and looked at Erbach again. "We need grace. Someone to tell us the truth."

The businessman frowned. He rubbed a hand on his face, a bit like he was waking up and then squinted at her. Finally, he shook his head.

"Get out of my car." He sounded utterly disgusted.

Samira looked hopefully out the window. Jesus was walking away, hand in hand with the skipping little girl. They passed Ata. He had his head cocked sideways, gazing through the windshield.

Fear seized her heart. "Umm," she sputtered. "Perhaps—"

"Out." Erbach didn't even look at her.

Reluctantly, she opened the door and stepped out into the chaos of the camp. As she tried to disappear into the crowd, she prayed desperately that Ata hadn't seen her.

Samira wove between tents. There were people everywhere. She wasn't looking at faces, just darting through gaps. *Jesus, please would it be so much to ask to be invisible? Just for a few minutes?*

She was so tense. Her body vibrating, she could hardly breathe. Sucking air in, she broke into a run. Ata had seen her. She was sure of it. He would be behind her, following. She couldn't go back to her tent. She had to lose him somehow.

Everyone was staring. *This is a terrible plan,* she thought. A few people who knew her well called out to ask if she was okay. She stopped her legs pumping. It wasn't reason or logic. Her limbs were animated by terror.

Looking behind her for signs of pursuit, she whipped around a corner and slammed into something. She thought it might have been a wooden post. It was completely solid. She barely kept her feet, head spinning. She tried to focus on what she'd hit.

"Hello, Susu."

Ata stood before her.

Oh God, she thought, *why couldn't it have been a wooden post?*

She whipped her head around looking for a way to escape. He blocked the way forward. There was a chain-link fence to one side and buildings to her right and behind. The only way to go was back the way she'd come.

She took a step back, but he grabbed her, pulling her into a tight embrace. It was completely unexpected. Tender. Not gentle. Ata was never really gentle. He used his strength to show his passion for her.

"Why did you run?"

It felt so good to be in his arms again. Suddenly, a weight of loneliness she hadn't realized she was carrying sloughed away. It lay like a corpse on the ground beside her. Something shot through her, like lightning, filling her with a sudden giddy energy. *Is this real? Is it possible? Does he really love me?* It made so much sense. His love had always caught her by surprise.

Even when he'd bought her from Mahmoud, she'd fought him. She'd tried to run and he just held her. Loved her.

He tipped her head back, his hand cupping her cheek. It was such a familiar gesture. A longing for him warmed her. She bit awkwardly at her lip. She'd felt half a widow for so long. A refugee from her violent, terrorist husband. But here he was. Still strong and passionate. Holding her. Comforting her.

Oh, Jesus, thank you! She prayed silently. A little worm of fear wriggled in her chest at the prayer. *Will he still love me when he knows?* She stomped on it. There was no room for such doubts. This was a moment to celebrate.

"I know it was hard for you," he said. There was a richness to his voice, a wealth of wisdom and understanding. She wanted to bathe in it. "I asked too much. I know that now."

Asked too much... Something about the words landed oddly within her. She brushed the feeling aside. A fountain of hope was in her heart.

"Are you..." she stammered, uncertain how to put her feelings into words. "Can we..."

"We can be like we were, Susu. You remember? How in love we were?" He looked a little uncertain. She could see her hope reflected in his eyes. He wanted her again. His wife. She smiled.

"I've been so alone," she said, closing her eyes. She pressed her cheek against his strong chest. He caressed her hair, softly.

"You aren't alone anymore, my jewel."

She nodded, relief like cool water on her skin.

"I'm sorry that I ran, Ata," she confessed. "I saw that girl," the vision of it threatened to break her, to steal the hope away and she rushed past it. "All I could think of was Yasmeen."

Feeling him move, she looked up into his smile. He was nodding. He understood.

"I needed to be more cautious," he agreed.

She smiled, relaxing. He understood. Whatever had happened to him, he was changed. After all, Ata never would have come to Europe, not the way he was before.

"I'm so glad to hear you say that." He had given up on his violent caliphate. She was more important to him. He'd pursued her.

"It was a mistake," he continued, "to leave you alone."

That landed oddly again. Did he mean that he'd taken too long to pursue her? Or was he saying he should have sent a minder with her when they attacked the checkpoint?

She pulled back, trying to look into his eyes.

"But you have survived the Westerner's cage," he gave her an encouraging smile. "You can see it for what it is now. It's just as I told you. The promise of Europe is a lie."

Hope died. The corpse of her loneliness grabbed onto her leg and began to climb.

On the other side of the chain-link fence, an American woman's voice called out to her. "Hey Sammie. Everything okay?"

Samira looked at the woman. On the other side of the fence, she could be of no help. *And if she were on this side? What then? What might Ata do if she tried to interfere?* Samira gave the other woman a wave and a smile.

Ata's eyes followed the American woman as she walked away. He grimaced in disgust.

"These Jesus worshippers corrupt even our names." He turned back to Samira. "I hope you have not let their lies change you." She felt terror now. Genuine fear for her life rushed into the vacuum where her hope had been. Her mind played through the coming days. When he discovered she was a follower of Jesus — and he would discover it. Everyone in the camp knew! *He's going to kill me.*

"What is it?" His voice pulled her back into the present. His expression was changed, growing concerned. She was stiff as a board in his arms.

He offered her another smile. "Come," he said. "It's been too long since we were together." He started to lead her away, one hand still gripping her arm. He was headed for a nearby tent. *His tent,* she realized. Panic had a hold of her again. She struggled to breathe. Two minutes ago, she could have imagined nothing more lovely than sharing his bed again. Now it was unspeakable.

She shoved his arm away. He stopped and turned to her, anger flashing in his eyes. He calmed himself with a deep breath and gave her a smile.

"Do you have remorse for the little girl?"

He chided her, "We must let the past go. This is our chance to begin anew, Susu." He cocked his head, as if suddenly understanding was coming to him. "Do not fear. I will not hold against you what you have done to survive here. We will start fresh. Both of us."

"Why have you come to Europe?"

He was annoyed, she could see it in his face. He wanted her to fawn over his generosity, not question him.

"We are winning in Syria," he leaned in, a mad glimmer in his eyes. "But the Westerners, they meddle. They can't abide the Caliphate. They fear us. So I will bring the war to them."

She jerked back from him.

"If you wish to be with me, Ata, you must forget this fanatical campaign—"

He exploded, "Fanatical?"

Spittle flew from his mouth, spattering her face, and he grabbed her with both hands, squeezing her arms painfully.

"Our righteous war to restore the Caliphate is just! We are taking back what Allah always meant to be ours."

That was the moment when he realized he was shaking her. She saw it in his eyes. His grip loosened, but she could see the zealot just beneath the surface.

She placed her hands gently on his arms.

"There is no justice in your dream, Ata." A terrible weariness settled on her. Ata's arrival, her flight, Suzi's return, meeting Erbach, the false feelings of hope for her marriage… it was too much. Too many emotions. Too much change. She didn't want to spar with him. The idea of their marriage restored was a beautiful dream. The moment she was in now felt like the bottom of a refuse pit. Everything beautiful was hopelessly mired in offal. "There's no room for me in your life so long as you pursue it."

Gently, she removed his hands where they gripped her arms. He didn't resist. *Why should he,* she wondered. *I cannot possibly escape him.* Stepping around him, she walked away.

"You are mine!" he shouted behind her. "You cannot escape me." She trembled at the echo of her own thoughts. "There is nowhere you can hide. I am your husband!"

twenty-four
Mahmoud and Samira: Freedom?

Fall 2015

The streets of Izmir were disorienting. Despite being in a Turkish city, Mahmoud found himself pressed together with Arabic speakers. His heart language seemed to be on every tongue. The streets of Basmane were warrens, narrow and crowded. Mahmoud wasn't sure who to talk to, and the wads of Turkish lira stuffed into his shoes left him feeling vulnerable. He let the crowd buffet him out of the center of traffic until he was pressed against a shop window.

Nearby, he watched a young woman rush up to a young man, whose confused expression mirrored how Mahmoud was feeling.

"I spoke with a man in the shop over there." Her wave was so vague Mahmoud had no idea to which shop she was referring. "He said the prices have gone up, but it is still possible to get to Greece."

The young man scratched at his beard, like it was new grown. He squeezed his eyes shut. "Where will this man take us, Lina?"

The girl, Lina, tipped her head back, so she could look down her nose at the taller young man. Mahmoud was reminded of Samira. A flutter of uneasy grief ripped through him.

"Lesvos is the closest of the Greek Islands," Lina lectured. "We can travel there in less than two hours."

Her brother, for he was surely a brother, was already shaking his head.

"Why are my ideas never good enough for you?" Lina demanded. "If you want to lead, then lead. Don't stand here like a lump!"

The crowd around them eyed the boy. Mahmoud could see his question reflected in their eyes. Was this young man going to let his sister berate him like this in public? Mahmoud understood the boy's paralysis. His sister simply couldn't understand the gravity of their situation. If she could, she would be struggling as well.

"Lesvos is a prison." Mahmoud had to strain to hear the boy's soft voice. "If we go there we will be stuck."

Mahmoud had heard the same thing. On Lesvos they put everyone in camps and forgot them. It was hard to be grateful in these times, but he praised Allah his first crossing had gone awry.

"So what?" the girl demanded. "We stay here? Do you think these Turks will treat us better than the Greeks?"

Mahmoud sighed. He smiled when he realized his sigh and the young man's had been synchronized.

"What about Cesme?" The girl continued, "We could see if there is anyone there who will take us to Chios."

Mahmoud could hear her desperation. The Basmane was a dangerous place these days. The smuggling trade had brought the worst of the criminal elements to Izmir. It was a hard place for a man. Terrible for a woman. Especially a young, pretty woman like Lina.

A dark-haired boy, perhaps 22, his face prematurely lined with worry, stopped in passing. "Chios is no good," he said. "You are better off with Lesvos. They are sending new migrants straight to Athens because there is no room for them in the camps."

This was exciting news. Mahmoud felt his eyebrows raise.

Lina and her brother barely acknowledged him. Strangers were dangerous here. And the brother and sister were too focused on their own conflict.

"Come," Lina demanded, bodily dragging her brother into the crowd. "At least listen to what this shopkeeper has to say."

Her brother allowed himself to be pulled away, his face a mask of long suffering.

"I am Mahmoud."

The boy with the deep creases in his face, turned as Mahmoud introduced himself.

The boy nodded politely. "Assem."

Assem had an easy manner, with a large smile, and a stylish black beard. He hunched his shoulders as though he was afraid of being hit.

"Peace be with you, Assem." Mahmoud tried to put the boy at ease with a smile of his own. It was hard to smile these days. "How long have you been in Izmir?"

The boy's grin slipped away. He looked around as though worried who might be listening. "Eight months."

Mahmoud nodded, but said nothing. He could tell the boy wanted to say more.

"I came with my sister. We attempted the crossing twice."

"Where is your sister now?" Mahmoud looked around. It was dangerous to leave a woman alone in this place.

Assem sadly looked at his feet. "She's... gone."

Mahmoud also looked down. He didn't know if the boy was saying his sister had died in the sea or been taken by slavers. It didn't matter. Flashes of light flickered through Mahmoud's mind. Pounding bass, old men and the stench of fear. Shame lit his cheeks, as his mind called up images of Tala, uncovered.

The men were silent. Perhaps Assem was also lost in memories of things long done. Mourning choices he could not take back. Mahmoud wasn't sure. For himself, he could not allow the past to distract him from what must be done now.

He put an arm around the young man's shoulder. "Come. I will buy you a coffee and you can tell me all you know of the crossings. I would be grateful for your wisdom."

The boy's smile came back, somewhat less broad. He led Mahmoud into the press of bodies.

"Oh, it was quite the spectacle," Suzi remarked as she pulled Samira through the camp.

"I don't... ahhh...." The unexpected girlfriend banter was disconcerting. However, it was the documents that had left Samira in an inarticulate haze. Suzi handed them to her several minutes ago and she still couldn't believe her eyes.

"He stormed into the office," Suzi continued. The German woman was smiling — actually smiling — she was so enamored with this story. "You've met him," she stopped for a moment, catching Samira's eyes. "You can imagine it."

Samira thought it was a question, even though it sounded like an order.

She could imagine it. She'd been in the tiny UNHCR office countless times. The force of Dominic Erbach's personality would overwhelm the room, especially if he was in a temper.

"He demands to know your asylum status." Suzi's voice was near laughter as she started pulling Samira along again. "They tried to tell him they were 'processing you as quickly as possible.'"

Samira looked at the paper again and nearly tripped.

"So then, Dominic says," Suzi proceeded to speak in a ridiculous, deep voice that sounded nothing like Erbach, "'What detail needs to be confirmed for Ms. Mohammed's application?'"

Samira felt a little flinch at the name. It was the name she'd given at the UN office — at least in the way Westerners reckoned names. That didn't make her any more comfortable. *I am Samira Masoud. When will I stop hiding and face my family?*

"What did they tell him," Samira asked cautiously. She felt certain she knew what was holding her application. She wasn't sure she wanted to hear it out loud, but… on some instinctual level she needed to know.

"They are unable to confirm whether or not your husband is a dangerous radical."

Samira nodded. Not what she'd feared. She been convinced they thought *she* was a dangerous radical. *I did participate in that attack.* Shame heated her cheeks. She needed to change the subject.

"So then what?" It came out harsher than Samira intended. "Mr. Erbach said, 'I don't care. Push it through. Here's twenty thousand Euros!'"

Suzi chuckled, "Dominic doesn't work that way. People who take bribes are weak." Suzi made a sour face. Samira wondered again what had gone wrong with her expense reports.

"No," Suzi continued. "Apparently, Dominic demanded your husband's name. Then, he punched it into his phone." Suzi stopped in front of the same black Mercedes Samira had sat in previously. She turned to Samira sticking her cell phone out like it was a sign. Once again, she spoke in her fake Erbach voice, "Does the UNHCR not know how to use Google?"

Suzi laughed. "Oh, Sammie. You should have seen that guy's face."

She turned and opened the car door. Samira slid in, relieved to see Erbach's seat was now empty. Suzi closed the door and walked around to the other side. As she entered, she waved to the driver. "Airport," she said.

"But…" Samira was confused. "What was on his phone?"

Suzi looked taken aback. "You don't know?"

Samira was immediately distracted. As they passed through the gate, she saw Ata. He blew her a kiss.

"Your husband is Abu Anas Al-laziky. Interpol has issued a Red Notice for him," Suzi explained. "He's one of the most wanted terrorists in the world."

Cold terror shot through Samira. *And a week ago, I nearly went to his bed.*

"Sammie," Suzi asked, "are you okay?"

Samira just stared back into the distance, watching the camp disappear. In her mind, she saw Ata blowing that kiss again and again.

She understood Ata's meaning perfectly. No matter where she went, he would follow. Hide how she wanted, he would find her. She was his. He didn't let people take his possessions.

Sucking in a deep breath, she nodded and offered Suzi a brittle smile. "Fine. Where to now?"

"Berlin," Suzi said, giving Samira a critical eye. "But first, I think we need to go shopping."

Twisting in the mirror, Samira eyed the skirt. It was too tight. It hugged her hips and her back side. Even alone, in a changing room, she felt embarrassed. *And I'm supposed to wear this in front of people?*

"Tell me again who I'll be meeting?" Samira was stalling.

On the other side of the curtain, Suzi sighed. "The board of Eurescue Syria. They're sharks."

Samira wasn't certain what that meant. *I can't keep putting this off.* She stepped out of the changing stall, giving Suzi an uncertain look.

"It's a shapeless sack," Suzi announced, "you need to go a size smaller."

"What happened to mystery?" Samira asked. "Shouldn't I leave something to the imagination?"

Suzi shrugged. It emphasized her visible cleavage. "I have a secret tattoo," she replied. "Only my lovers get to see it."

"Let's try something else," Samira said, blushing furiously.

Suzi held up another suit. "Pants."

"They're still going to be skintight on my…" she gestured at her rear end.

Suzi gave her an evil smile.

Samira took the suit.

"Compromise," Suzi said.

"I *am* compromising," Samira replied through gritted teeth.

"Sharks," Suzi replied as Samira stepped back into the changing stall.

As she started to wriggle out of the skirt, she called to Suzi, "what does it mean that they are sharks?"

"You've seen the type, I think," the German woman replied. "They aren't on the board because they're deeply concerned about refugees or making a difference in the lives of people. They're on the board because they have a lot of money. Donations look good in the press."

In her mind, Samira saw herself addressing a board room full of grey, toothy mouths. She snorted and looked in the mirror. The pants were far too tight. *But they did cover my legs.* She sighed. *Compromise.*

"They respect power," Suzi explained.

Samira frowned. *I look ridiculous,* she thought. "How many of the board members are from the Middle East?"

Suzi was silent for a moment. Samira stopped looking in the mirror and turned to the curtain as though her invisible attention would prompt Suzi.

"None."

"Muslim?"

Suzi snorted.

I need to see myself through their eyes. Samira turned back to the mirror. She'd read a thousand business books and magazines in her life. She'd seen the ads. Confidence. Making a good first impression — she understood all the core concepts. She'd dreamed of this moment. Imagined herself, garbed in a power suit. It just felt different when it was actually on her skin. Reality wasn't like the fantasy.

She pulled on the jacket. The neckline on the silk camisole slid down as she pulled the jacket over her shoulders. *This isn't me,* she thought. *I need them to see me.*

"Find me a shirt with a collar, please. And buttons."

"Wow, going all in on the power thing," Suzi muttered. Samira realized how commanding her voice had been. She wanted to apologize. Instead, she smiled.

It's confusing. As a girl, this was how she'd imagined herself. Firm. Addressing boards of influencers. Giving commands. But her life experience taught her to listen. To serve. *Who am I?* The woman in the mirror looked shy, uncertain. *I look weak.*

She turned and poked her head out of the stall. Suzi was nowhere to be found. A man was sitting on a bench, flipping through a magazine. He looked up at her, and she recognized him. Jesus. He smiled, giving her an encouraging nod.

She pulled her head back into the stall and looked in the mirror again. "I am Samira Masoud," she whispered to herself. "Beloved bride of Christ. I have survived war, human trafficking and imprisonment. And I am not alone."

A smile curled the edges of her mouth. Then she couldn't control it and all of her teeth were showing. She felt suddenly radiant. *I am powerful.*

"This work?" Suzi's arm appeared through the curtain, dangling a lovely cream satin shirt. Stripping off the jacket, Samira removed the camisole. She put on the satin shirt, hastily doing up the tiny buttons. Then she donned the jacket again. Even with the top button undone, the neckline was higher. She ran her eyes over the image of herself in the mirror. *I look silly,* she thought. She pursed her lips, gently correcting herself. *I am fearfully and wonderfully made. This look is simply wrong for this culture.*

She touched her hijab. She could see herself through the eyes of the board members.

"I'm going to need a hairdresser," she announced.

"Really?" Suzi sounded shocked.

Samira started removing the pins that held her hijab in place as Suzi's head suddenly appeared.

"What's going on?"

Samira continued pulling the pins out, slowly unwrapping her hair. She smiled at Suzi in the mirror.

"Doesn't that…" Suzi struggled to find the right word, "mean something?"

Samira laughed. *She doesn't have the slightest qualm about cramming me into a push-up bra and a skintight outfit, but she's uncomfortable when I remove my hijab?*

The last pin removed, she freed her hair. It hung about her face in waves, dropping in a bundle all the way to her waist.

"To me," she explained, holding up the hijab, "this was always a symbol of my modesty. It says that I'm a woman of good character." She turned to look at Suzi directly. "But in that board room, through their eyes, it will be a symbol of my oppression. They will see me as less."

She pulled her hair around in front of her and looked it over, biting her lip.

"It's too long, isn't it?"

Suzi chuckled, shaking her head.

Samira watched her. This severe woman, of whom Samira had long been afraid, was laughing. It didn't look right on her face, to Samira. Suzi was so strange. So alien. Culturally, they couldn't be more different.

"Are we friends?"

Suzi stopped laughing, raising both eyebrows. For a moment, she just stared at Samira. Finally she raised her hands in mock surrender, shaking her head.

"We have a mutual interest."

"Oh," Samira replied, amusement pulling at the corners of her mouth, "I'm glad we cleared that up then."

twenty-five

Mahmoud and Samira: Hoping

Mahmoud was elated as they piled from the back of the truck. The journey had been terrible. A mirror to the previous smuggling. But the sight that welcomed him was new — and joyous. *All of that money has bought us safety,* he thought. *A real chance.*

Beside him, the boy from the market, Assem, nodded his head. The boy looked to be reassuring himself more than encouraging Mahmoud.

The beach ended in an adhoc pier. Made up of wooden pallets and pontoons, it looked like the last steps of his journey from Turkey would be treacherous. However, at the end of the pier a ship — large, steel hulled, painted in glorious blue and white — sat solidly, unmoved by the waves.

The crowd on the beach was massive. They'd been forty to a dinghy before, and it appeared the smugglers intended to proportion this vessel similarly. Mahmoud didn't care. This was a ship, with a captain. *A greater legal risk, perhaps, but we will survive the journey.*

"I will go first," Assem volunteered. "There's no harm if I fall."

Mahmoud smiled. "We will not be the first, my friend. We can watch many people walk that pier before it will be our turn."

Assem flushed. "Thank you, again."

Mahmoud waved a hand. He'd paid the young man's passage. It seemed right.

As he anticipated, getting aboard the vessel was perilous. The smugglers packed them in cheek by jowl. The first families to board were sent into the hold. Women, children, crying babes, and wild-eyed young men descended into darkness. Mahmoud didn't need to enter the hold to know how it would feel. Like the back of the truck, they would be shoved in too tightly to move. Women would be pressed to men without a thought for modesty.

When it was Mahmoud's turn to board, he praised Allah for granting him a place on the deck. The sun was gone. Fragile moonlight illuminated the deck. There would be no more personal space above the hold — the only open space on the entire ship was around tiny cabin from which the captain steered the ship — but there would be blessed fresh air. The Aegean sea smelled like freedom and hope.

The ships engine fired up with a diesel roar. Mahmoud cheered. He couldn't help himself, and he wasn't alone. There was an ecstatic energy on board.

I am not alone. Others had failed the crossing. Others understood the blessing of a ship like this.

They accelerated away from the Turkish coast, the ship building speed. It carved through the waves with a relentless strength. Mahmoud felt the engine thudding away in time with his own heart. *This is life.*

He laughed and smiled. Across the water a new life waited. There was no war, no disappointed father, no long lost sister, no dead children. He was leaving behind the shadow of his wife's suicide. In Greece, he had never been drunk, never visited a brothel, and never shamed his family. He was free. Truly and completely free. The consequences and pains of his past were left behind. Escape was a drug in which he reveled. This new Mahmoud, the European Mahmoud, would be different. The crippling insecurities of Syrian Mahmoud were gone. The wounds of war were as nothing. Allah had given him a ship and the promise of new life.

"Do you hear another motor?" Assem asked, breaking his reverie.

It took a moment. His hearing was not equal to the young man's.

At first, fear wriggled through him that it was the coastguard. He tried to turn, to see. But the press of bodies was too much. Their ship didn't slow. It continued to build speed.

"What's happening?" Mahmoud couldn't see the questioner, and didn't recognize their voice.

Murmurs rippled over the deck.

"He's leaving."

Who is leaving? Mahmoud thought. It was ridiculous. They were in deep water. No one was leaving.

"The captain. Their taking him away in another boat."

Mahmoud could differentiate the sounds now. The other motor fading into the distance.

"Who," Mahmoud felt his mouth go dry as he voiced the question, "is steering the ship?"

There was no reply. The answer could not be given voice. Far from a safe ship, they were now on a steel torpedo, rocketing toward the jagged coast of Lesvos. Suddenly the weight of steel felt less like armor and more like a stone tied around their necks.

What will happen when this ship smashes into the rocky coastline at fifty? Sixty miles per hour? Mahmoud couldn't gauge their speed.

Their voyage proved blessedly short, straining Mahmoud's ability to continuously panic. When they approached Lesvos, lights from houses along the beach gave a pale orange complement to the strained blue moonlight.

Praise Allah! Mahmud thought. The beach ahead of them looked like it was mostly sand. By some miracle, their captain had set them on course for a place that might not kill them all.

He heard the motor slow. Someone had found the controls, and eased their pace. The ship would run aground, but they would survive.

There was arguing somewhere behind him. Some thought it best to keep the ship at full speed, run as far up the beach as possible. Others thought that would be certain death. Mahmoud wasn't a sailor. He didn't know.

Aching, his lungs filled and emptied as though air was something new. The beach was coming up fast. *But it is sand! Sand!* He closed his eyes.

There was a terrible sound, metal grinding against stone, and the deck tilted upward for a moment. Then it crashed back down. People all over the deck lurched and slammed against one another. Collision with the railing drove all the breath from Mahmoud's lungs.

Mahmoud heard the engine as whoever had the throttle drove it back to maximum. But the ship wasn't moving. They were trapped. In shudders and jerks, the ship began to rotate. Waves battered them, pushing the ship. Metal groaned. The ship rocked and turned and rocked and turned until they presented the side of the boat to the beach. And then the ship seemed to lock in place. Some magic of metal and stone had them in its grip.

Again, Mahmoud praised Allah. Again, he taught himself how to breathe.

The first wave came rolling in on a susurration of uncomfortable moans. The worried tones grew and grew, finally striking the ship. The ship listed heavily toward the beach. At first Mahmoud thought they were free of the rocks, but then the wave retreated. The ship lurched back the other way, too far, tipping everyone back toward the opposite railing.

As the tide rose, the waves crashed against the ship, rocking them side to side, ever more. Slowly, it dawned on him that they were not out of danger.

"If we stay here, we will all die." Again, Mahmoud heard the voice of someone he didn't know.

"Someone must get help," a woman cried.

Assem looked out at the lights along the beach. He took a deep heavy breath. "I'll go."

Mahmoud slashed a hand across his chest. "How will you reach the beach?"

"I'll swim," the boy said. The determination of his voice struck an odd counterpoint to the terror painting his features.

"How will you reach the water?" Mahmoud demanded. *This is ridiculous.* "We are trapped on rocks you cannot see. When you jump into the water you will break your legs or your skull."

Assem looked over the rail. It was hard to judge the distance in the dark, but they were easily twenty feet above the sea foam.

Turning, the boy met Mahmoud's eyes. "There are women and children on this ship. Some are trapped in the hold. If the waves push us over — when the waves push us over, they will all die. I can't do nothing."

He flung a leg over the rail, rapidly climbing to the other side.

Mahmoud grabbed his shoulder. He wanted to argue. To beg the boy to let someone else do it. But the words died on his tongue. "Allah be with you."

Assem smiled and then leapt into the darkness.

Staring at the massive expanse of wood that separated her from the

Eurescue Syria board, Samira smiled. *You could park a car on that table and have room to spare,* she thought. Every board member wore a suit that looked expensive and tailored. They all bore stoic expressions, giving no feedback on what she was saying.

She could feel the sweat beading on her brow. This room was designed for a multimedia event. Samira paced with her back to a massive television screen on which nothing was displayed.

"Refugees will need three things," she explained. Her voice sounded small and weak in her ears, but she pushed on.

Suzi stood at the back of the room, perched on a windowsill. She gave Samira an encouraging nod.

"A sense of purpose," Samira ticked off a finger. "You and I have a reason to get out of bed. We have something we're driven to do—"

"That's internal," an intense, hawk-faced woman remarked. "You don't give people ambition. They either have it or they don't."

Samira nodded. "Yes. But ambition and possibility are separate. For example, I knew a man in Aleppo — a young father. During the war, when he was unable to get to his job, he started a business making coffee for people in his community. I met him again in the camp, there he repaired phones and laptops. He doesn't lack ambition. But as a refugee, he's precluded from working. He's got hours of discretionary time every day, and no meaningful place to focus his energies. Instead of being a provider, he's a beggar and he hates it."

The woman frowned. She didn't like the answer. *But does she understand?*

Samira made a V with two fingers. "The next thing a refugee needs is—" She stopped. Suzi was holding up her thumb and first finger in the back of the room. Samira smiled and changed her fingers. "There I go, demonstrating cultural misunderstanding."

No one reacted. She swallowed.

"Refugees need a way to interpret your differing cultural values. They need to be prepared for how those values will affect them."

Her English felt fluid to her, but she was uncertain. *Am I making sense?*

"Each of us has an intuitive grasp of our culture. We don't have to think about it — in fact, we don't even recognize it most of the time. Middle Easterners — particularly Syrians — are coming from very different cultural assumptions than Germans."

Scanning the room, she met the eyes of a man in his fifties with steel grey hair and eyes to match. She looked for a sign her words were clear to him. He didn't blink. *Is he breathing,* she wondered.

Holding up a third finger, she continued, "We need a community."

The challenge wasn't just communicating the ideas. She had to explain them in English to a group of Germans. They all understood English. However, it was her second language, and in many cases theirs as well. Trying to be understood presented unique possibilities for misunderstanding.

"What do cultural values have to do with getting a job?"

Samira met Suzi's eyes and smiled. "This is Erbach Tech," Samira said opening her arms to the room, "so let's say we're opening an electronics shop."

The room seemed just as nonplussed with her hypothetical, but Samira felt a surge of confidence.

"We want our shop to open at 9am, so we tell our refugee worker to arrive at 8:30."

It came to life in her mind as she spoke. The tiny shop, crammed with all manner of tools and gadgets. A solid wooden table set with a soldering iron and a huge magnifying glass. Cell phone cases on spinning sale racks and a little bell over the door.

"Our employee arrives a few minutes before 9. He's not ashamed that he's late. In fact, he is smiling, gregarious, excited to chat and catch up on what's happening in your life."

A few board members leaned forward. This was especially mysterious to the industrious Germans.

"You feel frustrated," Samira continued. "He's late. That means he doesn't respect you or take the job seriously." There were nods around the room. She let her voice echo their frustration. "This is reinforced by his frivolous chatter."

She could see them scowling as they engaged with her story. She paused, letting them wind themselves up just a bit more.

"Because, for you, time is of a high value."

She'd worked with enough volunteers in the camp to have a thumb nail sketch of this problem. It was still nerve-racking trying to lay it out for a collection of power brokers like this. They valued time and she was taking it.

"To him," she explained, "he *did* arrive on time." That had them blinking and looking at one another. "He isn't trying to disrespect you. In fact, all the chit chat is aimed specifically at telling you that you are important to him."

"For him, the value is the relationship," a dark-haired woman said, her voice conveying the dawning realization.

"Exactly," Samira replied.

"Dogs wag their tails to say they want to play," Suzi muttered. "Cats lash their tails to say 'go away.' How could it possibly go wrong?"

The grey-haired man Samira had looked at before, lowered his brows. "What do we do about that?"

"The first step is housing," Samira explained.

"Dominic has an apartment complex for us," Suzi shared.

"We pepper the apartments with Arabic speakers, immigrants who have already adjusted to life in Germany and understand the cultural differences. They form a community with our refugees. They understand the struggles our refugees are facing and can mentor them in interfacing with the new culture."

"That won't work," the dark-haired woman said. "We've seen that. Ethnic ghettos where people isolate from culture and never integrate."

"You're right," Samira replied immediately. "We have to get them into the broader community. The next step is language classes. They need to get enough of a start in German that they can build relationships with Germans and keep growing their language skills."

"The Federal Government is putting together programs, contracting with language schools," another gentleman in a rumpled grey suit said. He looked at Samira through horn-rimmed glasses. His salt and pepper hair framed a precise frown. Whip thin, in his middle fifties, he could have been a white version of Mahmoud. Samira struggled to control a sudden surge of hatred.

"Good," She nodded. "But we need our people to be fast-tracked in language. We may need to create our own program."

Horn-rimmed glasses frowned. He didn't like that. She smiled.

"Once they come through their basic, intensive language training, then they go to work in our shop."

"We train them to fix computers, repair cell phones, that sort of thing."

"Initially," Samira said. "The goal is to get them at the counter, interfacing with the community. The relationships they build with customers are the way they move out of the," she looked at the dark-haired woman, "'ethnic ghetto' and start becoming German."

twenty-six

Mahmoud and Samira: We Have People

Some odd trick of the waves buried the sound of Assem hitting the water. Mahmoud's anxiety for the young man stretched. Like a worn-out elastic band, it eventually gave way into a limp exhaustion. Mahmoud felt dizzy. He was uncertain which direction was up. His whole world felt canted oddly to the side.

The ship should have meant safety. Buying Assem's ticket should have been a gift, not a death sentence.

Absently, he took a baby, the woman beside him handed over. He cooed for the little boy. The ship did the rocking. Each push of the waves felt bigger. More dangerous.

Like a good soldier, Mahmoud's stomach continued its anxious lurching. His emotions couldn't march on, though. They were spent. Even looking into the face of a sweet baby, he felt numb. They were all going to die. Nothing.

Someone found a switch for the steering cabin light. A tiny box on the deck lit up the deck of packed refugees and made the beach disappear.

Mahmoud wondered how they looked from the houses. Was anyone awake, watching them from the windows? What did they see? Little bobbing squares of light from the cabin? Or could they make out the crowded decks? Could they see hundreds of Syrians, slowly sinking into the sea, just shy of the coast?

With a sigh, the Diesel engine gave up. Out of gas. It felt like hope, fading into nothing.

Dawn took its time. It painted a golden eyeliner over the horizon, and then gradually crept up behind Mahmoud. He handed the woman back her baby. People moving into the lit cabin reduced the human tension on the deck. Mahmoud leaned a hip on the rail, straining to see the beach. At first it was little more than a different sort of darkness.

As the sun rose, the beach gained color. A pale khaki strip of sand, narrow and long. It stretched off along the coast, pointing at the curl of a highway. Cars and trucks occasionally rolled past.

"Surely someone will have seen us by now," the woman's words were hopeful, but her tone spoke of betrayal. Mahmoud understood. They'd all heard the ISIS propaganda. *The West hates you. They wish you would die.* Is that what the drivers thought as they passed on the road?

Mahmoud couldn't help but marvel at how close they were to the beach. Anyone could swim the distance. He thought he could do it, even holding a baby. But the sunlight had given shape to his fears. They were in a tiny bay. Rocks curling around them at both edges of the beach. The rocks, visible above waves, looked cruel. The distance was short, but perilous. If they tried to swim, many would die. Their only hope was rescue.

After a time, a car pulled onto the beach. Mahmoud narrowed his eyes. It was a light-colored VW Golf. The driver pulled right out onto the sand way down at the opposite end of the beach. The car stopped. On the aft part of the ship, refugees waved and screamed at the car. It was a strain to see from Mahmoud's position. He couldn't make out the driver. But no one left the vehicle. It just sat there. Pointed squarely at them.

The standoff reminded him of a moment when his boys were young. Jaber was stealing candy in the middle of the night. Esme had been angry and Mahmoud was sleeping on the couch. Not sleeping so much as lying there, rehashing the conflict again and again. He was nursing the hurtful words she'd said, and smoothing over his own. Jaber didn't see him. And he watched the boy. As Jaber finished extracting the candy from Esme's hiding place, he turned and crept back out of the room only to run into his older brother. The two froze. Staring at each other. Neither one wanted to move first. They were locked in an odd tableau. Mahmoud understood. Both were too concerned with the other tattling to realize the other was also transgressing.

This felt like that. He couldn't guess what was happening with the driver. Two vehicles, frozen where they shouldn't be. Neither one able to make a move.

Mahmoud's reverie was broken when the car suddenly reversed and drove away. *No help from him,* Mahmoud thought, bitterly.

Dawn gave way to morning. The sun climbed higher and higher into the sky. Hope made a brief appearance in the form of Assem. The boy trotted onto the beach, emerging between some trees no more than 20 meters from where Mahmoud stood. Mahmoud raised a hand. Cheers erupted from the deck. Assem waved back, but his shoulders slumped in defeat. He didn't need to reply. He'd found no one to come help them.

After a time, the young man retreated back into the shadow of the trees, his black clothes making him invisible.

Waves continued to assault the ship. Shoving them ever more urgently. Rocking the huge vessel. Mahmoud couldn't believe the waves were able to move the large ship so much. The light gave new perspective. They were definitely listing heavily toward the beach. Either the rocks were pushing the ship to the side, or there was a hole in the hull and they were sinking. He wondered about the people packed in the hold. *Are they standing in water?*

The day crept on. Hours passed. The sun was brutal, baking. High overhead, the relentless heat mixed with their exhaustion and fear to make a cocktail of misery. There was no denying it, at this point. Cars drove past regularly on the road. The houses and hotels along the beach were clearly visible. People knew they were here — had known for hours. *Help isn't coming.*

Sometime around noon, Assem reappeared. He was with a bearded man, too pale to be Greek. Mahmoud could see Assem, pleading with the man, gesturing at the ship. It was too far to hear the words, but Mahmoud could imagine them. Assem was telling this potential rescuer about the women and children trapped in the hold. The man raised a camera and began snapping pictures.

No one will help, but by all means, capture the moment. A Greek man in a dark pea coat appeared further down the beach. He glared at the ship, like it was blocking his view. He didn't speak to Assem or the photographer. Eventually, he left. Assem and the photographer stayed on the beach. They spoke occasionally, but mostly they watched the ship rock in the waves. And the photographer captured the moment.

Time dragged, and Mahmoud could see Assem's frustration. People had come. But they weren't helping.

The next arrivals were the most shocking. The whine of an outboard motor announced them. They appeared around the near edge of the bay, skirting the rocks. From his position in the bow, Mahmoud could see them clearly. A black dinghy. It was horrifyingly familiar. One of the cheap boats the smugglers sent with refugees. What sort of insult brought a dinghy to this beach when Mahmoud couldn't make the journey on a ship?

Why, Allah? Why taunt me like this? Have I not suffered enough? Mahmoud's lament slowed him down. He missed the key details. There were no orange vests in the boat. It didn't contain forty exhausted Syrians. Four fishermen ran the dinghy right up onto the beach in front of Assem and the photographer. *Are they here for a photo op?* Mahmoud felt blood rush into his face. He was angry. They'd literally driven around the ship to get to the beach.

Two of the fishermen jumped out and began waving their arms, pointing and arguing about a piece of fencing running along the back edge of the beach. It was mystifying to Mahmoud. Here in front of them was a terrible human tragedy. The solution was there. A boat! And they ignored the ship — the women and children.

After a time, one of the men ran over to the fence with a rope. They spent a terrible amount of time knotting it to the fencing. *Aren't fishermen supposed to be good with knots?* Assem and the photographer watched the fishermen intensely, and then two of the men shoved off in the boat again. They came straight for ship. Straight for the rail. And they threw up the other end of the rope.

The fishermen gibbered and shouted in a language Mahmod didn't understand. The men closest to the boat got the idea. They quickly knotted the rope onto the railing. Mahmoud wasn't certain whether it was in coordination or opposition to the shouting and arm waving of the fishermen.

Are we to slide down the rope like some Hollywood movie? It wasn't near taut enough, if so. Two men lowered an older woman down to the fishermen and Mahmoud finally caught on. They were using the rope as a guide for the dinghy. They didn't trust the outboard motor — wisely. He'd learned the smugglers hid small motors in plastic casings for larger, more powerful outboard motors to fool refugees. And he knew from experience that they frequently didn't have enough gas. If these fishermen had commandeered this boat from another group of arriving refugees, it was a miracle there'd been enough gas to even get it here.

A young woman and her husband were next into the boat. The fishermen didn't take on 40 people like the smugglers would have. They ferried back and forth groups of six to eight. As the refugees began arriving on the beach, so did others. Relief workers carrying shiny silver blankets and bottles of water appeared out of the shadowy trees. They met each boatload, helping people step onto the beach. More photographers appeared.

When it came Mahmoud's turn, he felt weak, being lowered to the boat. They settled him beside the woman and her baby. When he reached the beach, the photographer, the one who'd been speaking with Assem offered him a hand out of the boat. He looked the bearded man in the eyes. There was guilt and shame there. A helplessness that mirrored Mahmoud's own.

As he emerged from the boat, a blanket was thrown around him, and Assem appeared at his side with a smile.

"I was so worried. I tried knocking on all the doors. No one spoke English. Then he showed up. He said he'd tried calling the coast guard and the relief agencies — but he doesn't speak Greek either."

"So he called the coast guard, and four fishermen came?" Mahmoud asked. The ridiculousness of all of it, the suffering and anxiety broke him. He started to laugh uncontrollably. *We're safe. This is Greece. Europe!* Tears tracked down his cheeks and he gripped Assem's shoulder hard. *We made it!*

Summer 2015

The sound of plastic bristles scraping over concrete was soothing somehow — almost a *shhhh*. Repeatedly brushing the floor with the broom was helping Samira to relax. Once the shipping center for a long defunct tech firm, the warehouse, was vast. ErbachTech had acquired the building in a merger years ago. Too valuable to sell for a loss, the building sat. Squatters moved in, filling it with trash and human mess. The human labor costs of restoration got out of hand. A real estate pariah, it had fallen through the cracks. The board was ecstatic to foist the problem off on Samira.

Since she wanted all of their funding to go to refugees, she did the cleaning herself. The first days had been terrible. Discarded needles. Rank blankets, the smells of which took her back to the camp. Human feces. All of that was gone now. Now, she was sweeping up the dust of renovation. Bits of wallboard, saw dust, the final bits of the old and broken.

An Egyptian man, one of her volunteers, did the vital repairs. Broken windows were replaced. The stairs were reinforced where old wood was rotting away. Walls were scraped, sanded and graffiti painted over. At some point, Helmy, her volunteer, had brought a television and wired it to an aging Satellite dish on the roof. It burbled in the corner.

The news looped endlessly. Generic stories told about mobs of refugees. *It could be the zombie apocalypse,* Samira thought as she watched a wide shot of a massive crowd of refugees cresting a hill. The pretty green disappearing under thousands of feet. Dark clothing blotting out all that was bright. On the news, the refugee crises was hordes of faceless people blanketing Europe like a plague of locusts. Not that they were unsympathetic. *They utterly fail to see individual human beings.*

"…many are making the long trek across Hungary…."

The words washed over her, and Samira buried them in the soft susurrations of the broom.

The heavy metal door creaked open behind her. A moment later, she heard it slam shut. A tiny thrill of fear ran through her. *What if it is Ata? What if he has found me again?* But the rhythmic click of high heels on the concrete announced Suzi long before the woman spoke.

"This is going to be the processing center?"

Samira shrugged, not looking up from the ancient detritus she was scraping into an ever-growing pile. "Give it time."

"You know," Suzi gave Samira a critical look, "we have people for this."

Samira glanced at her friend, raising an eyebrow.

Suzi blushed and sighed. "They aren't *all* immigrants," she said. Samira scraped the pile into a dust bin.

"You can't do everything yourself," Suzi lectured. "I mean — you decorated the apartments. How many were there? Seventy-five? You'll burn yourself out."

Samira just smiled and kept sweeping.

Suzi grimaced. "No one wants to work for the person who micromanages everything."

Gunfire and explosions screamed from the television, demanding attention like a tired toddler.

"...bombing devastated Aleppo. Hundreds are dead, the nearest hospital a crumbling ruin..."

Suzi touched Samira's shoulder. Until her brain processed the touch, Samira didn't realize she'd frozen.

"It must be hard," Suzi said.

Samira wasn't sure how much time had passed. Enough for Suzi to close the distance between them.

"Your family is there?" Suzi asked.

Samira pulled her eyes away from the television and leaned the broom against an old crate. Reflexively, she put a hand in the pocket of her jeans and began rubbing her scrap of scarf.

"I," she stopped before she was even started, shaking her head. "When I think about my father or my sister..." Tears filled her eyes. She sucked her lips into her mouth. Suzi didn't move, eyeing Samira uncertainly.

Samira's hand tightened on the scrap, her fist squeezing painfully, knuckles white.

"I can't think about that," she said, voice going cold. She looked up, meeting Suzi's eyes. Suzi took a step back, her mouth slightly open, eyes wary. "So, I think about my brother."

Samira narrowed her eyes, but tried to smile. It was a weak effort. The tense moment stretched. Suzi looked away and expelled a heavy breath. *She thinks I'm a time bomb,* Samira thought.

"You have the furniture?"

Suzi nodded, and Samira started for the door. Suzi grabbed her arm, shaking her head.

"We have people for that. You just tell them where it all goes."

twenty-seven
Mahmoud and Samira: Unhappy Meetings

Fall 2015

Mahmoud entered the registration office with a deep sense of dread. On his first visit, they demanded far too much information about him. They asked about Tala and his baby. Esme's death came up, as did Ismaeel's sectarian connections, and the murder his brother, Ali, had committed decades ago. They'd wanted to know all about his association with Atallah Mohammed Tareq — who apparently was now a dangerous terrorist. Mahmoud flashed again to the confrontation in that alleyway. Ata waving a rifle in his face. The officials told him Ata had been seen in the camp days before Mahmoud arrived. It was terrifying.

And now Mahmoud was back. Once again called into this office. *Will they ask more questions?*

Mahmoud wondered, *Will they put me on a boat home? How will that affect my family? Or will it be worse? Prison? Is there some secret assassination squad that will murder me and then claim I was a dangerous terrorist? The West can live in freedom and peace now that Mahmoud Masoud is dead!* He'd heard rumors like that. Harmless men sacrificed on the altar of Western propaganda.

Mahmoud looked at the UNHCR official with eyes that were too wide.

"I was told to come here today," Mahmoud said.

"Have a seat," the official said, gesturing at an empty chair without really looking up.

Mahmoud sighed into a chair. The official's voice was perfunctory. *I'm safe,* he thought.

"Name?"

Mahmoud was thrilled, of course, to be informed that Ata was no longer in the camp. They'd told him that the first visit as well. Ata had fled somewhere. He'd not seen his brother-in-law since Ata had attacked him in an alley in Aleppo, but he hoped to never see the other man again.

"Hmm?"

Still, knowing Ata was out there, he moved carefully through the camp, checking faces. *What if he comes back?*

The official looked up over his glasses. "What is your name?"

He doesn't know who I am. Maybe it's not okay. Maybe once he knows it's me....

It was hard not to shake. Mahmoud found his nerves were especially hard to deal with lately. The boat crossing, the smugglers, escaping Syria... All of it had been terrifying. In so many cases, he'd survived on chance. He felt his nerves would never calm again. This constant, jumpy fear was a part of him now.

"Mahmoud Masoud," he whispered, his voice hoarse. He cleared his throat. It didn't help, so he tried to clear it again.

The official stared at him, narrowing his eyes. *I should have given a fake name! What have I done?* He could imagine the headline: brother of dangerous terrorist taken to Guantanamo. When Mahmoud thought he couldn't take it for another second, the official glanced down at a paper. The man muttered to himself.

"Masoud.... Masoud... yes!" He looked up at Mahmoud, a smile opening up his face. "I have good news for you, Mr. Masoud."

He seemed to expect a reaction. Mahmoud wasn't sure what to say. *Is it a trick?*

"You are going to Berlin."

He swallowed uncomfortably. "As a prisoner?"

The official looked shocked. "No. Of course not. Your travel documents have been provisionally approved."

Mahmoud exhaled a long breath. He closed his eyes, quietly praising Allah. No more living in a tent. He would be free. *Germany!* He smiled, eyes going blurry with unshed tears.

"Thank you," he gushed. "You don't know what this means to me."

"Yes, yes," the official waved a hand. "Please, there are others waiting."

"Of course," Mahmoud said woodenly. His entire consciousness was rapturously repeating the word 'Berlin' over and over again. "Thank you." He folded his hands in front of him and gave the official a small bow as he exited.

Winter 2016

Apartment buildings loomed over the narrow streets. Light spilled from the windows too occasionally, emphasizing the darkened apartments like lost teeth. Sporadic streetlights made little sanctuaries on the otherwise dark street.

Samira walked swiftly, one hand steadying the heavy canvas bag of groceries over her shoulder. She didn't like to be on the street, alone, in the night. For all of its European flair, Berlin wasn't a safe city. She was uncomfortably aware of how fitted the skirt was on her suit. It forced her to walk more slowly than she wished. She'd felt wonderfully glamorous — powerful — in this new suit while at the office.

She smiled to herself. Every hair in place, the eyes of her staff fixed on her in admiration. For a fleeting moment she felt... exalted. Fantasies of her younger self momentarily realized.

It all felt hopelessly impractical at the grocery store. And now.... now she felt half-naked rushing down the street in the dark.

It was all going well. Their center was running. Refugees were being housed and taking their first fledgling steps into German society. Everything was going to plan. Her plan.

Her apartment was just a few doors away now. She started hunting for her keys, not slowing. She extracted them from her bag. There were so many now. The warehouse, the main office door, her personal office door, the unclaimed apartments — even the filing cabinets had keys. *If it were safe, everything wouldn't need a lock.* She flipped through the keys. *Not apartment. Also not apartment. What is that one? Doesn't matter, not apartment. That's a refugee apartment, not mine.* Head down in the keys she became completely oblivious to her surroundings.

As she crossed into another patch of shadow between streetlights, the shadows seized her. Her groceries crashed to the sidewalk. She was pulled into an alley between two buildings. Her assailant pinned her to a wall, pressing his body against hers. She couldn't breathe. Her worst nightmares were alive.

A fickle sliver of moonlight gave her a glimpse of her assailant's face, but she didn't need it. She knew his smell.

"I've missed you," Ata said.

Frozen fear turned to violent panic. Struggling and squirming, she flailed her arms. It didn't matter how she moved. He just pressed himself against her more firmly, trapping her against the bricks.

"I was angry," he confessed, "when you left." She stopped fighting. His voice was soft, soothing. He sounded calm and a hint dispassionate. Something in his eyes was especially terrifying.

Her breath was coming in harsh gasps. His gaze stayed fixed on her eyes.

"Now, you're parading around like a harlot." His hand reached up, tenderly stroking her cheek. "But it's okay."

She started squirming again, trying to throw him off. *He's going to kill me,* she thought. She sucked in a breath of air to scream.

"Shhh," he said, his hand closing on her throat. "I know how to bring you back to Allah's truth." His voice was tender, excited. Like he was sharing a gift with her. His hand was choking off her windpipe.

"I will show you how to be a proper wife again."

I'm about to die. Please, Jesus, not like this!

He leaned forward, nuzzling and kissing her neck even as he suffocated her with his other hand. She squirmed and struggled. He just kept going, strangling and kissing. Blackness swam in at the corners of her vision. She twisted her body and he shifted his weight to keep her in place. Desperately, she pulled up her knee with all the force she could muster, exploiting his changed position. The hard bone of her kneecap smashed into his swollen genitals, and he staggered back, releasing her neck.

She didn't pause for air. She didn't counterattack. She just ran. Where she was going was immaterial. Anywhere was better than here. She needed to get far away.

Behind her, he shouted. All of the gentleness was gone from his voice. It was just a harsh, croaking. "I know where you live!"

Samira's shoes clicked on the Berlin sidewalk. She might have taken the U-bahn, but this morning it felt good to be out in the air. Fresh air felt like freedom. She'd spent the night huddled — hiding from Ata. Today, she needed to feel free. *He will not cage me!*

Her phone buzzed. She glanced at it. A speech bubble labeled Suzi demanded to know why Samira wasn't at the office yet. *She's worried about me.*

The pulse and energy of the city was exciting, but it was also cool and aloof — so alien compared to the loud and wild streets of Latakia in her childhood. It was so German. In many ways, German was the polar opposite of Syrian.

"I'm fine," she texted back. "Just getting some air."

Three young girls in hijabs huddled in a doorway. They looked hungry. Biting wind whipped Samira's loose hair as she approached them. They were whispering quietly to one another.

Samira studied them. The girls wore cast off Western clothes, ill fitting. Refugee centers often handed out donated clothing, but they were cleaner and less ragged than what these girls wore. The oldest was perhaps fourteen. She wore a pink hijab. The two younger girls, likely her sisters, weren't yet teens by Samira's estimation.

"*As-salamu Aleykum.*" Samira greeted the girls fluidly in Arabic. She smirked. They were taken aback. Women in a designer business suits with uncovered hair didn't speak Arabic in Berlin. Samira spoke Syrian Arabic without an accent.

"*Aleykum As-salam.*" The older girl responded, her younger sisters echoing her.

"Do you live in this building?" Samira continued in Arabic.

The girls glanced awkwardly at one another, uncertain how to answer.

"Do you need help?"

The older girl quickly lifted her head and clicked her tongue in the negative. One of the younger girls gave her a desperate, hopeful look.

"You can't stay here." Samira explained. "Are you living in the Ohlauer Strasse refugee center?"

"We... were." The older girl responded. Fear drained the color from her skin.

"Eurescue Syria has an aid station nearby. We can find you food and a place to stay."

The older girl was shaking her head. Samira understood her reluctance. Stepping forward, she crouched down so she could meet the girl's eyes. "We can help you reconnect with family."

The two younger girls looked wide-eyed at their older sister. She bit her lip. Closing her eyes, tears leaked out at the corners. Tension gripped her body. Finally, she nodded emphatically, all the air and tension bursting from her. Samira put her arms around the girl, sweeping her two siblings into the embrace as well.

This isn't Yasmeen, she reminded herself. But then she argued back. *It's three little Yasmeens. Someone's Yasmeens.*

"It's going to be alright. I'll help you."

Samira was supposed to be at the office, but... *It's never a bad thing to make a surprise inspection,* Samira thought. *I'll take the to the processing center and the go to the office.*

After a moment, their breathing began to settle. Samira led them down the street. She slipped her phone out of her purse and placed it against her ear. "Hello, Suzi? Yes. I'm going to pop in at the Center. Oh, right. Can you push that back one hour? Yes. I'm fine. Yes, really. Just fine."

The magic powers of fresh air were fading. A rough night of poor sleep was asserting itself. She'd gone straight to Suzi's apartment after fleeing Ata. As usual, the German woman saw a single answer to how the situation should be handled. Hanging up the call, Samira relived the argument from the night before in her mind.

"You need to call the Polizei!" Suzi ordered.

Samira sat on Suzi's couch. The apartment was dark, the city sounds distant and muted. Adrenaline was still rushing through her. She felt invincible and completely drained at the same time. She held a cup of schnapps Suzi had insisted on pouring her. Samira couldn't bring herself to drink it. Every time she saw alcohol, she felt a little sliver of shame for lying to Baba about Mahmoud.

"Why?"

The German woman gave Samira an exasperated look. "You were accosted on the street. You're afraid to go home. When that happens, you call the Polizei."

Samira looked Suzi in the eyes. "And then, *Der Spiegel* runs another article about Belin women being accosted by refugees. Think what that will do to our work?"

Rolling her eyes, Suzi took the schnapps from Samira's hand and drank it herself. "You're sure it wasn't someone you recognized?"

Samira sighed. Her wild energy drained away. She shook her head. *Why am I protecting him?*

"There's something you're not telling me."

It's not for him.

Samira gave Suzi a smirk. "Just one thing?"

"Is this about preserving mystery again?"

Samira laughed. The release felt good.

"Then, let me take you home. Two of us—"

Samira raised her hands. "Please. Just let me sleep on your couch tonight." She exhaled heavily and waved a hand vaguely in the air. "Tomorrow, I'll go to the office. Maybe I can work out a way to call the police without terrifying half the refugees in Berlin."

Suzi sat down on the couch next to Samira, her brows contorted with frustration. "I'm sorry," she said. "Of course, you can sleep here. I'm really sorry this happened."

Samira nodded.

"Whatever you need," Suzi said.

Samira looked up at her and smiled.

It was still hard to fathom having Suzi — cold, imperious Suzi — as a friend. And yet, Samira was learning that many of the things she found cold and distant in Suzi were simply a difference of understanding. German's didn't pretend they were happy. They didn't say they were fine when they were not. They didn't feign interest when they had none. They valued honesty. They saw it as the greater kindness.

Samira blinked her tired eyes, trying to stay focused on the present. She was on a street, shepherding three lost little girls.

Yasmeen came again to Samira's mind. She missed her sister. Worse, she was missing her sister's life! *How many years since I've even seen her?* Anger flashed through her. She shoved it away. *This isn't about Yasmeen.*

"Are you okay?" The youngest of the girls clutched Samira's hand and looked up at her with vulnerable eyes.

Not trusting herself to speak, Samira plastered a smile on her face and nodded.

The Center was only a few blocks away, but the journey felt eternal. These girls were exposed. Ata was out there. He killed a little girl not so different from these. Fear and anger warred in Samira. Wave after wave crashing over each other in an exhausting wind up. There was nowhere to release it. Nowhere she could let it go.

Scanning the street for dangers, she saw a familiar man on a street corner. Jesus. He looked ragged, as though he was living on the street. His eyes mirrored the little girls, looking at her with a question: *Are you okay?*

She shook her head, walking faster. Visions and superstitious nonsense wouldn't help these girls. Hallucinations of Jesus hadn't protected her from Ata. Not outside her apartment last night, and not in that cafe in Latakia so many years ago.

"Tell me your names," she said absently. The girl's responses barely penetrated her desperate fugue.

Samira walked into the Center, practically dragging the young girls. She felt groggy and unclean. *This is ridiculous,* she thought. *Two years living in tents, and* now *I feel filthy?*

She'd had a shower, of course. But she was in yesterday's clothes. Adrenaline and her frantic walking had worked up a sweat. Today's grime pooling together with yesterday's. Suzi's couch was the usual boxy IKEA sofa. It looked lovely and modern in the German woman's living room. However, it was uncomfortable for sitting and, as it turned out, for sleeping as well. The combination of tired and filthy were like sandpaper on Samira's nerves.

The Center was swarming like a kicked ant hill. Over the six months since they opened, traffic was steady. This was new. Many people were lined up at the tables. The play area in the corner was a madhouse of children and their mothers. Streams of conversation were deafening.

"...want to begin with language..."

"...family watch your baby..."

"...two daughters living..."

"...a different camp halfway across the country..."

Samira took a deep breath. Her heart was pounding. The sensory overload was winding her up even more. She gave the three girls a smile. It felt brittle, false. A rictus caricature of the real thing. All three girls stared at the room in wild-eyed silence.

"*As-salaam 'alaykum,*" an Egyptian man in his mid-thirties wearing jeans and a t-shirt greeted Samira and the girls.

"...too small. For four of us!" At a nearby table, a woman

complained. Her face looked desperate. Hopeless. Samira dragged her attention away. She met the eyes of the Egyptian man purposefully.

"Aleykumu salam," she replied. Helmy was a top worker from the mentoring program. He'd lived in Germany for four years before Samira recruited him. He was tremendously hardworking. When he wasn't at the apartment building, interfacing with refugees, he was here at the Center, translating for the volunteers and aid workers.

"Two busses just arrived," he explained. Samira shifted awkwardly. Yesterday's clothes itched. *Surely, Helmy will notice these are the same clothes.* Her clothes felt too stiff. She felt like someone was watching her. *Ata could be anywhere,* she thought. *He could be in this crowd.*

She tried to shake off the feeling and pay attention to what Helmy was saying. "…everything under control," he said with a smile.

"Wonderful," Samira said. "This is Samira, Adela and Eman. They need some help reconnecting with family here in Berlin."

He nodded. "Another Samira, eh? We're a little shy on translators today," he paused at her sharp look. His hands raised defensively. "I'll get them connected with Birgit, she'll be able to help them."

"You girls go with Helmy, alright?" The girls nodded. Emani, the youngest, didn't release Samira's hand. The sense of paranoia wasn't leaving. She scanned the crowd again, looking for a familiar face. The oldest girl pulled Emani away. Samira barely registered the little girl's hand slipping from her own.

Helmy started to shepherd the girls away. He stopped, turning back to Samira. "Are you alright?"

She shook her head. "It's nothing. Go ahead."

He nodded, but didn't move.

She saw something across the room. Her gaze fixed on the furthest table from where she was standing. A volunteer sat there, talking to a man. It was the man who caught her eye.

Exhaustion dragged at her as she squinted across the space. In reality, Suzi's couch had been fine. Terror was what kept Samira awake. Finally — *finally,* she'd made it. She was running a company. Making a difference in the lives of the people around her. *Surely, Jesus must be proud of all the work I am accomplishing in his name. This is the promise.* She was *exalted.* And then, Ata showed up. Now, she just felt terrified. Weak. Small. Everything she hated about herself was front and center again.

It was like her life was an old record. Just as she leaned into God's promise, just as the fruit was sweet in her mouth, the record skipped.

She was back in the cafe in Latakia. Being sold. She had no agency. Samira Masoud was a mere commodity to be tossed about and traded at will.

I'm tired of being afraid, she thought. *Tired of being the one who runs. Tired of seeing the wicked prosper.*

The fear, shame and discomfort suddenly imploded into an unquenchable fire in her chest and she launched herself across the room.

Everything about it felt surreal. She was watching herself from a distance. Feeling things, people, hearing sounds and voices but nothing really registered. Then she was standing in front of him, blocking the table. She glared up into his thin, old face. Her brother took a step back, raising his hands.

"Did he tell you to come here?" she demanded.

"Ahh," he looked around like he was hoping someone else would answer. "I was told to come here."

"How dare you!" Samira jabbed him in the chest with her finger. He took another step back, looking completely bewildered.

The power felt incredible. She wasn't afraid, Mahmoud was afraid. It was like a drug. Bitter delight burned in her veins.

The world began intruding into her dream. The constant buzz of conversation had subsided into something hushed. Where before she'd felt a vague paranoia that she was being watched, now she felt the full force of hundreds of gazes. The whole room was watching her.

"Perhaps," he suggested, "you have me mistaken for someone else. My name is Mah—"

"I know who you are!" His denials served only to rekindle her rage. She didn't care who was watching. Let them see. She would serve justice, just as she had to the rapists in the camp. "What game are you playing?"

Mahmoud opened and closed his mouth like a fish. Looking around, his eyes locked on something behind her. Relief washed over his face and it filled her with dread. Ata, she thought, *he's here.* She spun around and nearly clobbered Helmy.

"Maybe," Helmy suggested, "we can take this into another room?"

Samira brushed him aside. She turned back to Mahmoud. Angrier now because he'd tricked her. She saw Jesus, watching her from the crowd. Her rage waned. Mahmoud's confusion looked so genuine. *Is this how he always fooled father,* she wondered. *Am I being taken in?* The idea of letting him fool her rekindled her fury. She wasn't falling for his act.

"You know who I am!"

He looked her up and down, shaking his head. "I'm sorry. I've never seen you in my life."

She clenched her fists. *It's not possible.* Jesus was moving toward her through the crowd. Her tunnel vision was fading. *Everyone is watching us.* Hundreds of people were watching her scream at Mahmoud. Realization hit her like a freight train — she'd shoved her way through all the people to get to him, heedless of who she knocked aside. She looked away from Jesus not wanting to meet his eyes. Guilt flooded her with a sick feeling.

Mahmoud was still talking. "If I've offended you in some way, I'm very sorry."

Her rage flared to life again. Why should she feel guilty? *He* sold *me!*

"You will be," Samira muttered. At that moment, Jesus stopped, his hand on Mahmoud's shoulder. Suddenly, Samira couldn't stand the sight of her brother. She turned her back. She couldn't see him. Couldn't see Jesus standing with Mahmoud — *how could he!*

She avoided the look of shock in Helmy's eyes. This was a PR disaster. One newspaper article or even a blog post and everything they had built — everything *she* had built would be swirling the drain. Images flashed through her mind, newspaper headlines conflating refugees and criminals. She blinked them away.

Her phone was out of her pocket and to her ear in a moment. A part of her was screaming, begging her to stop. "Hello, yes. I'm calling from the Eurescue Syria center on Erich-Kuttner Strasse." The phone conversation was entirely in German, but around the room she could see people whispering, translating for those who couldn't follow.

Helmy was trying to get her attention. His eyes were wide. His lips moved in a silent plea, begging her to stop. On some level she understood the catastrophic consequences of what she was doing and she didn't care. She could punish Mahmoud.

"We've got a gentleman here who is a known associate of someone on your watchlist," she continued, waving a hand at Helmy. He was insistent and she turned away from him as well. "He's a human trafficker."

"Sammie! What are you thinking," Helmy's whisper quivered harshly at her ear.

"Please send someone quickly," she finished and hung up.

She looked at Mahmoud. His jaw was hanging open, his hand

clutching at his chest. She doubted he understood much German, but "watchlist" and "human trafficker" were easy to pluck out. The smile she gave him was cruel. Triumphant.

Helmy grabbed her shoulders turning her to look at him. "I don't know who this guy is, but you've just convinced several hundred refugees that we're going to have them arrested for no apparent reason."

He continued turning her, revealing the rapidly emptying room. She felt all the air rush out of her lungs. She could see it. Every person who'd seen this would tell… everyone they knew. Eurescue Syria would be handicapped. No one would come to them for help. No one would trust them now. *This is a disaster,* she realized. She shook her head, willing it all away, but nothing changed. Around the room, volunteers stared at her aghast.

She firmed her jaw. It was difficult, but she managed to swallow. She met Helmy's gaze directly. "I'm protecting them," she said with absolute conviction.

twenty-eight
Samira and Mahmoud: Interrogation

Samira watched Mahmoud shifting in his chair. His eyes were wide. She could see the sweat on his brow. She wanted to feel vindicated, avenged. All she felt was restless and unsatisfied.

A sheet of one-way glass separated her and her brother. She saw the bitterness in her half-reflected face. *When I know he's in prison,* she thought, *then it's done. Then I can feel better. Safer.*

She turned to the Interpol agent in the room with her. He was medium tall, with espresso-colored skin and dark, curly hair. He'd introduced himself as Carlos.

"He confronted me in the street. Threatened me," she explained. "And then, immediately afterwards," she pointed to Mahmoud, "he shows up."

Carlos cocked his head to the side, his face scrunching up. "You saw Abu Anas Al-laziky in Berlin? Yesterday?"

She nodded.

"Why didn't you report it?"

She opened her mouth to respond. No words emerged. Her reasoning from the night before swirled through her head again, the job, public perceptions of refugees.... It all crumbled to dust before she could speak. *What am I supposed to say?* She closed her mouth. *Why didn't I report him?* She opened her mouth again, but still had no words. She should have called the police as soon as she'd seen Ata. He'd assaulted her. The simplicity of it was heinous.

All I felt was terror. It didn't even occur to her that Ata was a danger to more than just her. *But he is,* she reminded herself, *he told me as much in the camp.* She sighed. Looking through the glass again, at Mahmoud's wide-eyed face. She felt pity — which she instantly replaced with rage. *When is he going to interrogate Mahmoud and stop grilling me,* she wondered.

"He knows him!" She slammed a finger into the glass right over Mahmoud's face. It made a thunk. Mahmoud jumped. "They probably arrived together."

Carlos didn't react to her yelling or her pointing finger. His voice sounded like a late-night radio host, all buttery calm. "Why do you think they're connected?"

"He sold me to Ata!" she shouted.

Carlos raised a hand for her to calm down. Her eyes flickered to Mahmoud. *Can he hear me through the glass?* Everything was so unfamiliar. Rage dipped into a gnawing worry. Her situation was precarious.

"I thought you married Abu Anas—" He cut off at Samira's eye roll. "Sorry, Atallah Mohammed Tareq before he was a terrorist?"

Does he think I'm the criminal here? She shook her head, burying her face in her hands. Emotions warred within her. She felt a wild rage at Mahmoud, a quivering terror of Ata, pity for the jumpy hunted creature in the interrogation room, love for the tender man who had shared her bed — all of it slammed together inside her again and again. It was pulling her to pieces.

She needed an anchor. If she could cling to one thing, maybe she could keep the rest from shattering her. A memory of Kelsey, the smell of burned coffee and Jesus's eyes twinkling popped into her mind, but it wasn't the anchor she wanted. She embraced the rage, forcing it into a cold, controlled burn. She raised her chin and stared Carlos in the eyes, her nostrils flaring.

"Why are you interrogating me?" she demanded. "He's the bad guy."

Carlos was unfazed. "I'm just trying to understand your story."

"My brother," she said, pointing at Mahmoud. She spoke slowly, like Carlos was an idiot. "Mahmoud, sold me to Ata. Ata married me. I…" she stumbled. She couldn't express this without letting herself feel it. The feelings were so raw and confusing. "I tried to make a go of it," she croaked out. She took a deep shuddering breath. "But Ata…"

"Radicalized?"

Her rage wall collapsed. Underwater again, she struggled to get a breath. She nodded, unable to look at Carlos now. She didn't want him to see her like this. Arms wrapped around herself, she clutched her own body for some semblance of comfort. She felt tiny. Weak. Scared. And brutally lonely.

Carlos turned away, pulling the door partway open. She heard his hushed whisper to someone in the hallway. "I need you to warn our field office that Abu Anas Al-Laziky is in Berlin."

Samira slumped into a chair, her face leaning against the cool glass. Somehow, she'd found her scrap of scarf again. Her thumb ran back and forth over the fabric. The gesture was familiar, calming. She looked up. Mahmoud's face was drawn. Thinner and grayer than she remembered, the years had not been easy on her brother. *I will not pity him! He sold me!* She let the rage take her, her hand balling into a fist over the bit of scarf.

The door clicked shut and Carlos turned back to her.

"I need some answers," he said.

She lurched out of her chair, animated by wild frustration and exasperation. "Ask him!" She waved at Mahmoud, and bulged her eyes at Carlos. "I don't know anything. They're friends. You want my help? I'm giving you him. That's how I help!"

Carlos watched her tirade unmoved. He took a slow breath, held if for a moment and then let it go. He blinked. Finally, he shook his head, shrugged and walked out of the door without saying a word.

Since the ominous thud from the mirror, there was only silence. Mahmoud fidgeted in his chair. *How long have I been here,* he wondered. It felt like hours. His throat was sore and burning. His leg bounced endlessly. He thought if he stopped moving for even a moment, he might pass out. *Or perhaps I will never sleep again.*

He heard footsteps. Hope thrilled through him like a furious river. He looked at the door. The sound moved past. That quickly, hope was gone. He let out a slow breath, trying to calm himself down. He couldn't. In the wake of hope, he felt utter despair. *When someone does come through that door, they will haul me away to prison. After all, I entered Europe illegally. Smuggled other people here.* He pictured the official in he camp: the man's beady eyes blinking behind his spectacles. *Sending me to Berlin was a colossal mistake. Now, I will pay for my crimes.* It was just. Fair. Right.

He hung his head.

Then, he jerked his head up again as another set of footsteps made their way down the hall. Instead of hope, this time, he felt like a hunted animal. The footsteps stopped. Mahmoud felt the muscles in his shoulders knotting. The door opened. It was a terrible sound. Hollow and metallic.

The man who strode into the room looked almost like an Arab with his dark skin. However, his curly hair was more African looking. His features were wrong. The slacks and blazer he wore were cheap. Working in the silk trade, followed by years of living with Nabil, gave Mahmoud a comprehensive education in quality menswear. Even across the room, he could recognize poor weaves and bad stitching. Mahmoud had watched Western television. He knew that a cheap suit was the hallmark of the hardened lawman. *Dirty Harry, Lennie Briscoe, John Casey…*

The door clanged shut with an echoing finality. Mahmoud tried to swallow, but he didn't have any spit. His throat just hitched. He tried again, nearly choking on obstinate phlegm.

"Please," he croaked. "She is mistaken. I don't know that woman."

The interrogator carried a folder marked with the Interpol logo. He laid it on the table.

"You have the wrong man."

It was worth a try. *What other hope do I have? Either they have mistaken me for someone else, or my life is over.*

The interrogator didn't look at him. In fact, there was no indication he'd heard Mahmoud speak. The lawman set a small video camera on the table. He worked methodically through getting it adjusted and pointed at Mahmoud.

Mahmoud watched every detail of the action: the adjustment of each leg of the tiny tripod, the flipping out of the screen, rotating the camera…. Then the interrogator turned away. He removing his sport coat, folding it carefully so the shoulders touched, and then in half over his arm.

Mahmoud's leg was going again. He tried desperately to generate some spit, but his mouth was completely dry.

The interrogator hung his coat over the back of a chair and unbuttoned his right cuff. Mahmoud couldn't take his eyes off the action. Sweat was rolling down his brow, as the interrogator began rolling up his sleeve. *He's going to beat me. I've seen the movies. This is how they prepare to beat me. He doesn't want blood on the cuffs of his shirt or his jacket.* The interrogator moved on to his left sleeve and Mahmoud wanted to wet himself. It was hard to breathe. He shook and quivered and gasped.

"Please," Mahmoud begged, "I am not who you think."

The interrogator picked up the folder and shuffled through some papers. Suddenly he looked at Mahmoud for the first time. Mahmoud felt like that look saw to the depths of his soul.

"Are you Mahmoud Masoud?"

Mahmoud grabbed both sides of his face and pulled hard, trying to squeeze away the desperate anxiety. He willed himself to be anywhere else. He could feel the skin on his face stretching, but it failed to distract. Nothing changed.

Defeated, he nodded his head.

"I need you to answer audibly for the recording," the interrogator explained. His voice was calm. Smooth. He spoke English with a neutral American accident which did nothing to inform Mahmoud of his ethnic origins. "Are you Mahmoud Masoud?"

"Yes," Mahmoud said, wondering suddenly why an audible answer was necessary for a video. He rubbed his face. It didn't matter.

The interrogator went back to the folder. He perused its contents with no sense of urgency.

"What is the nature of your relationship with Abu Anas Al-laziky?"

Mahmoud raised both his hands. "I don't know him at all."

Like a striking snake, the lawman whipped a photo onto the table with an audible smack.

"You don't know this man?"

The agent stared into Mahmoud's eyes. It was an intense, piercing gaze. It was an effort for Mahmoud to tear his gaze away and look at the photo. When he did, he felt all of the blood leave his face. *I am going to prison forever.* His vision grew blurry as tears filled his eyes. He nodded again, then shook his head. *Audible.*

"Uhh, yes. Yes. I know — well, I knew him many years ago. I didn't know he was… Al-laziky. He…" Mahmoud choked a bit, "married my sister."

The interrogator nodded as though he knew all of this already. "What is his name?"

"Atallah."

The interrogator stared at him and Mahmoud struggled to understand the problem. Westerners were funny about names. *They always want more names.*

"Atallah Mohammed Tareq." *Was that enough? Father and grandfather?* He hoped it would do.

The interrogator gazed intently into his folder. When he made a little clicking sound with his mouth, Mahmoud jumped in his chair. The interrogator paced, his head swiveling from the folder to Mahmoud and back — like he was comparing Mahmoud to something in his folder. Then he faced Mahmoud, cocking his head curiously.

"Did he pay for your sister?" His voice was casually curious. There were no moral indicators in voice or posture. Mahmoud felt his stomach lurch. Bile filled his mouth and he struggled to choke it back.

"I did not sell her," he shook his head wildly. "It was a dowry."

"Don't those usually go the other way?"

Mahmoud looked at the lawman in confusion. "No. The groom's family pays to honor the bride and her family. This is how it has always been done."

"And how much honor was afforded your sister?"

Mahmoud looked away. "It was many years ago…"

The lawman glanced at his folder. "Was it five hundred pounds? Paid in a single note?"

Blood drained from Mahmoud's face. "You have that in your file?"

The interrogator just stared at Mahmoud, unblinking.

Mahmoud shifted in his chair. "That is the correct amount."

The lawman nodded. "In 2011, that would have been what? Ten U.S. dollars? Would that be a normal bride price for a woman like your sister?"

The ground seemed to disappear from under Mahmoud like sand through an hour glass. He grasped for some stability, something to cling to.

"Ata's family was very poor."

"So, the marriage was advantageous because of your close relationship?"

Mahmoud's hands went up and his eyes widened dramatically. "No! No. I hardly knew him. It…"

Mahmoud had been lying to himself for years. His justifications shredded like paper. His body shook. He collapsed onto the table into a puddle of tears and snot.

"It's true," he blubbered. "I sold her."

Unmoved, the interrogator responded in his completely calm voice. From the interrogator's voice, Mahmoud might think they were friends, chatting over coffee. "I'm sorry. You're voice was muffled by your arms."

Mahmoud looked up, gasping, trying to control his sobs. His voice came out quietly.

"I sold my sister." He swallowed hard, his throat now clogged with mucus. "I married her off to a stranger to get rid of her. There can be no forgiveness for me." He met the interrogator's eyes. Mahmoud firmed his jaw. "I am guilty. I have done so many terrible things. She was always spying, making up lies about me, and I wanted to please father so badly," the confession tumbled out of him in an endless jumble of words, "but he could never see me. He only saw her. I knew she would follow me to the cafe that day..."

Mahmoud grimaced. *Where has she gone?* Susu was following him, just as planned and then... she wasn't there anymore. *She's going to ruin everything, just as she always does.*

He tried to feign indecisiveness as he turned and walked back down the street a third time.

What if I run right into her?

Mahmoud walked purposefully down the road. *This pretending is not for me. Let Nabil have his intrigues, I just want to protect my family.*

Out of the corner of his eye, he saw Susu poking her head around a corner. He felt a huge swell of relief that she'd found him. She'd thrown a ragged old abaya and scarf over her regular clothes. *Does she really think I won't notice?* The disguise was ridiculous, her regular clothes peeking out at the edges. He held back a laugh as he made his way toward the cafe.

As he entered the cafe he took a deep breath, reveling in the scent of coffee and the anticipation of victory. Young Ata fidgeted at a table in the middle of the room.

"Ata, good to see you."

"Mahmoud, I'm honored you were willing to meet with me."

Mahmoud waved for the waiter to bring them strong coffee and then took a seat.

Mahmoud listened to Ata with only half an ear. He felt a giddy excitement as he contemplated his revenge on Susu. The wriggling hint of shame, he ignored.

Behind him, he heard the waiter ask, "What can I get you?"

There was a long pause. Mahmoud listened eagerly, ignoring the words spewing from his table companion. He could imagine her discomfort, her fear, and it was magnificent.

Finally, he heard her quiet whisper: "Coffee." He wanted to laugh out loud! *She's here.* A long, contented sigh slid from his lips, and he tried to focus in on Ata.

"…I'd like to be near my family."

"Of course. But you have career prospects…." Mahmoud blathered encouragement at the younger man. Ata looked ready to jump out of his skin with nerves. Mahmoud could remember that feeling, from his own betrothal. *My wife is terrifying,* he justified. He tried not to let his condescension show as he looked at Ata. *But then, this idiot will be stuck with Susu.*

Mahmoud needed to give Ata some advice, help him establish boundaries early on so Susu didn't walk all over him — advice Mahmoud wished he'd received before he wed. Besides, Ata seemed a timid young man. He needed to embrace his strength. "Some women think they can handle everything on their own. They need a strong hand to disabuse them of the notion."

The young man met Mahmoud's eyes. There was unexpected steel there. Mahmoud raised his eyebrows in surprise. "I'm not afraid to be firm."

Mahmoud chuckled. *Oh, Susu. You're in for it. This one is not as weak as I thought.* He turned to look at Susu. She was hiding behind a book like the protagonist in a bad spy movie. Patiently, he regarded her until she noticed him. Her eyes met his over the top of the book. Her reaction was incredibly satisfying. Entire body jerking backward, her eyes flared open. It took everything Mahmoud had not to laugh.

He invited her to the table, what choice did she have? *Everything is going perfectly.*

As she gathered her things, she slid the rag she was wearing off of her head, revealing that cursed scarf their father had given her. Mahmoud felt it like a slap in the face. It was a constant reminder of their father's love for her and by extension his complete rejection of Mahmoud. Mahmoud, who would inherit!

She flopped petulantly into the empty chair.

"I'm very interested," she said, snidely, "to meet the man who has you sipping coffee in a cafe when you're supposed to be supervising a delivery. I'm sure father will be interested also."

The words cut at Mahmoud. They reminded him of exactly why he'd orchestrated this meeting, why he'd loitered outside waiting for her to catch up before entering. The waiter appeared to place a coffee in front of her. Mahmoud just watched her and smiled for all he was worth. He didn't feel happy. At this moment, he only felt rage. *But let her see my triumph,* he thought.

He spoke slowly, relishing the words. "But I am supervising a delivery, Susu."

She looked calm as she sipped her coffee, blissfully unaware of what was coming.

Mahmoud continued, "Ata, my sister, Samira Masoud. Susu, meet Atallah Mohammed Tareq, your husband-to-be."

Satisfaction warmed Mahmoud's belly as coffee spewed out of her nose. She struggled to react to his pronouncement and the mess she'd just made on the table at the same time. It was delicious. She was usually so smugly perfect. He loved seeing her discombobulated. Without looking away from her, he opened his hand to Ata. The young man paid him the agreed sum. Mahmoud stood.

She was panicking now. "Baba will arrange—"

The words enraged Mahmoud. *She refuses even now to acknowledge that I am above her. I run the business, I hold power of attorney, I am the head of this family!* As she tried to rise, Mahmoud put his hands on her shoulders, locking her in the chair. He leaned over, whispering to her. "Baba could never see you for what you are. But I will not let an ambitious woman tear our family apart."

He'd longed to say those words to her for years. They were his mission statement. When she told father about her supposed prophesy that she would rule over him, he knew he couldn't wait any longer. Saying the words, though, being in the moment, he felt suddenly nervous. *What if I'm wrong? What if she comes back?* "She must never return home." The words weren't part of his plan. Once the marriage was consummated, Yacoob Masoud wouldn't dissolve it. He would be angry with Mahmoud for a time, but there would be no more talk of Susu running the business. That had been the plan. But in the moment, fear lanced through Mahmoud. *She has to disappear.*

Ata nodded.

Mahmoud looked at Susu again, seeing the hated scarf on her head, the sign of their father's blessing. He would take it back to their father and claim she'd run away, rejected the family… he would think of something. He grabbed the scarf intending to whisk it away, but she clutched it and fought him.

"Stop! What are you doing?"

It wouldn't come away. He refused to let her have a victory. This was his moment and he was the stronger.

"I made this! It wasn't intended for you."

He tore the scarf away. It should have been a marvelous triumph, but he felt suddenly empty and small. The scarf he'd worked so hard on was torn, ruined. He looked at his sister, desperately trying to cover her hair in a busy restaurant. Seeing her publicly humiliated didn't make him feel better. *I made this,* he thought and felt ashamed. *That's my sister. My blood. I am supposed to protect her.*

In a panic, Susu shrouded her head with the rag from her lap. *She will be okay.* He nodded to himself. *Even in this, she is quick and competent.*

"This isn't what's supposed to happen," she gasped. It felt like an echo of Mahmoud's own thoughts. *I'm not supposed to be worried for her or for me. This is my moment of triumph.*

He turned, hiding his grimace. She wasn't reading his mind. She was referring to her stupid dream again. It was a fabrication, just like her stories about his drinking. *She is so desperate to have what is mine, she will do anything.* His fist tightened on the ripped scarf in his hand. He walked away. As he reached the doorway, his doubts were already coming back. *Am I doing the right thing?* He looked back.

Susu looked small and fragile. *This is my sister. I must protect her. This is all a terrible mistake.* He determined to go back, to apologize and lead her from the cafe. He took one step toward the table. As he did, Ata reached out and tenderly took her hand. The young man smiled at her. The look was caring, gentle, reassuring.

"I promise," the young man said, "it is not so bad. They call you Susu, right? I like that. It's cute."

Ata was gazing into her eyes with warmth and passion. Susu wasn't immune to it. Mahmoud could see the tension in her shoulders relaxing at his touch. Mahmoud smiled. *She will be fine. He will take good care of her.*

Mahmoud turned and left the cafe.

twenty-nine
Samira and Mahmoud: Memories

Samira glared at the one-way glass. Listening to Mahmoud gush out his sob story in some perverse attempt to justify selling her was utterly disgusting. She wanted to storm into the interrogation room and choke him to death.

She felt no pity for him as he described telling their baba that she was dead. The image of the old man's hand, grasping a twisted knot of Mahmoud's hair, as her brother knelt… *I wish he were kneeling at my feet. I'd be less gentle.*

The endless victimology went on and on. Mahmoud saw himself as some tragic figure, misunderstood. Her brother couldn't conceive that he was the villain.

"When we lost our second son to the fighting," Mahmoud continued, his voice low and hoarse, "I lost myself."

Samira felt a moment of shock. *Jaber is dead?* Jaber was nearly her age. They'd played together as children. She could remember mischief sparkling in his eyes, as they crashed through the Masoud home. They'd made up games together and shared secrets. She'd loved Jaber. Seen him as a brother.

Then Mahmoud had grown jealous. Ismaeel was the first to reject her. Seeming to reject all of them, her older nephew spent more and more time away, running around with radicals. As they hit their teens, Jaber grew aloof. He stopped looking at her like a sister. His smile turned to a sneer. Mischief in his eyes became cynicism. She knew why. Mahmoud poisoned her relationship with her nephews. Jaber turning away from her had hurt the most. *And now he's dead.* Regret cut through her. She'd never pursued Jaber or Ismaeel. When they rejected her, she wrote them off.

This was all Mahmoud's doing, she reminded herself. *I didn't do this.* Narrowing her eyes, she shook off any lingering pity for Mahmoud. *You did this, brother. You suffer by your own hand.*

He rambled on.

"We went to the house to tell Tala the news."

Carlos perched on the edge of the table, seemingly paying more attention to his folder than to Mahmoud.

"Who is we?"

"My son, my wife and I."

"Your youngest son, Achmed?"

"Ahmad," Mahmoud nodded and then shook his head. "Yes. That's correct."

He's still nervous about not speaking for the camera, Samira shook her head. She couldn't decide if she admired the way Carlos was manipulating Mahmoud, or whether it repulsed her. She enjoyed seeing her brother discomfited. On the other hand, she couldn't help wondering how she would fare in that same position.

She returned her attention to the conversation.

"Why? Hadn't you promised," Carlos glanced at his notes, "Tala's father she would marry Achmed?"

"Ahmad," Mahmoud reflexively corrected. Carlos just blinked at him, not offering the correction.

"I thought," Mahmoud sighed. He shifted uncomfortably in the chair. "I was crazy. Paranoid."

"You wanted the girl for yourself."

Samira took a step back from the glass. Even Mahmoud wasn't that dissolute. *Agent Gutierrez is going too far.* She watched Mahmoud squirming in his chair. *Does it matter? I want to see him suffer like I suffered.*

"I wanted to protect my son."

"Because your other sons joining ISIS and accosting women in the street were your daughter-in-law's fault?"

"I told you," Mahmoud protested, "I was crazy. I thought somehow, it was better for both of them."

"You thought ISIS was better?"

Mahmoud shook his head. "Not Ismaeel and Jaber. Ahmad and Tala. I thought it was better for them for her to return home."

Mahmoud's endless tale of woes was exhausting. She didn't care what was in his head, it was clear enough to her that he'd discarded his daughter-in-law even as she was grieving his dead sons. It was hard to imagine both Ismaeel and Jaber marrying the same girl, or that Mahmoud had given any serious consideration to her marrying Ahmad as well — especially over an insane drunken promise. But then, she'd never imagined Mahmoud would sell her either.

That's when he launched into the account of Esma's death.

"I couldn't imagine going on," Mahmoud said. "And then, my wife…" He collapsed onto the table, sobbing and gasping. Samira barely made out his words. "…Gave up."

Samira couldn't really remember her brother before he'd married Esma. Mahmoud was nearly thirty years Samira's elder. A wild streak had kept him single long enough for it to be scandalous, but he'd been properly wed before Samira was potty trained.

Esma was a fixture in her life, especially after Samira's mother's death. For several years, Esma was the woman of the house. She'd been the example of womanhood for Samira — an example Samira wanted no part of. Esma was cold. Imperious. She ruled Mahmoud by manipulation. *Maybe that's why Carlos is bothering me.* Honestly, Samira had enjoyed the way Esma often demeaned Mahmoud. However, the woman was just as inclined to beg or wheedle. Samira couldn't stand that.

Esma's truly unforgivable sin, though, was the way she tried to manipulate Samira's father. She would make up the most outrageous lies…. Samira shook her head. She wasn't sorry Esma was dead.

She was surprised to hear how Mahmoud described his wife. In his retelling, she was some sort of saint. Generous and caring, even selfless in defense of her children. Mahmoud acknowledged that her efforts were sometimes misplaced. Nevertheless, he described a woman of unflawed heart. Samira had never met the woman he described.

Hearing the stories of all of the relatives she'd left to the war, was distracting. In many ways, Ismaeel, Jaber, Ahmad and Esma had ceased to exist for her years ago.

Once again, Samira focused in on Mahmoud's tale.

Mahmoud's sob story continued. He was describing himself walking through the decimated streets of Aleppo, hunting for Esma. It sounded like a scene from a movie to Samira — or at least a work of fiction. *You would never risk yourself like that, not for Esma.*

"And then the gunfire started," Mahmoud looked hollow. His eyes were open too wide and there was no longer any inflection in his voice. "I threw myself to the ground."

"What happened to bravely searching for Esma?" Samira snarked. It didn't matter that he couldn't hear her through the glass. She couldn't keep her sarcastic skepticism to herself.

"I lay there, arms clutching my head," he suited action to words, his arms awkwardly wrapping his skull. "The gunfire was everywhere. I knew I was going to die."

If only.

He dropped his chin to his chest, shaking his head. "Suddenly, it didn't matter anymore. Why should I live?"

"Good question!" Samira spat.

"I got to my feet, eyes closed. Slowly, I spread my arms wide," he mimicked the action seated at the table.

Is Carlos buying this? Samira looked at the Interpol agent. His face was completely expressionless.

"Go on," Carlos said.

"I felt the bullets. They were passing that close. But none of them hit me. It was a terrible miracle. Even when my wish was death, I could not have what I wanted."

"Oh, please," Samira huffed. "You have no idea what it's like to have choice taken away from you."

Mahmoud collapsed. His arms fell back to his sides, his posture slumped. Slowly, he shook his head from side to side. His voice nearly broke as he said, "I thought I couldn't possibly sink any lower."

And then he launched into a story so awful it silenced even Samira's commentary. He didn't spare them the details as he described the brothel. Samira could see the girls — the children — dancing in their caked on makeup and stripper attire. She wanted to scrub the images from her mind, but she couldn't. Unlike the rest of Mahmoud's story, she couldn't pretend this was made up. She couldn't remember brothels in the Syria she'd known. They didn't practice Mut'a. But she'd heard too many stories from the war, known too many women in the camp. She had no trouble believing this story was one hundred percent real.

As he described the mother peddling — peddling her daughter — Samira wanted to vomit. It was hard for her to believe even Mahmoud would stay in a place like that.

"I found even greater depths of depravity," Mahmoud shook, shame coloring his face.

He described seeing a beautiful woman across the room. That's where Samira's imagination failed her. She saw the brothel too clearly. All the lurid detail made it impossible for her to imagine anything beautiful appearing there.

"I was out of control," Mahmoud said. "A slave to my lust. It was like I was taken with a djinn."

Samira shook her head. Leave it to her brother to blame a fable for his bad behavior.

"I told myself it could not be her," he continued.

Her who? Samira thought. *Who did he meet in the brothel?*

"She would never…" Mahmoud's voice choked off again. He shook his head and then shook it a second time, as though the first shake hadn't done the job. "It had to be another woman."

He spoke as though he was trying to convince Carlos. *Who could he be talking about?* Samira felt a dawning terror.

"I told myself that… with a look-a-like," he swallowed, "it would be a harmless fantasy… not…"

He crumpled to the table. Samira experienced several minutes of absolute suspense. She had no idea who Mahmoud could be talking about. She was desperate for the answer. It was horrifying, but also intriguing.

From what Samira could see, Carlos appeared incurious. *He already knows.* And then it started to dawn on her. Carlos had already given her the answer.

She felt an irrational surge of relief. She should have felt pity for the girl, but in reality she was just delighted it wasn't someone she knew and loved.

"Tala!" Ahmad shouted, rushing into the room.

Mahmoud listened to his son, ranting. Watched the terrible realization bubbling to the surface. Nabil did his part. In Ahmad's eyes, Tala had betrayed him. *Ridiculous,* Mahmoud thought. *She's been the wife of both his brothers, and still he thinks she is his.*

It was an errant thought. A distraction from the moment.

Like a spurned lover, Ahmad continued to shout and pace. The moments streaked past. Time became stretched and sticky to Mahmoud.

"She could not provide a child to either of my brothers, but now she gets pregnant whoring?"

Mahmoud closed his eyes. *This anger is only directed at Tala because he has no one else on whom to pin it.*

"I would have married her, but Allah has protected me." Ahmad dropped to his knees before Mahmoud. Mahmoud didn't want to meet his son's eyes. He was afraid that his guilt was visible. "You protected me. You were right about her, Baba."

The words cut Mahmoud deeply. *When he knows the truth, he will hate me.*

"We should withhold judgment." *Please don't judge me, son. I have been a fool.* "She has been through a lot. Two husbands dead." *Two sons dead.* "Maybe…." *A wife dead.* "Maybe there is an explanation—"

Ahmad sprung to his feet again, interrupting. "What possible explanation could there be? She has dishonored our family."

It was a childish hope. The idea that somehow he could curb Ahmad's anger.

"She is a young girl. She won't survive on the streets. They will—"

"Good!" Ahmad shouted. Just like that, the boy was championing Tala's death. *But it's my death he really wants. If he only knew.* "She deserves worse! She has betrayed everything!" Then, Ahmad asked the terrible question: "Would you go to a brothel?"

The boy couldn't have done more damage if he'd fired a gun into Mahmoud's chest. Mahmoud's every flinch and twitch screamed his guilt. *He knows! How? How does he know?*

Ahmad didn't notice. "Of course not! You are a righteous man, a man of honor." Mahmoud was frozen. "You uphold the dignity of your dead wife and your dead sons. You represent our community and our values."

Mahmoud slumped. *Mercy! Allah is good. He doesn't know. If I can only keep him away from—*

The servant girl appeared. "Tala bint Basem is at the door."

Nabil slipped from the room.

Mahmoud wallowed in miserable silence. Justifications bubbled up in him. He blamed Nabil.

Ahmad cut into his thoughts. "I can't believe Nabil is even speaking to her." It was a disturbing echo of Mahmoud's thoughts. "Does he care nothing for your friendship?"

Mahmoud wanted to turn the boy's ire on Nabil. If not for Nabil, he never would have been in that brothel. He looked up at Ahmad, opening his mouth to decry the corruption of Nabil. Nabil was standing just past Ahmad in the doorway. His eyes locked onto Mahmoud's. For a heartbeat, Mahmoud worried that Nabil knew what he'd been about to do. Nabil twitched his fingers, drawing Mahmoud's eye to the Masoud family ring.

The ring was gone before Ahmad saw it. Mahmoud said a silent prayer of thanks for Nabil's quick fingers.

"I will send her away," Nabil said. It was everything. Nabil would send the girl to her death, so no one would ever know Mahmoud's shame. It was a conspiracy to commit murder. All Mahmoud could feel was profound relief. He looked at Ahmad. *He will never know.*

Nabil turned in the doorway. Mahmoud watched. *I am free.* Out of the corner of his eye, he could see Ahmad nodding in approval. *I am teaching my son to hate and murder. Tala, sweet beautiful Tala, will die for my sin.*

Mahmoud lurched to his feet. "No."

Nabil turned back, arching an uncertain eyebrow at Mahmoud. Ahmad's eyes bulged.

"She is my responsibility," Mahmoud said. *And her baby — my baby.* He felt a thousand years old. The weight of his bad decisions dragged at him, but he straightened himself up. "I will speak to her."

As he moved past Nabil, the fat man slipped the gold ring into his palm. Mahmoud felt it heavy in his grip as he passed through the entryway and out the front door.

Tala stood in the street. Her abaya was ripped. Goose flesh pricked at all of her exposed skin. Marring her face, streaks of makeup, tears and snot scoured a complexion puffy and blotchy from weeping. She no longer looked desirable to Mahmoud. Broken. Pathetic. Ruined. *She is what I've made her.*

She shifted uncomfortably, one foot to the other as he stared at her. *What am I to do? What can I do? She is the only one who knows the truth. Who will believe her? I must send her away.*

He sighed. *It's the only way. Destroying my reputation won't fix hers. The child will always carry my shame. Better for them to suffer and die now, then to suffer and live in agony.*

Tala read the justifications on his face. He saw her eyes change. Something seemed to snap inside her. Righting her shoulders, she lifted her chin defiantly. Mahmoud felt the weight of her gaze. There was no hope in her eyes, only accusation. *She knows I won't help her. She knows I'm condemning her to death.* For the third time that night, Mahmoud wondered if someone could read his thoughts.

"I..." What could he say? *She will not survive the night and my secret will die with her.* Shame burned his cheeks at the thought. *To hide my shame, will I do something even more shameful?* But he knew it would be easy. Much easier than facing this. "I have wronged you."

She was shocked. She opened her mouth, but he didn't let her speak.

"The child you carry is..." he couldn't bring himself to finish the sentence, but he didn't have to. She nodded, closing her eyes.

Mahmoud didn't need to see Ahmad behind him. He felt the blister of rage on the air. Still, Mahmoud turned and looked at his son. The boy's face was nearly purple.

"This child," Mahmoud said, "will be my heir." He turned back to Tala. "As I promised your father."

Opening his hand, Mahmoud looked at the ring. She had returned it. She had asked nothing of him.

"Come inside," he told her.

She raised her head, looking at Mahmoud with a strange awe, like she had never seen him before. Ahmad shoved past him. Mahmoud's son snatched the ring from his still open palm. He looked at Mahmoud and Tala, shaking his head.

"Ahmad, my son, listen," Mahmoud attempted. "We live in complicated times."

Ahmad held up the ring like it was a weapon.

"You are not the man I thought." The boy's eyes were venomous. "Grandfather was right about you." The words plowed through Mahmoud leaving nothing but dust. Those were the most painful words he could imagine Ahmad speaking. "You were never worthy of this."

Ahmad stormed down the street.

It is done. I have chosen shame and pain. Goodbye, Ahmad.

Tears streaked silently down Mahmoud's face. Shame was piling on shame. *Tala will see my tears. Nabil will see them.* He smiled at Tala, careful not to touch her as he gestured for her to enter the house.

thirty

Samira and Mahmoud: Over the Wall

"I have hurt so many people," Mahmoud said. "I want to be a different person."

Well you can't, Samira thought, *there's no forgiveness for what you've done.* The echo of her own words so long ago brought Kelsey's response darting through her mind: "I'm not worthy either." She shook the thought away.

This is about Mahmoud. He'd impregnated his own daughter-in-law? Hired her as a prostitute? It was unbelievable. And… he was still talking. Still rambling out his skittering confessions as if Interpol was some holy priesthood of forgiveness. She shook her head. *What kind of Muslim reveals all of their shames to a stranger?* The memory of her conversation with Kelsey came again. She felt her cheeks heat. *That was different,* she told herself.

"The first leg of our journey was a bus," Mahmoud explained. "I settled the girls on the bus."

The girls? Samira realized she'd missed something. Was Tala's baby a girl?

"Tala needed help with the baby. I worried how Yasmeen would feel, alone on the bus with a strange woman and her baby. But there was no room. I couldn't stay with them."

Yasmeen? Samira was at the glass in an instant, pressing against it, almost trying to pass through it. *What has he done with Yasmeen?*

"Where did you go then?" Ever the interrogator, Carlos asked the question without curiosity. There was no inflection, merely a prompt to keep Mahmoud talking.

"All of the men were in the luggage compartment."

That got a reaction out of Carlos. "You mean…"

"Under the bus, yes. We were stacked on top of one another like firewood. I was fortunate I did not get in first," Mahmoud offered a half-hearted smile. "The oddest detail, I remember the man who closed the compartment was familiar, but I can't remember where I had seen him before."

"Ask him about Yasmeen," Samira demanded, willing Carlos to get the information for which she was desperate.

"The bus traveled from Latakia north to Turkey. The journey should only have taken a few hours, but we were on that bus all night. We would drive a few miles and then the bus would stop. I could hear the men shouting outside. Their boots were heavy when they would climb up into the bus." Mahmoud shook his head, his complexion paling at the memory. "I've never been so terrified."

"Why?" Carlos asked. "What were you afraid of?"

Mahmoud looked surprised at the question. "In Syria there are not two sides. There are many factions. The government, ISIS, the Kurds, the Iranians, Shias, Alawites and Sunnis, every group of rebels is splintered into a thousand subgroups. Do you know the uniform of Assad's military?"

Carlos shook his head.

"They wear black and mask their faces."

"Like ISIS," Carlos responded.

"Yes. And the rebels. Everyone. They all look the same. So imagine in the dead of night, a man dressed like that climbs onto the bus and points a machine gun in the face of a young girl and demands to know whose side she is on."

Samira felt dread building in her. It wasn't hard for her to imagine. She remembered being at a checkpoint, a machine gun pointed at her. *Yasmeen was on that bus.*

"And what happens if the girl answers wrong?" Carlos asked.

Mahmoud shrugged. "Maybe he takes the girl from the bus and she is never seen again."

Yasmeen! Please, no!

"Or," Mahmoud continued, "maybe he shoots everyone on the bus."

"Everyone's life depends on that one answer," Carlos nodded.

"The answer of a stranger. My daughter-in-law, my sister, my new-born son — their lives in the hands of a stranger, and I am trapped under a weight of other strangers, powerless to protect them."

Carlos opened his eyes a little too wide and blew out a slow breath. He nodded.

"What happened to Yasmeen?" Samira demanded. She slammed her fist into the glass. Both Carlos and Mahmoud turned to look at her. They couldn't see her. The sound drew their gaze none-the-less. Mahmoud looked frightened, of course, but Carlos looked angry. She took an involuntary step back from the glass. The Interpol agent's glare was fierce.

He turned back to Mahmoud. "Probably the cleaning lady getting a little too enthusiastic," Carlos said, smiling.

Mahmoud just stared at Samira. *Can he see me?* She felt a moment of confusion, but then Mahmoud blinked and the illusion was broken. He was staring into a mirror, seeing his own terrified face.

"So what happened?"

"Nothing," Mahmoud said. "We made the journey to Iskenderun."

"No one shot? No one taken from the bus?"

"No one from my family."

Carlos cocked his head. Samira could see he didn't understand, but she did. Mahmoud wasn't concerned with the strangers on the bus. He cared about his people. Caring about strangers was a luxury you couldn't always afford in war.

"You met smugglers in Iskenderun?"

Mahmoud shook his head. "We made our own way across Turkey to Izmir."

"You walked a thousand kilometers?"

"No," Mahmoud said as if that was ridiculous. "We walked, we took taxis and busses. Whatever we could find."

"In Izmir you met the smugglers."

Mahmoud nodded. "They were everywhere. We were everywhere. Lines of refugees wandering the countryside, but we were as numerous as the sand in Izmir. The smugglers wanted a huge price."

Samira could remember. They would set a price, and then when they'd taken you off into the wilderness somewhere they would suddenly decide it was extra dangerous and demand more.

The shared experience was another connection between her and Mahmoud. It made her angry.

"Did you buy the life vests?" Carlos asked.

"Not for myself. I worried for the girls."

Samira fumed. *Oh, you're* so *concerned and caring now.* She wanted to slap him.

Carlos looked at his watch and then down at his notes again.

"We made the boat journey twice," Mahmoud said. "Once, we were turned around in the dark and wound up back in Turkey."

Samira knew similar stories. She'd even heard a girl describe being robbed by pirates in the middle of the Mediterranean. Their boat was set adrift. Rescued by the Turkish coast guard, they were forced to start over again, or give up.

"When we arrived at the camp, there was no room for us. They sent us on."

Samira blinked. That was new. Well, there had never really been room for anyone, but sending people on was new. While she'd been there, they just crammed everyone into more and more tents out in the olive grove.

"Where did they send you?"

"I was told to come here, to Berlin," Mahmoud explained, "but we had to get here on our own. We crossed Greece into Serbia."

And then he launched into a description of the journey. Samira sighed.

Mahmoud wiped sweat from his forehead. It wasn't warm. He inched gradually to his right, body always touching the cement wall behind him. The baby boy, his baby boy, was swaddled tightly to his chest. On his left, Tala led the way along the wall, following a line of other refugees. To his right, Yasmeen sidled along after them, a similar line of strangers snaking behind her.

"I don't understand why they will imprison us for walking," Yasmeen whined. At fourteen, she was as insufferable as Samira had been. Certain that she was right about everything but utterly naive.

Mahmoud felt angry. He wanted to snap at her. *Complaining isn't helping anyone. We need to concentrate. This is very dangerous.*

"It only matters that they will," Tala answered her. "The wall hides us."

There was almost no warning. A rumble, like thunder from the ground. Mahmoud threw his arms wide, slamming both girls into the concrete wall, and flattening himself against it as tightly as he could. He didn't even allow himself to breath.

A train rocketed through, passing so close to them its wake tugged at their clothes. In an instant, it was gone again, disappearing into the distance. Mahmoud collapsed forward off of the wall, gasping for breath. He clutched the baby. Closing his eyes, he rocked his body forward and backward.

To their left, a woman screamed. It quickly turned into a familiar keening wail.

This journey is loss, he thought. *We were promised hope, but there is only death.*

He looked to his left and right. Both girls wore grim expressions. Tears tracked down Yasmeen's face. Tala looked hollow. *They are unharmed.*

"We have to keep moving," he said. They nodded and continued inching along the wall. It was an effort not to look down when their feet touched anything soft.

Lowering Tala to the ground, Mahmoud looked past her. The sky was nearly dark, the faint midnight blue outlining Yasmeen, perched on the wall above. Mahmoud's jacket was tangled in the razor wire so it would not cut her. Yasmeen held his son, softly cooing to the child. To her nephew.

He let go of Tala and reached up to Yasmeen. She handed him the baby.

Looking over her shoulder, Yasmeen grimaced. She spoke in a near whisper. "It seems safe here."

Mahmoud smiled down at his son. The child was beautiful. An unexpected blossom in the desert of his life. He would be different this time. Better. Mahmoud didn't know how. He wasn't a new person. He didn't have a new example of fatherhood to follow.

Messing up again isn't an option. This child will have the chance that Ismaeel and Jaber didn't. A father who doted. One who loved instead of one for whom nothing was good enough. *I will do it… somehow.*

He handed the boy to Tala. Reaching up for Yasmeen, he remembered her comment.

"Maybe," he said. *Maybe I'm being a fool.* "I can't help feeling that if we stop here, we won't ever leave."

Yasmeen dropped into his arms. He lowered her to the ground. She looked regretfully back at the wall. He knew what she was thinking. They'd had beds and shelter in this camp. He followed her gaze, but his regret was mostly the coat still caught in the barbed wire. The night was getting cooler.

"Or we'll be sent back," he finished.

He jumped for the jacket, but it was too far out of his reach. He couldn't possibly get ahold of it.

"Leave it," Tala said. "Someone will come looking soon and we need to be far away from here."

She was right. They weren't allowed to leave the camp — *no,* he corrected himself looking at the razor wire, *we aren't allowed to leave the prison.*

"Come," he said, and led them into the night.

"He's lying," Samira announced as Carlos came back into the surveillance room.

"He's just confessed to multiple crimes, including human trafficking and violating the terms of his asylum application. He doesn't seem like a guy who is holding a lot back to me."

She grimaced, shaking her head. *He is lying.* "Sounds like he has you fooled."

Carlos shrugged.

He flipped open his folder looking over his notes, perching one butt cheek on the countertop. Samira had seen this exact pose when he was interrogating Mahmoud. She turned to gaze through the window. Mahmoud was collapsed on the table, his head buried in his arms. He looked pathetic.

"I see you've been using a false name," Carlos said. "Mohammed. That's your husband's middle name, right?"

"His father's name," Samira corrected.

"Unusual for a woman in hiding from her husband."

Samira felt her cheeks color. Unlike Mahmoud, she was not comfortable sharing her shame with the Interpol agent. She glared at Mahmoud. *This is his fault. I wouldn't be here if he hadn't crashed back into my life. His plans for Tala and Yasmeen are just like his plan for me.*

"You see it, right?" She turned to Carlos. "He's just smuggling those girls here to make them prostitutes! He already admitted to it with his daughter-in-law!"

Carlos met her gaze without blinking. "You were Samira Masoud before you were married?"

Samira shook her head. "Bring in the girl. The younger one. Let me talk to her. She'll tell us. I'm sure of it."

Carlos set down the folder, crossing his arms over his chest.

"You've told us your husband is a dangerous radical. We think he's here to plan an attack," he paused watching her.

Is he waiting for a confession, she wondered. Her lips pursed in disapproval.

"An attack on Berlin," Carlos continued. "When you saw him, you didn't warn anyone."

Samira took a step back, her sarcasm evaporating. "Are you accusing me of something?"

Carlos raised his eyebrows. He waited. She didn't speak.

"You're well connected in the tech industry here," he said without inflection. "You have access to small electronic components and the power to place incoming refugees into positions where they can get their hands on bomb making tools—"

"Do I need a lawyer?" Samira interrupted.

Carlos sighed. "For now, I'm asking my questions on this side of the glass."

"I think I'm going home now."

She moved to the door. Carlos didn't move to stop her. He just watched curiously. As she grabbed the handle he mused.

"Hmm. I thought you were in danger. That *Ata* knows where you live." He emphasized her husband's nickname. Like he was calling her out.

Samira froze. In her rage at Mahmoud and then at Carlos she'd almost forgotten how this had all begun. She felt her heart pounding suddenly. She could imagine Ata lying in wait for her outside her apartment.

"I've been very patient with you. I've let you sit in and listen to me interrogate your brother."

She turned around, leaning her back against the door.

"My name is Samira Masoud."

"See, not so hard." Carlos smiled. "Why keep it a secret?"

"You would not understand."

"Try me."

"Because a Masoud," she paused, looking at him. His face showed nothing.

"You were saying?" He prompted.

"A Masoud would never break her marriage vows and I have fled half-way across the world to avoid my husband."

She didn't know if he believed her or even if he understood.

Carlos raised his eyebrows. "A man whose name you took when you were hiding your identity."

She threw up her arms. "Mohammed is the name of the Prophet!"

"You still call him 'Ata.'"

"I told you. You don't understand."

He shook his head. It was clear he thought she was lying. "Why can't we do this the easy way?"

"I'm trying. Let me talk to the girl. Please." She could hear she was begging and she didn't care. She had to see Yasmeen.

He shrugged. "I already asked my people to bring her in. I'll let you see her when she gets here," Samira felt a thrill run though her. Her back came off the door and she started to smile. Carlos raised a hand. "But." He looked her in the eyes intensely. "But then you're answering my questions. On this side of the glass or on the other."

thirty-one
Samira: Sister

"Trafficking, prostitution," Samira watched Carlos walk around Mahmoud. He sounded regretful, like he wanted to help. "You've confessed to so many violations of international law."

Mahmoud was shrinking in on himself. Samira knew him. She recognized the regret on his face. He'd admitted wrongdoing in a moment of passion and now he wished he could take it back.

"We have it all recorded," Carlos continued. "You're in a lot of trouble."

Mahmoud closed his eyes. He did that stupid thing he always did when he was really upset, grabbing the sides of his face and pulling downward. Samira shook her head. He looked like an idiot.

Carlos shrugged. "Someone has to pay for these crimes." He moved away from Mahmoud toward the bank of windows that ran along the wall with the door. The interrogation was a piece of theater. But suddenly the blocking didn't make sense to her. Every move was designed to push one of Mahmoud's buttons.

"You seem like a decent guy to me," Carlos continued. "You've gotten on a bad path, but you're trying to do the right thing."

Mahmoud looked up at Carlos, a sudden hopeful light in his eyes.

Carlos started turning the post that opened the window blinds. *Why is he opening the window shades? What button does that push on Mahmoud?* "You didn't commit your crimes alone. You have accomplices. People who can take the punishment for you."

It all looked causal, coincidental. Samira felt the blood drain from her face. On the other side of the window, an agent was escorting Yasmeen down the hall.

Samira felt her breath sucked away. Yasmeen was being held by Interpol. She shook her head. *Is this what he meant when he said he'd let me 'see her?'* It was all theater. She knew it. They weren't really arresting Yasmeen. They couldn't possibly mean to let her pay for Mahmoud's crimes. *Can they?*

Yasmeen turned to the window, seeing Mahmoud through the glass. She rushed to the window, touching the glass gently, her face etched with concern for her brother. Samira couldn't believe how much she'd grown. The little girl she'd known was nearly a woman. Tears tried to cloud her vision and she dashed them away with a hand. Mahmoud wasn't deserving of Yasmeen's compassion.

For his part, Mahmoud lurched from his chair toward Yasmeen.

"Do not," Carlos shouted with all of his authority, "get out of that chair."

Mahmoud sat down again, but now he was on the edge of his seat, quivering with a frenzied energy. Samira understood completely. She wanted nothing more than to rush into the hallway and pull Yasmeen into her arms.

"Please," Mahmoud begged. "You've heard me tell you about sitting with my father, having to tell him of one daughter lost." Tears poured down Mahmoud's cheeks. "Please. I promised him I would be responsible for her. I would see that she was safe."

Samira felt rage building in her. Who did Mahmoud think he was? *You're not the hero.* Yasmeen's clear concern for Mahmoud only made her angrier. His deception ran so deep. Samira couldn't see what Yasmeen was saying, but it was clear she was asking the agent to explain. She didn't understand why Mahmoud was in the interrogation room.

"I have confessed to many crimes," Mahmoud begged. "Just as you say. I deserve to be punished." He swallowed hard, took a deep breath, struggling to compose himself, and slowly met Carlos's eyes. "I will confess to anything you name without question," he continued. "Only, please, let my sister be free."

Carlos looked at him. It was the first time Samira had ever seen uncertainty on the agent's face. She wasn't sure what reaction Carlos had expected, but it wasn't this.

In the hallway, Samira could see Yasmeen, now livid. She was yelling at the other agent, pointing at Mahmoud. *She's demanding they release him.* Samira's nostrils flared. She couldn't believe her precious sister was so deep in Mahmoud's web that she would fight like this to protect him. It filled her with rage.

"Please," Mahmoud said again.

Carlos waved to the agent on the other side of the glass. The other agent took Yasmeen's arm firmly, leading her away even as she protested. Samira watched.

Thoughts and emotions swirled in her chest. Carlos had promised she would see Yasmeen. She thought they would be allowed to speak. He'd deceived her. Like Mahmoud was deceiving everyone. *Are there no honest men in this world?* It didn't matter anymore. She didn't care what Carlos did to her. Mahmoud needed to pay for his crimes. Yasmeen. *Sweet, innocent Yasmeen believes he cares for her.*

She stormed out the door of the monitoring room and into the hallway. She flung the door to the interrogation room open. She would be cold, imperious and clear. In no uncertain terms, Samira would tell her brother that he was a destructive parasite. He had wrecked his family and ruined Tala. She would tell him to leave Yasmeen alone. That was her plan as she burst into the room. The words that screeched from her mouth were less articulate.

"How dare you! Liar!" Carlos met her a few steps into the room. He hooked her waist with an arm, lifting her into the air. She hadn't realized she was lunging bodily for Mahmoud until Carlos stopped her.

She fought wildly. Battering the Interpol agent with elbows and knees, she was heedless in her desperation to reach Mahmoud and claw his eyes out.

Mahmoud jerked back trying to escape her. He tumbled over in his chair. Man and chair clattered to the floor hard.

"You can't be in here," Carlos hissed through gritted teeth.

"Who is this crazy woman," Mahmoud exclaimed, scooting backwards on the floor like a crab.

"Did you make her care about you with all your lies?" Samira demanded. Even to her the words didn't make a lot of sense, but she was so angry, she didn't care. "Does she know what you did?"

She'd lost the element of surprise. Carlos was both stronger than her, and trained. He started to pull her out the door, controlling her flailing arms.

With an effort born of desperate hatred, she managed to plant a foot on the door frame and stop him from dragging her out of the room.

"Stop!" Carlos demanded. "Stop it. He doesn't know who you are."

She turned to Carlos, desperate to spit some invective at him but unable to find any words sharp enough. Something in his eyes was too much. She turned away, seeing herself in the one-way mirror. Hair in wild disarray, she was red-faced, a finger pointed like a dagger at Mahmoud's chest. *What am I doing?* She shook her head, letting her rigid body relax. Carlos eased his grip on her.

"How," she panted, the words a flabbergasted whisper, "can you not recognize me?"

She felt disoriented. Adrenaline and shame beating against one another in time with her heart. The wild animal who'd crashed into the room bore no resemblance to her self-image. She was logical. Smart. Sensible. The ragged creature she saw in the mirror was something else. A trail of memory carried her through the events of the day, highlighting all of the moments she'd been anything but logical and sensible. From not calling the police after seeing Ata to calling the police in a room full of refugees because she saw Mahmoud it was too long and disturbing a list to take in. She tried to block it all out of her mind, but some part of her was insistent that she look at it. Look at herself honestly.

Mahmoud was getting to his feet, but his back was firmly pressed to the concrete wall. "You are the woman from the center. How could I forget?"

Samira pulled the scrap of scarf from her pocket, rubbing her thumb over it. She shook her head. *It's impossible.* Slowly, she raised her hand and held it open for Mahmoud to inspect.

"It won't be easy," Kelsey had told me. "He'll ask you to forgive people who have hurt and wronged you." But he deserves to be punished!

Mahmoud looked at the tiny piece of fabric, not daring to move a step closer. His brow crinkled in confusion. She could see him struggling to identify why it was familiar.

"I'm your sister," she said. "Susu."

Mahmoud's eyes shot open wide. He blinked, his jaw hanging slack. He shook his head, denial and disbelief working their way to recognition on his face. Then he moved. With swiftness she wouldn't have imagined he possessed he rushed around the table to reach her. Carlos was faster putting his body between them. Mahmoud fell to his knees, looking around Carlos to her.

"Samira," he said. His lip quivered and tears filled his eyes. "You are alive. Merciful Allah! Father will be so pleased."

He deserves to be punished! Please, Jesus.

Mahmoud turned his gaze to Carlos, nodding. "I can go to prison a happy man," he even smiled, "knowing that my father will have both of his daughters again."

Carlos looked perplexed.

Is Baba all that matters? He doesn't even care about what he did to me!

"I am so sorry," Mahmoud said, looking into Samira's eyes. "I can never make right what I did. I am so very sorry." His eyes fell to the floor. "I understand now everything you have done." He nodded to himself and then looked up at her again. "And it is right."

How did Kelsey put it? "But Jesus died for me anyway."

She turned away, unable to keep looking at him. She felt her fist, squeezing painfully on the scrap of scarf. *How dare he!* Sparks of pity tugged at her. The compassion filled her with self-loathing. *He's manipulating me now, just as he has Yasmeen.*

She looked out the window, wishing her sister would be there again. There was no Yasmeen waiting in the hall. In her place, a man stood, watching. The stranger. Jesus. He looked through her eyes, into her very soul. She gasped, seeing herself fully reflected in those eyes. Desperate love collided painfully with her pride and selfishness. Quickly, she turned away from him, facing once again into the room. Looking at Mahmoud.

"I know you will care for Yasmeen," Mahmoud nodded to her. He was openly weeping now. *My brother is weeping where people can see.* "And it is not right that I should ask anything of you, but I cannot help it. Please," the earnestness in his voice was like a dagger stabbing into her chest over and over again. "Please look after Tala and my son. Like you, they are victims of my failure."

She felt her teeth grinding as she raised her clenched fist. Tears blurred her vision, but they did not deter her. She met Mahmoud's eyes with the coldest most imperious glare in her arsenal. She felt more than saw Carlos react, his body tensing as he prepared to stop her from hitting Mahmoud.

No! Samira wrestled against Mahmoud's genuine contrition. He was literally verbalizing the things she meant to say. Her words intended to cut him apart were his words of confession. Even if she'd entered this room and said exactly what she hoped, she would simply have been telling him what he already knew about himself. *No! He doesn't….*

Slowly, more slowly than anything she had ever done in her life, because it was a fight, she inched her eyes closed. She couldn't see

Jesus. She could feel his eyes on her, his presence close to her. She could sense his strength offered to her. It took an eternity. Like prying open a steel door, she forced her hand open. She felt the scrap of scarf leave her hand, knew it would flutter away.

I'm letting go of my life, my past, she thought. *Give him everything, Kelsey told me.*

"I…" The words choked her. She coughed. Shaking her head, she took a deep breath and let it go, forcing some of the tension from her body. Opening her eyes, she looked at Carlos. She nodded to him and he seemed to understand. He looked confused, but he stepped to the side. She looked at Mahmoud, reaching out to him. Reluctantly, uncertainly, he took her hand. She pulled him to his feet. It was an effort not to grimace at the way he towered over her, even in heels. He was always disgustingly tall.

"I forgive you," she said. The words came out and she struggled to mean them. *I forgive you.* She nodded to herself, willing herself forward. "What you meant for evil, God has used for good. To help our family."

Mahmoud was dumbfounded. She turned to Carlos. Out of the corner of her eye she saw Jesus still standing in the window. His eyes twinkled like they had on the bus. She felt a rush of joy again, a shadow of that first time with Kelsey when she'd given him her life.

Carlos was staring at her. She bit her lip feeling awkwardly like the Interpol agent was catching her in an intimate moment. She squared her shoulders and met his eyes.

"My brother cannot help you capture Ata. If I will answer all of your questions, will you allow him and my sister to go free?"

This was important. Yasmeen must be free, and she did not feel right allowing Mahmoud to go to prison. Not when it was she who had called for his arrest. Not when he had brought her sister to her finally.

Carlos narrowed his eyes and shook his head. "It's going to take a bit more than that."

thirty-two
Samira: Facing Ada

Samira walked to the front door of her apartment. Her movements were swift. Small tremors in her hand jingled her keys as she sought the right one. She was distracted, rubbernecking. It was hard to focus. She was completely exhausted.

"It's strange for me, too," she said into the phone pressed to her ear with a shoulder.

Finally, the key slipped into the lock and turned. By rote, she slipped into the shadowy apartment. She kicked the door shut behind her with a click. There was a sense of finality. She could open the door from inside the apartment, but the magic of German doors was such that no one could open it from outside. It was a tricky business when you walked out the door without your key, but a comfort at a moment like this.

The apartment was a crosshatching of moonlight and shadows. She searched it with her eyes. Nothing was out of place. She lived minimally, preferring empty spaces to clutter. *There is nowhere to hide,* she thought. Relief rinsed the tension from her bones.

"I'm not sure how I feel about any of it, but…"

She tossed her handbag onto the low sofa. Looking at the keys still resting on her palm and realized she'd forgotten to put her keys in the bag. She felt so tired, the idea of reclaiming the bag was too much. With a shake of her head, she flung the keys after the bag. The untidiness was out of character. A little warning flag went up somewhere in her mind.

One night on Suzi's couch. Nearly twenty-four hours of interrogation. She was too exhausted to care. Her fastidious nature buried in a bone weariness she was having trouble shaking off. Some part of her rankled at the compromise. She hated disorder. *When you fail to do things methodically, you skip important steps.*

It was a fleeting thought. An interruption to what really mattered. The tension was creeping back. *It's okay. I looked. He isn't here.* They sounded like lies.

"You should get some sleep, Yasmeen," she said softly into the phone. "I love you."

She smiled sadly and hung up the phone. As soon as the candy-bar shaped device had left her ear, it happened.

Arms grabbed her from behind, knocking the phone from her hand. She flailed. Struggling to reach the door — she didn't have much left. Too long without sleep, too many emotionally draining events. *I even tried to out-muscle an Interpol agent.* She was no match for Ata.

She knew it was him. Berlin was a big city. Women got attacked by strangers. Men broke into apartments. But she knew. His scent told her. The sound of his breathing. The feel of him pressing against her back. It was all as familiar as her own face.

He flung her onto the couch easily. She crashed down. Her elbow jabbed painfully into her keys. She didn't have time to process her change in attitude. He was on top of her, holding her down with the weight of his body. Ata wasn't a large man. He wasn't tall like Mahmoud. But he was heavy with wiry muscle. With him on top of her, she could barely breathe.

He was grinding his hips against hers, pawing at her breasts. A lascivious smile twisted his lips. *He's going to rape me,* she realized.

"I was too gentle with you before," he cooed.

She squirmed desperately, adrenaline flooding her system. Fatigue was washed away in a torrent of panic. A wild elbow caught him in the jaw, knocking him onto the floor.

Scrambling desperately off the couch, she stumbled, stepping on his stomach. Air rushed out of his lungs. Her ankle turned. She fell to her knees on top of him. He grunted in pain. She fought awkwardly to her feet; launched herself toward the door.

All of the kicks and stomps didn't slow him. He was right behind her. She felt his fist close on the neck of her blazer. Time slowed down in her mind. She could see it playing out: His arm pulling, her being yanked back off of her feet, slamming to the ground. Her head would bounce hard on the floor and she would be disoriented, incoherent as he rent her clothes—

She flung both arms backward, like she was taking flight. He pulled hard on the blazer. It barely slowed her, sliding down her arms and off her body. A sound of flesh on wood and an exclamation of pain registered behind her for half a heartbeat. Then, arms still behind her, unable to protect her, she slammed face-first into the door. She lost a moment. Disoriented, she shook her head, trying to settle things. Her fingers found the latch on the door more by instinct than by any mental prowess she was capable of mustering in that moment. She fiddled wildly. She had no dexterity. Adrenaline and exhaustion created a wild and speedy ineptitude.

"You know now," Ata panted, "it is like I told you."

She glanced over her shoulder. Ata was on his feet, her blazer laying across the room. He was stepping over her coffee table, which looked out of position. His moves were slow. Unhurried. His eyes locked on hers.

"You are less than nothing to these Europeans. These Christians."

It was a small apartment. There was no way she could get out the door before he reached her. She continued scrambling at the latch, blindly. She couldn't tear her eyes away from him. He prowled forward like a tiger. His head was tilted down and he gazed at her through his lowered eyebrows. He looked evil. Demonic. She could imagine nothing more terrifying than his eyes.

Three feet away, he reached out an arm. *I cannot let him touch me.* Like a frightened child, she pulled on the door, dropping and huddling as she slid down the wall behind it. She pinched herself between the wall and the door, trying to use the now open door as a shield. Blocking her own escape. It was irrational. Idiotic. She felt her confidence implode. *I thought I was capable. Competent.*

"Going to church doesn't make you one of them," Ata continued. He was in no hurry now.

I'm a foolish child, hiding behind a door.

She shivered, pulling on the door handle. Anticipating him jerking it away from her. She could feel her sweat on the metal handle. It was becoming slick.

He leaned his head around the door so she could see his cruel smile.

"No one will protect you, little Susu. As the Surah says, 'good women are obedient,'" he quoted. "'As for those from whom ye fear rebellion…'" His cruel smile grew wider. "'Scourge them.'"

He curled his fingers slowly around the edge of the door. No quarter would be shown to an enemy, she knew. He would take his time. Build the drama. Let her fear rip at her before he took what he wanted. Their eyes were locked together. Wild shuddering terror met with vicious promises. There was a metallic click. Ata froze. Her terror suddenly reflected in his eyes. She watched his posture stiffen.

Relief flooded through her. Ata was turning, looking behind him. She didn't need to see to know what was there. He would be staring down the barrel of a gun. He would follow the barrel to the handle, to a hand, an arm, a face, a badge.

She could hear them now, the Polizei shuffling into the room. The clatter of guns and body armor. It was barely audible over the ragged sound of her own breathing. *Why is it so hard to breathe?*

"Abu Anas Al-laziky," Carlos said, "I've been looking for you."

She closed her eyes, nodding to herself. It was okay. She'd done it. Mahmoud and Yasmeen would be free. Carlos had his man.

Opening her eyes again, she slipped around the door. She got to her feet. Nothing prepared her for the army in blue, or the arsenal of semi-automatic rifles. *They are here to protect me.* It was a strange comfort.

She watched as Ata was shoved roughly against the wall, his hands cuffed together behind him. They began to pat him down, hunting for weapons.

Carlos gave her a smile. Relief corroded the last of her adrenaline. Suddenly, it was all she could do to stay on her feet.

Finished searching Ata, one of the Polizei grabbed his arm and pulled him away from the wall. He spun, facing Samira.

"You don't know your place," he spat.

Her face reddened. Rage gave her new animation. She stepped up to him, her face nearly touching his.

"Actually," she said, savoring his powerlessness, "I'm exactly where I'm supposed to be."

She turned on her heel and walked dramatically away. It felt so good to have turned the tables on him. There was a rabid joy to it. *I beat Ata. He holds no power over me now. I get to see him brought low.* A grim satisfaction quirked her lips into a smile. The feeling was familiar, reminiscent of how she'd felt watching Mahmoud struggle in the interrogation room.

"I do," her words from nearly a year ago came floating back to her. "I forgive them all."

She stopped. She felt cold. Closing her eyes again, she expelled a slow breath. *Please, no!* She prayed. *Not him.* She opened her eyes, looking at the ceiling. But she found no relief there.

"Wait!" She shouted turning back around. Ata was out the door now, but they hadn't yet put him in a car.

Everyone looked at her. Ata's face was twisted with contempt. The unflappable Carlos looked fearful, uncertain, after her performance at the interrogation, what she might do. The German policemen were idly curious.

She felt the weight of every eye on her like she was an ant under a magnifying glass. Heat burned her neck and her cheeks. Sweat broke out on her brow. It was cold in the Berlin night. She quivered with tension. Then she saw the policeman holding Ata's arm by the car. He met her eyes and she knew him. His eyes sparkling with delight at what he knew she was about to do.

"Ata," she swallowed hard. *I don't want to say these words, Lord, but I know I need to.* "I forgive you."

Ata looked incensed. He sputtered, but didn't manage to say any actual words. The Polizei dragged him out and shoved him into a car.

She felt relief again. Different. This relief wasn't debilitating. It gave her life. She felt free.

Carlos moved to stand beside Samira. They watched together as the car door was closed, the policemen piled in, and the car drove off down the road, flanked by several other police vehicles.

Carlos turned to her.

"Are you sure you're alright?"

She wasn't. Completely drained, she could barely stay upright. She didn't think she'd even manage to get out of her clothes. Her emotions were such a tangle. *Like bubblegum in my hair,* she thought, a memory of a mean prank Jaber had played years ago suddenly vivid in her memory.

"Mahmoud is out there?"

Carlos nodded to a car parked down the road. *I have family again,* she thought.

"I told him we'd leave an officer, but he refuses to leave."

Samira smiled and couldn't stop. Growing wider and wider, the smile blazed out of control.

"Then it sounds like I'm well protected," she said.

Carlos looked at her like she was insane. She just kept smiling.

He shook his head, chuckling to himself. He escorted her back into the house and then left, pulling the door shut behind him.

Samira bolted the door and headed for her bed. She felt lighter than air. *I have a family again.* There was no chance of sleeping now. But she would lay in her bed and pretend.

Epilogue

Spring 2016

Mahmoud felt the cold air on his face. He was still adjusting to the sensation. It wasn't that air in Syria was never cold, only that it was never *this* cold. Berlin had many attractions, but he considered the cold to be its most intriguing. He enjoyed the feel of warm clothes enfolding him.

He stood on the tarmac near a private hanger at the Berlin airport. Tala stood close by, using him as a wind break for her and the baby.

A little more distant, Susu — Samira! He still couldn't believe she was here — stood with Yasmeen and the very attractive, but cold German woman who often accompanied Samira. He watched them.

Yasmeen shivered and huddled in her coat, pressing into Samira for body heat. Samira danced from foot to foot, keeping warm. Mahmoud saw she also struggled with an uncontainable energy. *Nerves.* He understood. What she'd done…. It was inconceivable. Unforgivable. *But who am I to judge?*

The German woman — he thought her name was Soozee — just stood, wind whipping her shock of blond hair. She glared as though she could grimace the cold away.

Mahmoud smiled.

They heard the plane first. All of their eyes tracked it as it touched down distantly and taxied across the long network of… Mahmoud didn't know the term. *Are they roads when it is an airplane? Is everything a runway?*

He found that he too was dancing foot to foot. It was not the cold. He, too, was filled with an uncontrollable jittery tension. He willed the plane closer. Faster. The impending arrival was all he could think about. Yacoob would come off the plane and… *what?*

Now, finally, Baba will be pleased. Their family was reunited. Both of Yacoob's beloved daughters were here.

The thought drew his eyes to Samira even as the plane rolled to a stop in front of them. She was biting her lip, fussing at her uncovered hair as it blew in the wind.

"Do you think," she started to ask Yasmeen. But then her words trailed off. She was unable to finish the thought.

"I don't know," Yasmeen, still modestly clothes in an abaya and hijab, replied. "It's a lot."

She wasn't wrong. Mahmoud wasn't sure what to think of Samira's following Jesus. Thrilled as he was to have his sister back, he considered what she'd done a deep betrayal of the family. At the same time, it was her new beliefs that led her to forgive him. She claimed Jesus had appeared to her, in visions and even in person. Mahmoud shook his head. *What am I to make of it?* A weak, ugly part of him hoped that their father would be livid. It was in character. Yacoob would see this as a betrayal of all he believed, all their family stood for. But Mahmoud's heart wasn't in that. Not anymore. His deepest desire now was for complete reconciliation.

Samira nodded sadly to Yasmeen. Mahmoud could see Samira struggling to accept the worst. His heart went out to her. For so long, she had been his adversary. Wishing ill on her was easy and natural and… He didn't want to do it anymore. He wanted to see her smile. joyful.

"Everything will be different now," he told her, smiling. He wanted to reassure her, but the look she gave him was at first surprised, then suspicious and finally resigned.

The door of Dominic Erbach's private jet folded down into a set of stairs. For Mahmoud, the process felt eternal. He watched the slow operation of the mechanism desperate for it to complete. He was swollen with a painful desire to see his father's face.

When the steps locked into place, a figure appeared at the top of the stairs. Mahmoud looked up eagerly. But it was wrong. Too tall, too broad. Stepping from the shadowy interior onto the lit stairs, Mahmoud saw his brother Omar and then Ali descending from the plane.

He gave Samira a shocked look and she smirked at him with a twinkle in her eyes. *I guess she did remember,* he thought.

He looked back up at the stairs and then flinched back. It was Ahmad, his son.

When Mahmoud visited the family home in Latakia, before he left for Europe, he had spent hours arguing with Yacoob. Convincing him to let Yasmeen join Mahmoud's trek was nearly impossible. Mahmoud hoped that Ahmad would come as well. Perhaps, the journey would allow healing between them. Ahmad refused even to see him. Now the boy — no, the man — was here. At the head of the stairs, gazing down at Samira, Yasmeen and Mahmoud.

Mahmoud was conflicted. *What am I to say?* He'd rehearsed too many apologies. He had no words. Ahmad's anger was justified. Sleeping with Tala, getting her pregnant was a deep shame on the family honor, one not easily rectified. Doing it after forbidding Ahmad to have a relationship with her only served to make the offense more personal.

Nothing in Ahmad's face or his eyes betrayed what he might be thinking, seeing his father waiting on the tarmac. Ahmad stepped back, disappearing into the darkened plane.

Ali and Omar reached Mahmoud each patting him on the shoulder in greeting. They grinned at him, joy softening the years from their faces. He tried to smile back, but it was a flickering thing, his mind consumed with Ahmad.

The brothers moved on to greet Samira and Yasmeen, but Mahmoud continued to stare at the doorway of the plane.

When Ahmad reappeared, he stood with Yacoob Masoud. Mahmoud smiled in spite of himself. His father looked just as he always had. White hair tousled and wispy. Frowning even more lines onto his face than age had placed there. The old man grimaced down at them. Lifting a hand, Baba gave a stately wave. Mahmoud was confused until the motion of Samira and Yasmeen's waves grabbed his eye. With a shake, Yacoob dislodged Ahmad's helping hand and started down the steps.

Mahmoud was beaming. This was it. The moment when their family fortunes were shifting forever. Finally, they could all be together. Nothing would stand in the way now. He would not battle with Samira. Now, it would all be okay. Everyone was happy. He quivered with excitement, desperate to hug his father. As Yacoob neared the bottom of the steps, he tottered.

Concerned, Mahmoud rushed forward. He offered a helping hand to Yacoob. His father didn't even look at him. He batted the hand aside and rushed past Mahmoud to pull Samira into his arms.

Mahmoud felt the sting deeply. No greeting. Not even a nod. *He hasn't seen Samira in years,* Mahmoud thought, *it is only natural he would rush to her.*

But then the old man was hugging Yasmeen to him. He pulled back from her putting a hand on each girl's face. There was no hesitation, no moment of pause as Yacoob considered Samira's uncovered hair. Even Soozee received a polite handshake. And then his arms were wrapped tightly around Samira again. Her head cradled on his shoulder, she closed her eyes, a tear rolling down her cheek.

It was a beautiful picture. Mahmoud was moved by it. A father's unconditional love for his child. It cut all the more because it was his father, loving someone else.

The space between them felt as wide as an ocean to Mahmoud. *Can I ever bridge it?* Was there any hope he might be a part of the loving family that stood a few feet away from him? Suddenly, he wasn't sure.

Ahmad stepped up next to him. Mahmoud turned. His son was also watching Yacoob clutching Samira in his arms. He saw his own thoughts reflected in Ahmad's eyes. Ahmad met Mahmoud's gaze. There was still anger there, but it was muted, awash in a deep sadness. He extended a hand to Mahmoud. The family ring sat on his open palm.

Mahmoud pulled his son to him, hugging the boy tightly. After a moment, Ahmad reciprocated. Mahmoud still had no words. Nothing he could say could make up for what he had done. But there was understanding between them. When their hug came to an end, Ahmad once again offered the ring.

"You didn't give it to..." Mahmoud looked at Yacoob.

Ahmad glanced at his shoes. "I tried. He said it belongs to you."

Mahmoud took the ring and smiled at his son. Mahmoud looked back at his father.

Yacoob held Samira's face cupped in his two palms. "You are safe," he said, delighted.

She blushed and smiled. A brief glance at Yasmeen showed the younger sister bouncing on her toes, intoxicated with the thrill of the moment. Ali and Omar stood with them. They hadn't stepped back from Yacoob Masoud.

"We all are," Samira responded.

Mahmoud smiled, a tear tracking slowly down his face.

What Now?

Thanks for reading *What You Meant For Evil*. There are a lot of books you could be reading. I'm grateful you took the time to read this one.

If you've been moved by Samira or Mahmoud's story and you want to do something more, there's a number of ways you can get involved:

First, I hope you'll share this book with friends and family. We've got zero marketing infrastructure. I'm terrible at marketing anyway. So the best hope for folks reading this book is you. Please share it. Gift a copy to a friend, talk us up on social media, leave our website conspicuously open on your work computer... whatever sharing looks like for you.

Second, would you consider hosting a discussion group? This wasn't written in a vacuum. It's based on the story of Joseph as told in the later chapters of Genesis. As such, we've got a whole study you can do with friends and neighbors talking about the book and the scriptures it's based on. You can find that study here:

https://whatyoumeantforevilbook.com/discussion-guide

Third, we'd really like to see the *What You Meant For Evil* film. Film reaches a broader audience than print. However, films cost a lot more money. Your purchase of the book has already made a contribution to our film fund. However, if you would like to do more, you can make a tax-deductible contribution here:

https://whatyoumeantforevilbook.com/donate/

Fourth, the Kelsey character in this story (along with many of the other camp workers) is based on a real person. You can get involved in the life of refugees and make a real difference. If you'd consider making a short term trip to Lesvos or to serve the needs of refugees in Europe, please reach out to my colleagues at Greater Europe Mission here:

https://gemission.org/refuge/

If travel doesn't fit for you, you can still get involved by joining in the work of How Will They Hear. You can help out with a refugee bible study online. More information on that is available here:

https://www.howwilltheyhear.net/

Again, thanks for reading. I'm grateful for you!

Acknowledgments

I've been writing books my whole life. In first grade, I put together a series of books about a dog finding a bone, through which my poor mother suffered. In fact, Jim and Phyllis Cox have been huge supporters and cheerleaders of everything I've ever done in my life. (Thanks, Mom and Dad). By the eighth grade, I was churning out a hybrid Sci-Fi/noir mafia story. I've never stopped writing. Somehow, though, I've gotten through 46 years of life without ever trying to publish anything. That's where this gets ironic, because this is exactly the sort of book I never wanted to write.

Despite a career working in missions and the church, I've taken a snooty view of Christian fiction. I've always felt that writing a book for Christians limits the author from reaching our primary audience. The great commission isn't a calling to go out and encourage all the Christians. And yet, here we are. You've just read a book written for North American Christians. Of course, there is value in encouraging the body. I'm still trying to repent of my pretensions.

I also swore I wouldn't self-publish this book. I'm terrible at marketing. My passion is the storytelling part. So, please tell everyone you know about this book.

To complete my hat trick of thwarted expectations, this was never meant to be a book. I set out in 2017 to make a film retelling of Joseph set in the refugee crisis. I expected a project that ambitious might take me several years.... You can't see the look on my face right now in 2021, but it tells a story all it's own.

This journey began on a beach in 2015. Sounds lovely, right? The Greek Islands. The gentle patter of the Adriatic Sea.... Except that the sea was pattering at a ship, filled with hundreds of refugees. I was standing on the shore, watching, powerless to help as the sea was slowly sawing the ship to pieces on the sharp rocks of the bay. You've read a bit of this story. I contrived to put Mahmoud on that ship.

You can read the full account of that day online (https://whatyoumeantforevilbook.com/wrecked/) but the important person at that event was a young Syrian guy whose name I've lost. In this book I called him Assem and invented a backstory. In other writings, I've called him Abdullah. That morning, in the dark, he jumped from the ship into rocky waters. He swam to shore. Going house to house, he knocked on doors, trying to explain in Arabic and English to Greek speakers that there were women and children trapped on that sinking ship. I'm confident that the fishermen, who finally arrived to rescue the trapped, came because of his efforts and bravery. Thank you, Abdullah.

Michael Knowlton, thank you for sending me to Lesvos to film refugees. Kim Garrity and Fred Naff, thanks for helping me get my feet on the ground when I arrived.

The next critical step was a short film I wrote called (in English) *the Family Home*. I was showing the final cut of the film to our two actors, Wessam and Abdul Hakim. Since I don't speak Arabic and neither of them speak English, it was a difficult conversation. Wessam was doing his best with his limited German to help me understand what Abdul Hakim was saying to me. The message I got was simple enough, "tell our story." I doubt Abdul Hakim will ever read this, but if you do, I hope you're satisfied with my attempt. I also need to mention Chris Tweedy who heard about that meeting and was the first person to tell me in English, "You have to make this!"

This sounds a bit like the setup for a joke, but try to imagine this scene:

Two Americans, two Canadians and a German walk into a coffee shop in Greece. It's 2018. All five of us are utterly shell shocked. It's cold out. A young girl from Australia is puttering about making us coffees as we eat cheese pastries from a bakery up the road. We have to decide what to do. See, we spent a bunch of money to be here, on Lesvos Island. We've got a script for a trailer. That trailer belongs to a film that hasn't been written yet. It revolved around a single actress… and she isn't in this coffee shop. You see, a family emergency put her on a plane home the night before. We were supposed to start filming today. So here we sit. What are we to do?

Those moments in that coffee shop are treasured memories for me. Every day, for a week, we met in that shop. Ate pastries. Drank coffee. There was never anyone else there. Mostly, we fought despair. We sought ways to keep this dream alive. How could we tell this story?

So, Jonathan Roth, Neil "Sport Mode" Zubot and Ed McKell, thank you for dreaming with me. Thanks for believing. I love you guys. I wish many a morning we could meet up again in that coffee shop. And thanks to our Australian barista. I've forgotten your name, but you made a great Chai latte!

Yes, dear reader. You can do math. I said five and then thanked three people. Even including myself, that's fuzzy math. However, I can't just toss this last person in. In that coffee shop, we were being filmed by my intern. A brilliant engineer, he'd finished his studies and thought, "I want to change the world. I should go be a film-maker." While he started as an intern, he's now my chief partner-in-crime. Without him, there's little hope you would be reading this book. He's read so many drafts, shot down so many terrible ideas, and brainstormed, challenged, and wrangled this story to be better in countless ways. In fact, at this moment, he's keeping a horrible GANTT chart that says I have to finish writing acknowledgements today. Alex Reimer, thank you!

Our trailer was brought to life thanks to assistance from Yann, Kelsey, Dorcas and Medhi. Thank you for taking a chance on us. In Kelsey's case a huge one (jumping into an unmarked white van with a group of guys you'd never met to go make a movie).

* * *

Returning from Lesvos we got a huge assist from Elena Diaz Gonzalez, Miette Bretschneider, Jeremy Pusey, Carmela Bonomi, Ben Kommerau, and the Familie Stadler. I would also be remiss if I didn't thank Faraj, our amazing Ata. I still can't picture anyone else as that character. For anyone who is worried, Faraj is a gentle and friendly soul, who just did a great job bringing our villain to life.

I need to make a brief interlude here to again mention Jason Clegg and his amazing wife, Amy. They were a huge support on this and other projects. Notably, they were instrumental in helping me to gather the harrowing refugee stories which appear in this book. I owe a debt of gratitude to many brave refugees who shared their stories. Thank you!

Our trailer launched to huge fanfare thanks to my amazing FUEL cohort. I think of you all whenever I'm eating crenelated bacon. I definitely owe a shout out to Andreas Kranzler who was encouraging at many points in this journey. My dear friends Tom Hawkins and Stephen Coney have been relentless cheerleaders through the process from the first airing of my initial idea. Thanks guys! To Robert Diaz Gonzalez and Eric Gibson I owe a huge debt. You guys kept me sane through a great deal of this process. I miss hanging out! Thank you also to Richard Brohammer for your endless social media commentary and enthusiasm.

I also need to say thank you to Aaron & Andrea Boyles, Roger & Marilyn Blake, Kay & Ray Baker, and Courtney & Krista Roes. Each of you came along at a vital moment, and encouraged us to keep going, to keep trying. Jill Corley, Eric & Susan Eklund and Bob Ewell thank you for being a part of our team!

Many of my early alpha readers are already mentioned above, but Jeff Gage and Tom Khazoyan are not. Thanks guys. I'm grateful for your feedback and willingness to push where you think I'm wrong.

I'm also grateful to my wonderful beta readers. Bruce Penner, David Kroeker, Katrina Smith, Jesse Simmons, Tim Cougar, Bill Lucas, Richard Krahn, Peter Kroeker, Edith Peters and Serge & Andrea Varga. Your feedback made this book better.

Immediately prior to COVID, we were struggling to solve all of our financing and distribution challenges with a team of dedicated and hardworking folks. Cori, Jonathan G., Jordan T., the Deckers, Patrick and Jonny S.: thank you! I'm grateful to each of you for what you've contributed to my understanding of this story and how to bring it to life. Thank you also to Laura Davis at theD3.com and to Miriam Griffith. When our website is good, it's all Laura and Miriam. When it's not, it's probably my fault.

Throughout the development of this story, I've turned to my dear friend, Freddy Labib for his expertise on Arabic culture. He's been merciless about everything I've done wrong. So, if it's still wrong, blame Freddy. Just kidding. I've also received a ton of help from Jeffrey Hayes. His expertise on Syrian culture and Islam added accuracy and detail to this narrative. Dr. Wes Theisen also contributed his expertise at several points in the project where we were struggling with tricky cultural questions. Though Freddy, Jeff and Wes have worked hard to keep me accurate, I'm stubborn and a bad listener. So any mistakes are mine. However, if you walk away from this story with a deeper understanding of Arabic or Muslim culture, these guys are a huge part of that success.

I owe a special debt to each of my children. Brittany, thank you for fearlessly sending me a book on how to write better sentences. You're writing inspires me. I look forward to reading your book one day. Isaac, thanks so much for your work on our discussion guide. I'm so impressed with your commitment to scripture and truth. Thank you for being a part of this project! Faith, I so appreciate all of your quiet encouragement. You've lived through more stages of my insanity with this story than either of your siblings, but you're first response to seeing my book on Amazon was "Can I tell all my friends?" You rock!

As I write this, my dear wife, Brandy, is upstairs sorting through Beta reader feedback in preparation for yet another draft. My love, you're amazing. Thank you for all you've done for this project. Thank you for ceaselessly asking me questions I can't answer, like "Why wouldn't Suzie call the Polizei?" Thank you for putting up with me when I'm in the fog of other worlds. I love you. You bring delight to my life.

I want to write a huge non-thank you to Brent Weeks. I don't know Brent, but he does an excellent job writing entertaining acknowledgments. I've utterly failed to meet his challenge, but it has added days to Alex's GANTT chart.

Thanks to you, dear reader, for taking a chance on this book. I hope you've been entertained. It's my prayer that you've been surprised in places both by what we've found in the story of Joseph, but also by what's really happening with refugees in Syria and Europe.

Finally, I'm grateful to God for bringing me together with each one of you. This book has been a long and sometimes painful journey, but He has carried me through. When I've wanted to quit, He's encouraged me, often through the people mentioned above. Thank you, Lord, for continuing to press me to keep going.

God bless. Thanks for reading.

Theodore D. C. Cox - August 16, 2021